Travis walked to the shoreline. He stood shoulder to shoulder with her, staring at the water slogging slowly past.

"I reckon you wish someone else was the heir." It bothered her to think that he did, but she couldn't blame him for it. "I'll do my best not to shame you."

"Shame? I'm so damn grateful for you, Ivy."

He turned to face her. Those lush green eyes all but made her weak in the knees. They reminded her of home...of the river and the trees. He tugged gently on her braid, then let go so quickly that it was as if her hair had burned him.

"I'll teach you everything you need to know," he said.

Author Note

Do you sometimes feel like Cinderella, staring out of your turret window and watching your dreams ride off without you? I think we all do in one way or another. Perhaps you did not get a job you had your heart set on? Perhaps your prince was not charming? The home you made an offer on went to someone else?

Ivy Magee knew for certain what she wanted from life...until the dream of her heart was snatched from her. Like Cinderella, she never cried, "Oh, poor little me." She didn't jump into a lake of woe. She smiled, she worked hard and one day her cowboy-prince noticed her...fell desperately in love with her. Not that he could claim her, of course. Travis Murphy was a man bound by obligation. He understood that the woman he loved was meant for another. This was a problem that not even a fairy godmother could fix. But true love could. Given the courage of Ivy and the devotion of Travis, old dreams fell away and new ones blossomed.

Life happens that way sometimes. The things we want most don't happen but something better does.

So, my friend, be open to new dreams, because you never know when the glass slipper will fit.

THE COWBOY'S CINDERELLA

CAROL ARENS

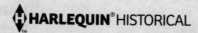

Recycling programs
for this product may
not exist in your area.

ISBN-13: 978-1-335-46757-7

The Cowboy's Cinderella

Copyright © 2017 by Carol Arens

Printed in U.S.A.

www.Harlequin.com

Carol Arens delights in tossing fictional characters into hot water, watching them steam and then giving them a happily-ever-after. When she is not writing, she enjoys spending time with her family, beach camping or lounging about a mountain cabin. At home, she enjoys playing with her grandchildren and gardening. During rare spare moments, you will find her snuggled up with a good book. Carol enjoys hearing from readers at carolarens@yahoo.com or on Facebook.

Books by Carol Arens

Harlequin Historical

Rebel with a Heart
Dreaming of a Western Christmas
"Snowbound with the Cowboy"
Western Christmas Proposals
"The Sheriff's Christmas Proposal"
The Cowboy's Cinderella
Western Christmas Brides
"A Kiss from the Cowboy"
The Rancher's Inconvenient Bride
A Ranch to Call Home

The Walker Twins

Wed to the Montana Cowboy
Wed to the Texas Outlaw

Cahill Cowboys

Scandal at the Cahill Saloon

Visit the Author Profile page at Harlequin.com.

Dedicated to the memory of "The luckiest man in the world"...my father, Glenn Lester Ebert.

"love you I."

Chapter One

Coulson, Montana, June 1882

"Gull-durned female traps!"

Ivy Magee watched three women dressed in all manner of frippery stroll across the gangplank of the *River Queen*.

Leaning over the rail of the upper, hurricane deck, she observed their slow, sashaying mosey from the boat to shore.

With all the fussy petticoats, there wasn't room for all of them to walk side by side. They were trying, though, arms linked and giggling. One wrong step and someone would tumble headlong into the river.

While the image playing in her mind presented a humorous picture—with flailing legs getting all tangled up in ruffles, elegant hair dripping water and mud weeds—Ivy could only pity the woman who would have to launder the muck from the clothes. Sure as shootin' wasn't going to be those fancy ladies.

Wasn't going to be Ivy, either.

Just because she was a female didn't make her honor bound to clean up after folks. Uncle Patrick was training her to pilot the *River Queen*. She was happy as a fish in deep water to be his "cub."

For the life of her, Ivy couldn't figure the female species out.

Gosh all-mighty! Why would a soul want to stuff her body into whale bones and yards of heavy cloth that would only make her sweat and stumble? If she guessed right, the whole of female creation could not breathe.

"Gull-durned female duds…worst kind of a trap," she repeated, this time with a dash of scorn.

Sometimes she thought her fellow sex were touched in the head to willingly—even happily—submit to such abuse.

Once again, she was grateful for the soft cotton shirt she wore, for the durable denim pants. Even the belt that held her trousers up was just a strip of red cloth. Its flower print and the bow she fastened it with was all the adornment she needed.

The oldest of the three women, the one walking in the middle, lost her balance when the plank heaved with the current. The young ones tried to set her to rights but they all listed toward the water.

Just in time, young Tom, a deckhand, dashed across the plank to help them rebalance.

Ivy had grown up on this boat. In her twenty-two years, she'd seen that not all of the ladies maneuvering the plank were so lucky. Last fall, one had gone over and washed up half a mile downriver. A couple of roustabouts fished her out a second before her waterlogged skirts dragged her to the Great Beyond.

These ladies were luckier than some. At least they might be, were they not destined for a life of selling their bodies in this wicked town.

Ivy was glad the boat would dock here only one night

before turning east toward respectable towns…more profitable ones, too.

The *River Queen* was unique among the boats that did business along the Missouri. Most of them were work-horses, transporting goods and passengers.

But Patrick Malone, her uncle and the man who had raised her, had a different vision for his boat. The *River Queen* did transport people and their goods, but it was also a high-class gambling boat.

Like Ivy, Uncle Patrick had spent his life on a river-boat, but a grand one on the Mississippi.

Oh, the stories he loved to tell of a night, when the after watch took over and the boat grew quiet. He'd spend hours spinning yarns about the glory of the old days when floating palaces plied that great and peril-ous river.

He'd started as an apprentice, a cub. He'd gone on to become the highly respected pilot of the *Jewel of the Mississippi*.

The tales he'd spun about that huge boat left her breathless. The glitter of crystal chandeliers, the orches-tra playing and lots of folks becoming instantly rich, then just as fast, poor again…it was as though she'd seen it all herself.

The events she witnessed through his eyes had been beyond grand, the gentlemen and the ladies all rich and refined, the firemen and roustabouts not refined but strong as bulls, their mighty muscles glistening with sweat in the reflected heat of the fire that kept the float-ing palaces moving.

Ivy's favorite stories involved the river pilots, whose uncanny intuition sensed how the river changed, noticed every ripple in the current that might foretell disaster, could see below the water in their mind's eye, even on a pitch-dark night.

Lives depended upon their knowing when and where the riverbed shifted. If a pilot made a mistake, failed to sense sudden changes below the water, tragedies occurred.

Uncle Patrick remembered many such events. But none of them were of his making.

Even as a tot, no more than two years old, Ivy used to sit at her uncle's feet and listen to him spin his magical stories, fascinated even though she didn't understand much of what he said.

By the time she was four, she knew that she wanted to be a pilot, just like Uncle Patrick.

But time was running out for riverboats. Her uncle expounded on this very subject every time he saw her becoming breathless with excitement over piloting a boat.

The railroad had done in the Mississippi years ago. It would do in the Missouri as well.

Just last night she had argued with him over it.

To her way of thinking, yes, freight hauling and transporting folks would give way to train travel, but gambling would not. Folks were always in a sure-fired hurry to lose their money and there was romance in doing it on a steamboat.

But Uncle Patrick believed even this recreation would end.

She sure did hope he was wrong because she was set on being a pilot.

"The ladies invited me to the Sullied Gully tonight, me being their hero and all." Young Tom settled beside her at the rail.

"My uncle will have your hide, Tom." And he would. "He promised your ma he'd keep you in hand."

"I'm of an age." Tom grinned at her. Sunshine touched his nose, dotting it with fresh freckles.

"An age for what, you young fool?"

"Women." Just saying the word made him blush.

"Wait until you grow up a bit for that." Ivy knocked the cap from his hair with a flick of her fingers. "There's one of our passengers down there on her knees. Looks like she tripped over her fool skirt. I don't think she's a lady of the night, though. See if you can find her a safe place to stay."

Tom pushed away from the rail. "Sure won't miss that noisy green bird of hers."

She watched him cross the deck, disappear down the stairs then reappear on the stage plank.

He was carrying the woman's trunk across his shoulders. She indicated a spot on the ground for him to set it down. It looked like she handed Tom some money for his effort.

"Gosh almighty." She sighed. "Uncle Patrick will tan his hide if he spends it at the Sullied Gully."

All of a sudden her hat shifted, tipping toward her nose. She caught the small white mouse that slid from the brim.

"You little varmint, what's waking you so early? Sun's not even set yet." Ivy fished a peanut from her pocket and gave it to the mouse.

It sat on her shoulder nibbling the treat. After a moment she tucked the furry creature back into the special pouch under a large satin flower that was attached to the brim of her hat.

"Go back to sleep until dark. It'll be Hades own chaos if a passenger sees you."

To her relief, the mouse snuggled into his space and became still.

Not even Uncle Patrick knew that her best friend was a rodent.

* * *

Moonlight reflected off the liquid face of the Missouri River.

From the cabin deck of the docked *River Queen*, Travis Murphy watched the sparkling ripples gliding past, not in a straight line, but with the twisting tug of the current.

The sight kept him mesmerized, since at the moment, his life resembled those twisting ripples. It sure wasn't traveling the straight line that he hoped this journey would take him on.

The future of the Lucky Clover Ranch depended upon him finding Miss Eleanor Magee. But it seemed the harder he searched the more twisted the trail became, the pursuit more urgent.

At one point, he'd nearly caught up with the woman, but his horse had come up lame. It had taken some time for the poor creature to heal properly.

That delay had been frustrating, but he'd finally made it to Coulson, a day ahead of the steamboat.

Now, here he was, the boat finally arrived, but he sure didn't see anyone who resembled the woman's twin sister, Agatha.

Travis swatted a moth away from his face. The determined insect seemed intent upon incinerating itself on the lamp hanging over his head.

Where the blazes could Eleanor Magee be?

Hell, he'd only learned of Eleanor's existence when his boss, the man he loved as much as he remembered loving his own father, confessed on his deathbed that he had another daughter.

That revelation had nearly kicked Travis to his knees. He'd always felt like a member of the family, believed he'd known everything about them.

When, at six years old, his parents had been put in the grave, Travis had wanted to leap into the hole with them. But Foster Magee had been there, his big hand pulling him back from the shadow of death. He'd taken him to the big house and raised him as his own.

But another daughter? In the moment he'd demanded that Foster tell him why this girl's existence had been kept a secret, why she had not been raised at the ranch.

The reality was, he'd had no right to demand anything of Foster. But in that moment he had been a stunned son, not an employee.

The reason turned out to be a divorce agreement. He'd learned the full story while watching tears drip down his mentor's disease-ravaged face—his stand-in father's face.

He'd given up Eleanor in an agreement with Mollie Clover Magee.

"She was a beauty, my wife," he'd admitted.

The proof of that, her portrait, still hung over the mantel of the huge fireplace in the great room back at the ranch.

"She was a wild flower, a free spirit, the plain opposite of me. Fire and ice I reckon." he whispered, his voice hoarse, weak from the effects of his illness.

It was true. Foster Seamus Magee had been a man of purpose. His desire to have the largest and most influential ranch in the state had consumed him. A proper life of social niceties, all the rules of etiquette observed, this was what he'd striven for.

"My Clover, she was never cut out for that kind of life. I watched her dry up in front of my eyes. My pretty wife… The life I sought sucked the life out of her.

"Son, you understand that I never stopped loving her, but I had to let her go when she wanted to…just not all of her. I wouldn't let her have Agatha because of the two girls she's the one who reminded me of my Clover, with that blaze of red hair and those emerald-colored eyes. Turned out, though, she didn't have her mother's high spirit. The girl is sickly...well, you grew up with her, you know."

He did know. Agatha was a shut away. She was frail, retiring, and lacking the vigor that the demands of inheriting the ranch would place upon her. He only hoped that Eleanor was different from her twin.

A lot of livelihoods depended upon her being strong, but even more, that she was willing to step into her role.

Sweat trickled down the back of his neck, not with stressful thoughts of past and present, but because the heat of the day lingered on the land and shimmered over the water. In the mountains nearby the temperature would be different. He reckoned just a short distance away the night was getting cold.

Well, not the night so much anymore, but the wee hours. Even the gamblers had taken to their beds.

He swiped the ticklish moisture from his neck while he strolled to the side of the boat facing west. Maybe there would be a breeze off the water.

There wasn't a breeze...but there was a woman.

A naked woman.

Naked women weren't so unusual in Coulson. But here on the riverboat at this hour? Perhaps she'd been entertaining a gambler.

Propriety told him to look away. Nature urged him otherwise.

The woman stood on the lower deck, her back toward him and her arms reaching for the night sky. When she lifted her face toward the moon, he saw the slim line of her nose but nothing else.

He smiled, wished he was the moonglow. That elusive finger of light touched the curve of her hip, shimmered in the fall of blond hair tumbling down her back. It cupped the lovely round orbs of her bottom.

She bent her knees, pushed off the deck, and dove headlong into the water.

She came up, grinning, then went under again. Her fair-skinned body skimmed inches below the surface of the water as she swam alongside the boat.

Hell, now he wished he was the river, with the right to touch her so intimately.

Spinning about, he strolled toward the other end of the boat, hands shoved deep in his pockets.

Whoever the woman was, she was not Eleanor Magee. From what he'd learned from the Pinkerton he'd hired, Miss Eleanor was watched over by her uncle. It was hard to imagine the guardian who would let his niece loose at all hours of the night, who would allow her to leap into a river naked.

The fact that Patrick Malone was Eleanor's guardian, and that she'd grown up on this boat, was all he knew of Miss Magee. He couldn't be certain that she even lived here any longer since the Pinkerton had never actually laid eyes on her. For the price Travis had been able to pay, all he'd got for his investment was a bunch of the man's "educated guesses"…leads that may or may not find the Lucky Clover's heir.

If the investigator was wrong in his information, Travis had wasted a valuable month away from the ranch.

The nosey gambler was supposed to be abed but Ivy felt his gaze between her shoulder blades…and lower. She longed to twitch, to ease the burn on her back.

Gosh-almighty, she wouldn't give the voyeur that satisfaction. This was her boat and her time. To her way of thinking, swimming bare was no sin. Eavesdropping was. Let him be the one to squirm before the preacher of a Sunday.

Doing her best to ignore the intrusive gambler, who was probably too drunk to really see her anyway, Ivy dove into the cool murky water.

She burst the surface of the river, grinning. Wasn't this as close to paradise as a body could get?

Treading water, she inhaled, savored the scent of damp mud, of verdant plants growing at the water's edge.

"Howdy-doo, all you fine crickets…good evening, all you fat old frogs."

She stroked through the cool water, feeling the day's sweat and grievances wash off her skin. It was her custom to float on her back, watch the twinkle of the stars while feeling weightless, but the gambler was still up there.

It wasn't likely that he'd come out intentionally to spoil her solitude—chances were, he only wanted a bit of fresh air.

All at once, the man spun away. Shoving his hands into his pockets, he slowly walked toward the other end of the boat.

She stroked along through the water, this time she was the one watching him. There wasn't a whole lot she could learn in the dark, not until he passed under one of the lanterns hanging from the roof over the cabin deck.

Then—gosh all-mighty, he was handsome! Fine of figure, he had the stride of a man of authority, a fellow who knew where he wanted to go and how to get there.

He didn't seem drunk.

"Hey, mister!" she called up to him while treading water.

He stopped, looked down at her then came to the rail. Resting his arms on the balustrade, he gazed toward her.

"This here's my private time. I don't hanker to spend it with a Peeping Tom."

"Sorry, ma'am." Well, now she wasn't sure his smile said sorry or not. "I didn't know. I was only cooling some sweat, walking away some worry."

That was probably the truth. On a gambling boat, for every winner there was a loser worrying over his loss. Not that the wealthy clients of the *River Queen* needed to worry over the loss…most of the time.

As far as the knowing went, he probably didn't. There were no signs posted about Ivy's private time—it was just something that the men who lived on board knew and respected.

This fellow didn't live on board so she ought to allow for that.

And the river was a balm when one wanted to wash away a day's stress. She couldn't imagine living her life away from its soothing embrace. Often, she pitied land folks who never knew the feel of the river against their skin.

One more thing she ought to allow for was that the fellow up there was a paying customer. According to Uncle Patrick, those were soon to become scarce.

"I reckon you lost money tonight." It was not unpleasant carrying on a conversation with this handsome fellow. Not when she was hidden in the cool kiss of the inky water and he was up there sweating in his fancy duds.

"If it's a woman you're looking to sooth yourself with, I ain't her, but over yonder in Coulson you'll find what you need."

"I doubt it, ma'am."

He was still smiling in the way that let her know that in this moment, his stress was relieved, but under that half-lifted mouth, life was not grand. She saw this to be true even in the dim light of the boat's lamps.

It was her duty to make sure the passenger was happy so that tonight he would take a seat in the casino again.

"Look here, mister, if you agree to keep to the paddle side of the boat, I'll share the water with you."

"I'll need to strip bare. You don't mind?"

"I reckon I've got a peek coming since you were ogling me. Just keep to your side of the boat and we'll get on just fine."

The fellow pushed away from the rail. She heard his boots tripping down the stairs. He reappeared on the lower deck, his shirt in hand and his chest bare.

It wasn't uncommon for Ivy to see a man bare chested. The roustabouts often worked shirtless.

But there was something different about this man, something curious. He made her insides feel fluttery.

Why was that? Men were men. One was not so much different than another. Two arms. Two legs.

Two muscled buttocks. She could not help but notice when he turned his back to her and stepped out of his trousers.

He was giving her the same glimpse of him that he had taken of her.

That was not quite true. He turned his head to flash her a mischievous smile before jumping feet first into the water, his back still presenting.

"Looks like we're even, mister," she said when his face broke the surface of the water.

She felt safe enough even though she kept only a twenty-foot buffer between them instead of the boat length. If he made an untoward move, she'd be off as quick as a minnow.

"What's your name, gambler?" she asked then ducked under the water, surfacing a foot closer to him.

"Travis."

Travis went under the water then came up a yard closer to her. His handsome face was dotted with water. He shook his head, splattering droplets from his short brown hair. It stood up in spikes all over his scalp—gave him a real boyish, friendly look. That sure was contrary to her first impression of him being a no-nonsense man of authority.

"What's yours?"

"Ivy."

"Pleased to make your acquaintance, Ivy."

Naked sure was an odd way to meet a fellow, but the night was dark and so was the water.

"So, how much did you lose to keep you restless so late?" She ought to swim to the other side of the boat and float about gazing at the stars, but she was enjoying gazing at Travis's face instead.

"To tell you the truth, I didn't do much gambling."

"Most folks aboard the *River Queen* come just for that." A fish nibbled her toes. She kicked it away. "There's some who just need transportation, but mostly they're gamblers. Big money gamblers."

"Are you familiar with the ship?"

"A bit." She didn't want to say she knew every inch of it, every board and shadow. That she was training to be a pilot. A lady pilot tended to be frowned upon and for some reason she did not want Travis frowning upon her.

"I'm looking for a woman named Eleanor."

Her swim time was about up. If she didn't rap on

Uncle Patrick's door telling him she was safely aboard, he would come looking.

"A sweetheart?" Gosh almighty she couldn't swim away without knowing about that.

"No...not a sweetheart." Oh? For some reason she was relieved to know it. "She's inherited a ranch. I've got to find her and let her know."

"And you believe she's aboard?"

"I have reason to think so," Travis answered, parting the water between them.

Only ten feet of sparkling river lay between them. Just because the water was dark did not make her any less naked.

Her imagination saw a dozen things that her eyes couldn't.

It was time and past for her to be in her room.

She ducked under the surface and swam away. When she came up for air she looked back to see Travis on the deck, knee-deep into his britches.

Whoever this Eleanor was, she was a mighty lucky woman to have him looking for her, even if they were not sweethearts.

With the exception of one gambler, still in his chair but dead asleep with his head lying on the poker table, the saloon was empty.

The man's pockets were turned inside out. His heavy breathing stirred the cards in front of his mouth.

Travis figured the fellow must have fallen asleep over the losing hand in front of his nose. No doubt, the smile tugging his mouth meant he was dreaming of the winning hand for tonight's competition.

A lingering scent of cigars hovered in the corners of the large room. For all its size and elegance, the saloon was still cozy. The overstuffed chairs near the windows, the padded stools about the gaming tables, all invited one to stay and enjoy an evening.

With the piano covered for the night, the lamps turned low and everyone abed but the lone sleeper, Travis decided to continue his restless night right here, with his butt snuggled into a plump brown chair and his feet up on a gold ottoman.

For comfort, it beat the hell out of the cot he'd put up beside his horse on the main deck.

He'd taken only a small amount of money on his quest to find Eleanor. The more he left behind for the ranch to keep going, the better.

Since he was on his own, it would not be a problem to live frugally for a time. Even the little bit of gambling he'd done had been for the purpose of gaining information about Miss Magee. It sure hadn't hurt that he'd won a few dollars.

Hadn't gained a thing by way of discovering anything about Miss Eleanor, though.

At daylight, the boat was going to turn south. If the lady was not aboard, it would cause him all kinds of trouble. He only hoped the Pinkerton knew his business.

If Travis didn't come up with any information by nightfall, he'd try and get a moment of the captain's time, not an easy thing to do, he'd discovered, with such a busy man. But if he couldn't find out something about Eleanor from her own uncle, he despaired of finding it at all.

That was a notion he couldn't let his mind dwell on. Futures depended upon him bringing her home.

Hell, what he did want to dwell on was the magical water nymph.

Ivy. Even her name conjured up things fresh, green and growing with abandon, having no regard for rules.

He closed his eyes, reliving the memory of her diving into the water, of her face as she surfaced, so full of the joy of just plain living.

If only he could be more like her. Not that he wanted to run from his responsibilities, but if he could rise above them from time to time...

When Ivy invited him to strip down and join her in the water, he'd felt ten years old again.

He'd liked being ten. By then he was past the constant grief that his parents' deaths had caused and had come to love his life on the Lucky Clover Ranch.

For a few moments last night, he had been that boy again because looking at Ivy—and he didn't just mean in appreciation of her lovely body, but her smile and the love of life that shone from her eyes—he'd felt fresh. Renewed.

He'd come from the water full of hope and now he sat in this chair because the only way to hold on to that feeling was to hold her memory fresh. To keep her in his mind so that he could draw on that brief moment out of time.

When life was not so fresh, he would remember Ivy.

Too bad he would never see her again. No doubt by now she was back in Coulson doing whatever a free spirit like her did in the wee hours.

Turning frogs into princes, coaxing butterflies from their cocoons, maybe even leading a symphony of light with fireflies as her instruments, that's what he would like to think, even though he knew reality was certainly far different.

Reality or not, he was good and sorry he would never see Miss Ivy again.

Chapter Two

It was late the next afternoon when a storm swept in. The boat rocked erratically on the choppy water so the captain decided to set to shore and open the casino early.

As far as Travis could tell, walking past the open saloon door, the weather didn't dampen the gaiety of the games going on inside.

He worried his horse might be skittish though, so he clasped his hat to his head, leaned into the wind and took the stairs down to the main deck to check on her.

As it turned out, he needn't have worried. Through the dim light he spotted someone, a young man if he guessed right, speaking to the horse and petting her neck.

"Thank you," he said when he entered the stall. "I appreciate—"

"Howdy-doo, Travis. This sweet girl belong to you?"

"Ivy?"

The ethereal creature from the night before was still here? This earthy woman, wearing a huge floppy hat and dressed like a man was the same woman he'd fantasized over last night?

"Glad I came across you," she said. "I've been asking around and no one's claiming to be your Eleanor."

"Are you traveling on the *River Queen*, Ivy? I thought you might be from Coulson."

She snorted…through her nose. The image of the water nymph dissolved and no matter how he tried, he could not get her back.

"That snake pit? Why I'd just as soon live on the moon."

She looked at him for a long moment, her eyes squinting, judging him, he thought.

"I reckon we became friends last night, so I can tell you." She gave the horse one last squeeze about the neck then stepped closer to him. There was still something of the woman in the river after all—she smelled like cool fresh water. "I live here. I hope to pilot a boat someday."

She lived aboard and didn't know anyone named Eleanor? This was not good news.

All at once, the only thing he wanted to do was sit down in the straw and hang his head. So he did.

It seemed that finding the heir was beyond him, but giving in to a moment of private gloom was within his control.

Or not. The straw rustled beside him when Ivy sat down.

"You know what she looks like? Maybe she goes by some other name?"

"I don't. She's got a twin sister with red hair, green eyes, about as tall as you and about your age. They weren't identical though."

"I always fancied having a sister." In the subdued daylight he saw how blue her eyes really were. A sunny blond braid lay over her shoulder. "So much so that I dream of her sometimes. Why, when I was little I used to pretend to play with her. How's that for fancy?"

Ivy flopped back in the hay, stretched her arms over

her head and sighed. "Ain't this a fine way to pass a stormy afternoon? Tell me about this ranch of yours."

She patted the straw beside her, inviting him to join her in gazing at the rafters overhead.

Ivy was disarming, and unlike any woman he had ever met. He thought perhaps he liked her, liked her very much.

He lay down beside her. With his arms folded behind his head, he listened to the drum of rain hitting the deck several yards beyond the stall.

"It's not mine. Not in a legal sense. I started running the place a few years ago when my boss took ill. I kept on after he passed. I feel the responsibility for the ranch like it was mine."

"I'm right sorry, Travis. You loved him?"

It was easy to hear the regret in her voice. Spoken so softly, he knew she meant it.

"He became a father to me when I lost my folks. Gave me a home when I was a lost little boy."

"What a kind man he must have been."

"Kind, yes, and ambitious. It's a big spread. The biggest in Laramie County...one of the largest in Wyoming." He closed his eyes, picturing miles upon miles of grassland. How the scent was fresh and how the wind rolled over it in a whisper. "I swear, Ivy, it's the prettiest piece of land on God's green earth. You can ride all day long and not get from the east end to the west."

She eased up on her elbow, gazing down at him. "The land has your heart...just like the river has mine."

"The Lucky Clover is a special place."

"The Lucky Clover?" She blinked, grinned, and dug under the collar of her shirt. "Don't that beat all? Look, my ma gave me this necklace before she passed. It's got an *L* and *C* etched on it. The *C*'s a mite faded so it could be an *O*. My Uncle says it must be the initials of some long gone relative. But ain't that a coincidence?"

"It's pretty, even though it's faded…and I'm sorry," he said. When she looked puzzled he added, "About you losing your mother."

"I've been told I cried for a week solid, but I was only two years old and don't recall the event anymore."

"What about you father?"

"I never did recall him." Thunder rolled overhead. "So this Eleanor, she's going to inherit the whole ranch?"

"If I can find her."

"What happens if you can't?"

He groaned out loud. He didn't really want to talk about it, he'd prefer to just lie here in the straw and forget for a moment.

"The ranch will fail without her." Wind whistled around the lower deck blowing in a hail of raindrops, but they didn't reach inside the stall. "There's a big mortgage note coming due. If we can't pay it a lot of folks will lose their livelihoods, their homes. People who have lived on the Lucky Clover their whole lives will be put out."

"I can't imagine losing my home here on *River Queen*." She sat up, frowning and glancing about. "Some say the trains will be the end of the river trade, but I think folks will always want to gamble on a steamer."

"I hope that's true, Ivy."

"And I hope you find your heir."

All of a sudden, he wanted to reach up and touch her cheek. In spite of her boyish clothing, her skin was fair, pink cheeked with a light smattering of freckles across her nose.

He laced his fingers together behind his head.

"Even if I find her I've got to convince her to do something I reckon she won't want to."

"She might…if she gets a sister and a fine ranch for the trouble."

"She'll have to marry our rich neighbor. It's the only way to get the ranch out of the debt it's fallen into."

"Gosh almighty!" Ivy clasped her hand to her throat. "What are you going to do when she says no?"

"You think she will? I'm offering a lot in exchange."

"I think it depends upon her life. Maybe she'll be willing if she's a lonely spinster…but I don't see that she's old enough to give in to that yet. And what if she's married already with a pack of young'uns…but I wonder if she might be a widow…in that case you have some hope."

"I do know that she is not married. The Pinkerton I hired didn't know much, but he knew that, and that she is supposed to be living on this boat."

"Could be he meant the *River Belle*. She sails the Missouri." Ivy's hat began to tilt even though she hadn't touched it. "Good news if that's so. We're putting into dock beside her tomorrow night at Bridgerton Landing. Big gambling day for both boats with rich folks coming from all over."

Something…a mouse, tumbled from Ivy's hat! He swatted at the dirty vermin, anxious to keep it off Ivy.

She laughed, reached out and caught the creature in the palm of her hand.

She nuzzled its white head with her nose.

"Don't tell me you're skittish over a little old mouse?"

"Repelled more than—"

All of a sudden Ivy placed the mouse in his hand.

"Little Mouse is a sweet thing once you get to know her."

The "sweet thing" nipped his thumb.

"See? She likes you?"

"Where'd it come from?"

Ivy took the hat from her head, pointed to a pocket attached to the brim.

"She lives here in my hat when we're out. She's got her own little cage in my room." The mouse leapt from his hand and onto Ivy's shirt. It scrambled up to sit on her shoulder. "You will keep my secret, won't you? There'd be the dickens to pay if anyone but Tom knew about her."

"It can't be healthy, wearing a rodent on your head."

"Well, she's white, and not vermin. Little Mouse is as clean as you or me. And she's tidy of habit…goes off to do her business."

"Ivy, that's—"

"None of your business, Travis." Her eyes narrowed at him, daring him, he thought, to believe otherwise.

"Not my business to tell, is what I was about to say. But I still don't think mice ought to live in ladies' hats."

All of a sudden she started to laugh, deep from her belly.

"Can't you picture that?" she sputtered, trying but not able to control her giggles. "All the screaming and swatting…the fainting?"

He did see it, smiled, then burst out laughing along with her. He sat up, bent over at the middle. All of a sudden his worry felt twenty pounds lighter.

When the humor began to even out, she swatted his knee.

"It's a lucky thing I'm no lady. I'd sooner fall in the river and never come up than be like one of those poor females."

He'd always been partial to the sweet gender, enjoyed their delicate, flirtatious ways.

But he'd never forget Ivy. She was not the water nymph he'd fantasized over…she was so much more.

* * *

Morning dawned bright as a new penny. Climbing the outdoor stairs to the pilothouse Ivy breathed deep, savoring the fresh scent of river and pine.

This was going to be a good day filled with the wonder of learning the river, then come nightfall the excitement of games of chance.

"Howdy-do, Uncle Patrick!" She crossed the small space to give her uncle a hug around the middle. "Did we turn a profit last night?"

"Not much, my money-minded little love, but tonight we should earn enough to keep you happy."

"I'm only money minded so that we can keep the boat going. You know I don't give a fig about the fancy things to be had with it."

"Maybe you ought to." Uncle Patrick's bushy white eyebrows nearly touched when he frowned down at her. "How are you ever going to get a husband dressed like a boy?"

"Why would I want one of those?" Her uncle meant well, but his aim for her life was a mite different than her own. "I'm happy as a mudsucker here with you."

"A woman needs a home and family."

"Not this woman." She placed her hands on the wheel. It was so large it extended below deck. She felt a thrum pulsing through the wood. The power of the engine, the pull of the boat drawing through water, was right under her fingertips.

Exhilaration claimed her to her toes and back.

"No swimming for you tonight, young lady. The gamblers won't be abed at all."

"I hope not."

"And don't you go sneaking off to gamble, either."

"I'll keep my clothes on, but I won't promise not to

earn us a fistful of money." She nudged her uncle in the ribs, shot him a grin. He'd always claimed to disapprove of her gambling, but she was skilled at it. In spite of his duty-bound admonitions, she knew he was proud of her. "Besides, I'm looking for someone who might be on the *Belle*."

"A man?" Her uncle asked, overstating his hope.

"A woman…for a man."

"You matchmaking for one of the roustabouts?"

"There's a passenger, a nice, friendly fellow named Travis, looking for the heir to the ranch he ramrods. If he doesn't find her the ranch will be lost."

"And she's one of our passengers?"

"Not that I've heard of. Travis is under the belief that she lives on the *Queen*. But since I'm the only woman living here, I reckon he wasted good money on the Pinkerton he hired."

"A Pinkerton?" Uncle Travis mumbled, then grew silent, watching the river with a frown. He must sense some danger she did not yet have the skill to detect.

"The lady's name is Eleanor. If you recall someone of that name, it would help our passenger out a great deal."

Her uncle swung his gaze away from the river and settled it on her. She noticed his throat constrict, swallow hard.

"Eleanor?" Odd that his voice sounded unusually gruff…drawn tight in a way that was not common for him. "Girl got a last name?"

"Plum forgot to ask. Reckon it would help if she's using her true name but we can't be sure." She shrugged. "Could be we'll find her on the *Belle*."

Uncle Patrick grunted.

"You see some trouble out there that I don't, or you got a bellyache?"

He stood behind her, covering her hands with his strong, gnarled ones.

"Could be trouble," he said. "We'd best ready ourselves for it, just in case."

As hard as she stared at the water, she could see nothing but the calm surface. She longed for nothing more than the ability to see what a seasoned pilot like her uncle could in its murky depths.

Travis had sat down at a poker table in the casino of the *River Belle* at a little after nine. This early in the evening gaming was a social event, the bets low enough that the gamblers without much money could join in and hope to get lucky.

The luck that Travis was after was to find Eleanor Magee without losing too much in the process.

He'd been partially successful. In the three hours he'd been in this chair, he had tripled his money but come no closer to unearthing the elusive Miss Magee.

He'd met a lot of people from both boats tonight, deck hands, roustabouts and sons of millionaires. He'd been told that the fathers and boat owners would come later on when the losers had drunk their fill and emptied their pockets.

If he quit playing now, he'd be nicely ahead. But there were still plenty of folks visiting the saloon. One of them might know something.

The future of the Lucky Clover's cowboys and their families depended upon what happened here. What was walking away a winner compared to that?

A woman came into the saloon, her sparkling gown catching the glow of the lantern light. She was too old to be Agatha's twin. No doubt she was the wife of a rich

gambler, or perhaps the mother of one of the young men
at the table with him.

The dealer skillfully dealt the hands. Travis stared
down at the backs of his cards, wondering what they
would reveal. The only lady he was going to find was
the cold likeness of a queen.

He yawned. Couldn't help it. It was nearly midnight
and he, because of his years on the ranch, was an early
riser.

All of a sudden the scent of fresh water chased away
the stench of tobacco.

"Howdy-doo, gentlemen!"

"Miss Ivy!" exclaimed a young man sitting at the
table. He greeted her with a broad, friendly grin. "You
won't get my money this time!"

None of the men stood up like they had done when
the woman in the sparkling gown came in.

Just because Ivy didn't have an elegant bearing, did
not mean she was not a woman due respect.

Travis stood, pulled out the chair beside him. "Miss
Ivy," he said. "We'd be pleased to have you join us."

"Nice to see there's one gentleman present." She
slapped him on the back and sat down on the red vel-
vet stool. "Boys, hold on to your chips. Especially you,
Travis. Once a fellow begins to yawn, he might just as
well pass his money to the left…gosh almighty, I'm on
your left!"

Laughter rang out at the table. Clearly, Ivy was a
popular player.

Ivy's hat shifted. She reached for the pouch and
stroked it. He doubted that anyone else knew there was
a mouse living inside. For some reason it pleased him,
sharing that special secret with Ivy.

An hour later, Ivy had most of the chips in front of

her. Somehow, he had managed to only lose a small stack to her.

It was now one thirty in the morning. Back home everyone would be asleep except for the cowboys keeping night watch over the herd.

He tried to stifle a yawn but the urge to doze was too strong.

"Better get back to the *River Queen*, Travis, before all your chips end up in front of me."

She leaned closer to him and whispered. "I'll ask around after your heir."

"Obliged," he whispered back. And he was. In the shape he was in now Eleanor could sit down next to him and he wouldn't even notice.

He stood up, bid the men at the table goodbye then nodded to the man waiting to fill his spot.

From the doorway, he heard Ivy ask the newcomer if he knew someone named Eleanor…last name unknown.

Walking out onto the deck, he shook his head. How had he neglected to inform Ivy that Eleanor's last name was Magee? In the end, he reckoned it didn't matter since she might be going by another name anyway.

Fresh June air washed the scent of tobacco from his hair and clothes. He breathed it deeply to cleanse his lungs. While cowboys also tended to smoke around the campfire at night, the space was wide open and one did not become suffocated with the fumes.

It was a short walk from the gangplank of the *River Belle* to the gangplank of the *River Queen*. Walking between them, he gazed up at the stars, then lower at the lamps glowing cheerfully in the windows of the *Queen*'s casino.

It would be a profitable night for both boats.

For Travis, there was only one thing he wanted…well

two, maybe three…but just now, he was for his cot next to his horse on the lower deck.

Rounding a corner, he spotted Captain Malone. The boat owner stepped away from the shadowed wall and strode toward him, his pipe puffing smoke into the night.

"Mr. Murphy," the captain said. "I've been hoping to speak with you."

That was a bit of luck. He'd been eager to speak with Malone but had never gotten the opportunity.

"If you wouldn't mind?" Captain Malone indicated a bench with a swipe of his pipe. "It's been a long day and these old bones begin to ache, what with the damp and cold coming off the river. I ain't the man I used to be…not by a stone's throw."

"I've been hoping to speak with you as well." Travis sat then the Captain sat beside him. The boat swayed gently beside the dock. The splash of water against the side sounded gentle compared to the jovial laughter and the cries of dismay of the gamblers.

"Ivy tells me you've been looking for a woman named Eleanor. May I ask what her last name is?"

"Eleanor Magee, sir." He swiped his hand across his face, trying to rub away some of the weariness. "It's most urgent that I find her."

The captain sighed, shook his head.

"You have found her, son."

Chapter Three

The noon hour was later than Ivy liked to rise, but the sock in her drawer was stuffed with money so the late night spent on the *River Belle* had been well worth it.

While quickly plaiting her hair in a single braid, she imagined the happy look on her uncle's face when she handed over her winnings. If gambling kept up like it was, the *River Queen* could sail the Missouri for years to come.

She was smiling and tying the red-flowered belt through the loops of her pants when there came a vigorous pounding on her door.

She opened up with a grin on her face, ready to greet her visitor.

"Captain wants to see you in the pilothouse." Tom announced without his usual smile. "Like to know what you did to make him so out of sorts. We're all paying for it, so you know."

Generally, Uncle Patrick was a man of slow temper.

What in good glory could have happened?

She watched Tom stomp away without closing her door behind him.

Following him outside, she shut the door then climbed the stairs to the pilothouse two at a time.

"Uncle Patrick! Tom says you…oh, hello there Travis."

Uncle Patrick did look as glum as Tom described. He stood beside the wheel with his fist gripped tight on a polished spoke.

Odd that he didn't look up at her greeting. No…and neither did Travis.

That handsome fellow sat on the bench, his hands hanging between his knees while he stared at the high shine on the floorboards.

Something was wrong! Misfortune of some kind was about to rain down upon them. Sure did look like it had to do with Travis.

"Gosh almighty, Uncle Patrick, why the long face?"

Silence answered her question. Worry made her heart pound and her belly flip.

"Somebody sick?"

More silence.

"Dead?"

"We've located Eleanor," Travis finally said with a sidelong glance at her.

Blamed if that glum look didn't make her feel like she needed to run to the rail and vomit. His expression looked as miserable as hooves stuck in deep mud. Eyes that only yesterday shone bright green were the color of dull moss.

"She's dead?" Poor Travis! He would lose his ranch.

Travis shook his head.

With a nod, Uncle Patrick indicated that she should come closer to him.

Keeping one hand on the wheel, he circled her shoulder, tugging her close. His fingers bit to the bone.

Gosh almighty, his touch had never bit to the bone, even when he was in a temper.

"She's you."

"And you're the Queen of Sheba!" This was one grand joke that her uncle and Travis were playing, but she would go along, laugh out loud until they did too. "And I reckon Travis is your trained leopard."

She slapped her thigh, guffawed…but…something was still wrong. Humor had not brightened the desolate mood beating against the walls of the pilothouse.

The men were not laughing.

Travis stood up, shoved both hands in his britches pockets.

And just there, at the corner of Uncle Patrick's eye, a tear welled.

"When I went to bed last night, my name was Ivy… still was when I woke up this morning, far as I can tell." As much as she willed it not to, her voice quavered.

"Eleanor Ivy Magee," Uncle Patrick said, "is the name you were born with."

"You're making that up!" She gasped, but she couldn't imagine why he would. Unless—

"I reckon you're just wanting to get me married off to some rich fellow so I can't be a river pilot." Her voice was rising now…in anger, or panic, certainly denial.

She spun on Travis. "You can't just make up an heir. I'm not her!"

"Take out your necklace, the one your mama gave you." Uncle Patrick shoved his hand through his gray hair. "Read the back."

"I don't need to read it—I know what it says." She folded her arms over the ache in her belly. It was exactly thirteen stairs down and twenty-seven steps to the rail and a temporary relief. "Anyone can have a trinket with letters." Now she was grasping for solid ground and making no sense whatsoever.

She had always known the necklace was special. One of the memories she did have of her mother was of that necklace. She'd sit on Mama's lap and twist it in her chubby fingers.

"The ranch is yours," Travis murmured. The line of his jaw looked tight, tense. "All you need to do is claim it."

"You'll be secure, have the home and family you ought to have."

All of a sudden she could not feel her legs. She plopped down onto the bench. The hard wood slapped her bottom.

"I never wanted that, Uncle Patrick. You did."

"Maybe, but given that I raised you, I figure I have the right to determine what is best for your future."

"Gull-durn it, Uncle Patrick!" Yes, she did shout that. "If a home and family is all that grand, why didn't you marry?"

"My life was on the river. It would not have suited."

Suddenly her legs didn't feel weak anymore. Anger made them stiff and twitchy. She leapt up.

"So is mine!" She braced her feet apart, anchored her balled-up fists on her hips. "I'm of age. You can't force me to leave the *Queen*. You'd have to hog-tie me and—"

"I'm selling her."

Words of defiance, of independence died in her sagging jaw.

"You aren't! You love the *Queen*."

"No, Ivy, I love you. This grand life we've lived… it's dying. Captain Cooper of the *River Belle* has made me an offer. At this point in my life I'd be a fool to turn it down."

"You can't sell her. She's our home."

He shook his head. The sorrow in his expression crushed her heart. He loved this boat as much as she did.

"Mr. Murphy will take you back to your ranch. You'll marry and give me lots of grandbabies. You'll be surprised at how good your life will be."

"I'm piloting a boat. Maybe not this one...but I'll do it. Just you wait and see!"

She sounded like a twelve-year-old not getting her way; she knew that but could do nothing to act otherwise.

Uncle Patrick turned his back on her. Gripped the wheel he cherished in both fists.

"Be ready to travel at sunrise," he stated.

She'd be ready to travel all right, but not to the Lucky Clover Ranch.

She spun about, nailed Travis Murphy with a glare.

"Why you low-down—" She caught her breath at the brokenness of his expression. "I thought you were my friend."

"I never meant to hurt you, Ivy. I didn't know who you were."

She lifted the necklace from her throat and shoved it at Travis's balled-up fist. It tinkled when it hit the floor.

While it hurt like a hornet's sting to give up the remembrance of her mother, the past was the past and she was headed to a future of her own making.

What Ivy needed was time, Travis decided. Time to think things through. That's why he didn't go after her when she ran out of the pilothouse yesterday afternoon.

That's why he'd spent fifteen minutes knocking on her door this morning only to discover that she had fled in the night.

Just when he thought his problem had been solved, he found himself chasing the heir to the Lucky Clover all over again...and rain was on the way.

Travis rode alongside the river, guessing that's the way Ivy had gone. The Missouri was her comfort and chances were that's where she would seek solace.

"I reckon if she's set on piloting a boat, she'll be looking for work on one," he explained to the horse. It made sense, when he said it out loud.

Late in the afternoon he came upon a small paddle wheeler docked at the river's edge. When he asked about Ivy, he discovered she'd been there.

It irked him that the men were still laughing at her... at a woman thinking she could do a man's job.

But it worried him too. Ivy had been sheltered, had grown up under the protection of her uncle and the men on the *River Queen*. She didn't know the dangers that could befall a woman alone. Sooner or later she would come upon a man who wouldn't be laughing.

At twilight, the rain began to fall. He reckoned he ought to seek shelter, but he'd rather be wet than sit inside warm and dry, worrying about her.

Could be he was a fool and she was the one who had taken shelter, the one who was warm and dry.

"Well, hell," he muttered, riding past an inn whose welcoming fire glowed through the big parlor window.

She might have taken shelter there, but he doubted it, given that she had left a note with her uncle, giving him all of her money and begging him to take it and not to sell the *Queen*.

In Travis's opinion, money had nothing to do with the sale. Patrick Malone, captain, pilot and owner of the *River Queen*, would be well set financially. But the man understood that the river life was taking its last gasp. He wouldn't want his niece wasting her future on it.

Travis took off his hat, shook out the water gathering in the brim. His coat was not yet soaked through, but it soon would be.

If Ivy hadn't taken a room at the inn, she couldn't be far ahead of him, given that she was on foot.

He'd ride another hour before he sought shelter.

As luck would have it, fifteen minutes later, he spotted a campfire among the trees. He tethered his mount to a bush beside the river, then walked fifty feet through the woods toward the fire.

Ivy sat with her back toward him, huddling under the shelter of a tarp that she had strung across some branches. She must have heard him crunching across twigs and fallen leaves, because she turned her head, glanced at him then back at the flames.

"I'm sorry," he murmured.

"I reckon I was harsh on you. This isn't your doing."

It felt to him like it was all his doing.

Maybe he should go home and try once again to convince William English to marry Agatha instead. She was a Magee, just as Ivy was.

But Agatha was not the heir. She was an invalid and not the sort of woman the neighbor needed to promote his political career.

"I'll take your word that she is a lovely person, Travis," William had argued the last time Travis suggested Agatha instead of Ivy. "But as far as I can tell, she never comes out from the shadow of her balcony. The couple of times I've seen her she just sits in her chair watching the world go by. There is no spark of animation in her. I need a woman who is genteel, gracious—ready to get out among the people, shake hands and win votes."

And have children. It was William's firm belief that a man without children was unelectable. All of Travis's arguments ended there. No one would expect Agatha to fulfill that demand.

"There's an inn a ways back," he said, crouching beside her. "It'll be warm and dry. We can talk."

"I'm dry enough where I am." She looked at him then. "But you aren't…if I were you I'd scoot closer to the fire."

"All right, I reckon we can talk here. But if you start to shiver, I'm hauling you back to the inn whether you want to go or not."

She glanced at the dreary sky and shook her head.

"Did my uncle change his mind about selling the *Queen*?" Her eyes seemed red and swollen. It cut him to the quick to know she'd been weeping. "I reckon he was threatening to sell in order to get me to leave with you."

"I'm sorry, Ivy. He went to the captain of the *Belle* this morning…they made an agreement, shook hands on it."

Rain tapped on the tarp. Ivy drew her knees to her chest and hid her face. When she looked up a single tear rolled over the curve of her cheek.

"The *Queen* is his life." She wiped her sleeve across her face. "Can't imagine what he'll do now."

"Look, Ivy, I spent a long time talking to your uncle the other night. The boat is not his life…you are. The decision he made, it was because it was best for you."

"That's not for anyone but me to decide."

"As right as that sounds, sometimes life decides for us."

She reached across the distance separating them and squeezed his hand briefly. Maybe she forgave him…a little bit anyway.

"Reckon you didn't feel so in control of life when your folks died and left you alone."

"I wanted to crawl in the grave with my ma and pa." Even now it was hard to think about the desolation he'd felt. "But your father was there with his big hand on my shoulder. After a while I was glad to be alive after all."

"Well, ain't I a sniveling ninny?" She straightened her shoulders, flashed him an unreadable glance then wriggled her fingers at the flames. "Boohooing like a spoiled child."

"Not a spoiled child, Ivy. The life you wanted has just been taken from you. You've a right to your grief."

"I tried to get a job on a boat, got laughed at all the way back to shore…and all because I was a woman."

"I know…I spoke with the crew. I believe you could put their skills to shame seven days a week—I reckon that's what scares them…having a woman do a better job would shame them. It's easier to hide behind laughter."

"Sounds like you know something about that."

"Your father raised me like I was his son. There were some early on who thought I got my position because of it. Thought my job ought to have been theirs."

"I bet you worked twice as hard just to prove them wrong."

"And you know something about that."

She nodded, gazing quietly at the fire.

"I have a sister?" she murmured at last. "I ought to have known it…the way I always felt a part of me was missing. Sort of like, a person standing in the sunshine and not seeing her shadow…if that makes any sense. All those years I thought it was just dreams and child's play because I wanted a sister so badly. Now I know all along I was missing Agatha."

Ivy's hat lay beside the fire, she turned it so that the pouch was away from the heat.

"Even hearing her name…it doesn't sound like a stranger's name. Uncle Patrick should have told me."

"Right now, I guess he wishes he had. But all he ever wanted was to protect you and honor his sister's last wish for him to be the one to raise you."

"Don't see why he couldn't have done both," she grumbled then sighed deeply. "Can't see the harm in telling the truth."

"At first, when your parents divorced, there were plenty of hard feelings. Your father wouldn't let your mother take both of his girls. Your uncle says that your mother was afraid that if your father knew where you were, he'd take you back. He had the money and the power to do it. It was your mother's dying wish that Patrick raise you…so he kept your past a secret from you and everyone else."

"All I ever knew was that my pa was a good man, a rancher who died young. How is it that you know so much when the only thing I know is a bald lie?"

"Like I said, your uncle and I talked for a long time. Everything he did was out of love for you. Even selling the boat. He didn't come to his decision to do it without a lot of thought. I told him all about the ranch and about William English."

"Who's that?" she asked, her expression suddenly wary.

"The man who hopes to marry you." There was no point in denying it.

"Gull-durned fellow, doesn't know a whit about me!"

No he did not…and when he did, would the deal be off? William was expecting a high society bride, one of impeccable manners to charm voters and help accomplish his political ambitions.

Travis's stomach felt hollow at the thought. Ivy was not the type of bride English was expecting.

In the end, it might not matter since there was every chance that Ivy would refuse to come with him.

"I got any other relations I don't know about?"

"Only Agatha, but the folks at the ranch, they all feel like family."

"Tell me about them, might help if I know."

Help what? Her decision, he hoped.

"It's like we're a big family…there's a lot of people involved in running the ranch. In the house we have Maria, she's the head cook. Then there's the girls who work under her, mostly the daughters of the hands. There's Rebecca, the housekeeper who keeps things neat and tidy with her crew of girls. There's Master Raymond, the schoolteacher for the children…the adults too, when things slow down for the winter. There's Hilda Brunne, Agatha's nurse. We've got cowboys, most with families and we have caretakers who keep the ranch in running order. Arthur runs the stable along with the three boys he's training. Wouldn't want to forget Elise, she does the household laundry. We'd be ripe smelling without her, then—"

"I think I'm getting dizzy. That's a lot of folks. Reminds me of the *Queen* with everyone having a part to do."

"It's a lot like that, but on the land not the water."

"Got any rivers for swimming on all that land?"

He hated to dash the hope suddenly lighting her eyes, but, "There's water, we call it a river, but it's not anything like your Missouri."

"Don't reckon it's my Missouri anymore." She picked

up a stone beside her foot, tossed it into the fire. "Tell me more about Agatha."

"Your uncle says it broke your mother's spirit when she had to leave Agatha behind. Later on, your father told me he loved your mother, for all that they didn't suit. It wasn't for spite that he kept Agatha, but through her he hoped to keep part of his wife.

"I never met your mother. The two of you were gone when Foster took me in. From what he's always told me about her, I reckon you take after her."

"I don't recall much about Mama, just flashes of memory…a picture here and an image there. I want to know about my sister. What is she like?"

"She's something of a recluse…and shy. Not much for conversation. I've tried to engage her but she's just not interested in much of anything…especially lately."

"Was she always withdrawn?"

"When I was a boy, I never paid attention, really. She was just a little girl and I had my own growing to do. But I do recall one day asking your pa if she could ride with me. He said she was sickly and he would not risk her health for a bit of fun. Mrs. Brunne, her nurse, agreed with him. A few years ago, Agatha nearly died of a fever. It left your father shaken and even more protective than he had been. According to Mrs. Brunne, she became unable to walk. The things she likes are reading and sitting on her balcony."

"Gosh almighty, I know something about fevers, but I never heard of one leaving a person lame."

Ivy stared at the flames without speaking. Rain tapped on the tarp. Travis's heart beat triple time because he figured Ivy was going over what he had told her—possibly making up her mind about things.

"Unless I agree to go with you to marry that man…"

Ivy's voice was barely above a whisper. It almost seemed as though she was talking to herself. "...the ranch will be lost and my helpless sister will have no home."

Travis nodded his head. Losing the ranch would be hard on everyone but it would be especially ruinous for frail Agatha.

"I can't rightly say I want to get married, especially to some stranger." Ivy gazed over at him, her eyes narrowed. "Can't quite figure why he'd want to marry me either. Maybe he'll just give you a friendly loan, being neighbors and all."

"He needs the ranch. He's running for territorial legislature of Wyoming so being the owner of respected property will buy him votes."

"Gosh almighty," she murmured then gazed out at the rain dripping from the tree branches all around.

"All day long I've been walking and thinking, thinking and walking, my head all abuzz...and, Travis, I want to be with my sister."

His heartbeat raced, he began to sweat even though he was cold.

"And I sure don't want the two of us living in a tent beside the road." She took a deep breath, let it out slowly. "Looks like you've got yourself an heir, Travis Murphy. As long as I can bring my mouse."

He hugged her quick and hard, couldn't help it. "Bring a dozen if you want to!"

"One's trouble enough."

"Let's go back to the inn. It's not far."

"Your horse would appreciate it. Poor thing's getting soaked."

He stood, placed her hat on her head then gathered up the tarp.

"You won't be sorry, Ivy. I swear on my life you won't be."

"I'll ask one thing." She touched his arm. He liked the feel of her fingers there. He liked the way her eyes looked extra blue with raindrops spattered on her lashes. "Will you take me back to the *River Queen*? I need to make peace with my uncle. I promise I won't carry on and beg to stay. Just… I need to say my goodbyes."

"I'll do anything, Ivy…anything you ask."

Whatever was in his power, he would do it.

She'd vowed not to wail and carry on, but the promise was proving hard to keep.

"Goodbye, Tom," she said. Tom was the last of the crew she embraced in a hug. She held on a little longer than the boy might be comfortable with, but there was still one person to bid farewell to and she was putting it off.

Uncle Patrick. She was not sure she could do it.

The weakling in her wanted to run away and wave goodbye from a distance.

The one and only way she would be able to manage was to remember that this was what he wanted for her. What he wanted so badly that he was willing to give up what he loved the most…all right, what he loved nearly the most.

It had taken some time, and some talking with Travis on the way back to the *River Queen*, to be able to accept it because the way she had first looked at things, the selling of the *Queen* was a betrayal.

Ivy had always considered the boat to be her legacy… but maybe something else was her legacy instead.

Something big and vast. Acres upon acres of land.

To hear Travis go on about it, the whole time his voice filled with wonder.

And it was all hers until she married. Then, she reckoned, it would belong to her husband. That didn't set well.

A husband could do what he wanted where his wife was concerned. If he decided that she and Agatha ought to live in the barn he had the power to send them there.

Gull-durn it, that was a worry for another time. In this moment she had her heart full of saying goodbye.

Standing on the main deck, she looked up to see her uncle gazing down at her. He pushed away from the rail then began his descent down the steps. She listened to his footsteps, picturing where he was by the creak that each board made. Every sound this vessel uttered was carved on her heart.

She strained to hear because it was like the boat was talking to her, saying its own goodbye.

Travis stood on the shore with a pair of horses. All her worldly goods, which were not many, had been stuffed into the saddle packs.

Travis waved. She nodded back.

Too soon, Uncle Patrick was there, holding his arms wide for her to rush into them.

His embrace swallowed her, was nearly her undoing, but she held together, remembering that she was going to Agatha.

She wanted to say that she forgave him for keeping the secret of her past but her throat was too tight for words.

"I love you, Uncle Patrick," she managed to whisper against his chest.

"And I love you, my brave little love." He set her at arm's length but didn't let go. "This is for the best."

She nodded because her voice might betray her and she did not want him to think she believed otherwise.

"What will you do, uncle?"

At least Ivy was headed to a new future...whatever it ended up being. For Uncle Patrick, he'd never lived any place but on the water.

"I'll think of something." He patted her head and smiled. "Now that I'll be a landlubber, maybe I'll get married."

"That would be fine."

"I've got something for you, Ivy." He dug into his pocket. "Well, two things."

He slipped her mother's pendant about her neck. She reached up, closed it in her fist. It felt right to have the memento back where it belonged.

"And here." He pressed an envelope into her hand. "It's money. This marriage is a good thing—I want that for you—but a woman should have something of her own, in case of hard times. Your groom doesn't even have to know about these funds. Travis has agreed to store them for you should you need them...which I don't think you will, given that your intended is well-off."

Uncle Patrick stared at her for a long moment. She reckoned he was memorizing her face, same as she was his.

Slowly, he turned her about, his hands firm on her shoulders.

"Off with you now," he said. "Go with your young man and claim your future."

She wished Travis was her young man, she'd feel a sight more comfortable about this whole thing if he was. Travis was at least a friend, instead of a stranger.

Silently, she nodded then walked over the gangplank

toward the unknown, pausing for only an instant to feel the aged wood rocking under her feet.

"Goodbye, you wonderful river," she whispered.

Then Travis was there, offering his hand. She took it and stepped ashore.

Chapter Four

Ivy stopped on the gangplank. Her hesitation was slight, barely more than a couple of heartbeats, but in that second Travis felt the future balance on a razor's edge.

If she changed her mind—and no one would blame her for it if she did—the lives of those he loved would be damaged forever.

But then she came to him, taking the hand he offered, but more than that…accepting the future he offered.

"I bought you a horse," he said, stating the obvious because he did not know what else was appropriate to say. "But back at the ranch you own a hundred more."

Ivy narrowed her eyes at the pretty little mare that he had purchased. The horse was guaranteed to be gentle. He believed it; friendliness shone from her soft brown eyes.

"You want me to get up on that thing?"

"I thought you liked horses."

This might be a setback. It would be Christmas before they got home if they had to walk to Wyoming.

"I do. I like them fine. I was talking about the saddle. Never been on one before."

"You've never ridden?"

"Not much call to on a boat deck."

"I reckon we can lead them for a mile or two, then when you're comfortable, I'll show you what to do."

"Could take a lot of leading," she admitted.

"I know this is all so strange to you."

She nodded. "It feels like I'm going to live on the moon."

"You'll grow to like it. Everyone will welcome you like you are a queen."

"I never aspired to be a queen…not even a princess."

"I only meant that they will be forever grateful."

Ivy stroked the mare's nose, whispered something to her that he could not hear.

"Uncle Patrick is watching from the hurricane deck," she said with a backward glance. "I reckon it would make it easier for him to see me riding. That will make him think that I'll be all right."

"You will be all right, better than all right."

"Easy for you to say, my friend. You aren't the one marrying a stranger."

"Let's take this thing step by little step. Starting with learning to ride."

She took a breath, patted the pouch on her hat. "Sure is a long way up there."

"Nice view of things once you settle in, though."

"How do I go about settling in?"

The easiest way to get her on the horse would be to put his hands on her rear and hoist her up. But Patrick Malone was watching and Ivy's rump was—

He had to look away quick. The heir was not meant for him. He'd better not let ruinous thoughts creep into his mind. Better to cut them off at the beginning before they got out of control.

Making a cup out of his joined hands, he indicated

with a nod that she should put one foot in the cradle of his hand. "Hold on to the saddle horn and hoist your-self over."

"Here I go. Make sure you catch me if I start to topple over the other side."

"I won't let that happen."

But what did happen was that in rising, the ample curve of her breast, clad only in worn flannel, passed within an inch of his nose.

His heart thumped harder. He would not let that hap-pen either. She had called him friend and so he would remain.

Anything more and he might just as well not have ripped her from the life she loved.

Although, as ripped as she no doubt felt, she had made the decision to go with him of her own free will. Yes, it had been aided by the sale of the boat, but still, no one had forced her.

"You look fine up there, Ivy." He smiled up at her then mounted his horse. "You'll make a good horsewoman."

She turned in the saddle, waved to her uncle and gave him a big smile. "That's a bit hopeful. Critter hasn't even moved and I feel like I'm going to lose my breakfast."

"You won't." He urged his horse forward and the mare followed. "All you have to do is hold on—your sweet girl will trail after my horse."

"I'm putting my trust in you, Travis."

Somehow, that simple statement made him want to deliver her back to her uncle. Her life was about to be spun about in a twister. Riding a horse instead of a ship was the least of what was to come.

But for now, she meant that she was trusting him to teach her to ride. "The rocking of her gait isn't so different from the rocking of a ship. See how she rolls just like a deck."

"If I fall off the deck, I'll hit water. I fall off this saddle it's hard ground."

"This new life will be strange for a while," he said, glancing behind and seeing that the *River Queen* had disappeared from view. "I'm here, Ivy, you don't need to worry."

Ivy was worried.

No longer worried about falling out of the saddle, but on this second night camping outside, she wondered if she would ever sleep again.

The land, while not quite silent, was lacking in the comfort of human sounds. With the exception of Travis's deep, even breathing, that is. The man slept like a baby in his mama's arms.

At home on the *Queen*, Ivy had been lulled to sleep by the gentle rocking of the boat and the knowledge that someone was always awake and keeping watch. She would stir in the night to hear footsteps going past her door, then whispered voices as the watch changed hands.

Out here there were rustling critters in bushes, owls and bats overhead...worst of all were the howls of coyotes and wolves moaning over the land.

She sat up suddenly from her bedroll, too aware that there were no walls, no buffer of water between her and them.

"Travis?" she called. He lay stretched out, relaxed, on the far side of the fire.

He lifted his hat from his face to...yes, to glare at her. But, gull-durn it, it wasn't her fault that the wolf sounded closer and bigger than it had five minutes ago.

"That wolf's getting closer. Little Mouse is nervous about it."

"Not a wolf, a coyote, and it won't come near the fire."

He'd assured her of that three times in the past few hours, but in her opinion, it did sound closer.

"She's also cold. She's used to being in my room all warm and cozy." Truthfully, the mouse was probably toasty inside her pouch. It was Ivy who was cold.

And sore. Every time she felt a mite comfortable trying to rest on the ground, her muscles would begin to ache. One couldn't spend all day in the saddle without paying a price.

All right, Travis could, she would have to admit. But as much as he assured her that her aches would go away, she didn't believe it…not any more than she believed this little fire would keep a pack of hungry predators at bay.

Travis sat up, rubbed his hand over his face. Then with a groan, he reached for the woodpile and tossed two logs on the fire. Sparks crackled toward the treetops.

"That better?"

"Warmer," she admitted. "But it seems to me that it sends a big signal, letting those hungry critters know where we are."

"They already know it. Have you gotten any sleep at all?" he asked in a gruff, accusing voice.

She shook her head. Maybe it would help if she loosened her braid like she did at home.

Untying the leather thong, she shook her head then ran her fingers through the messy hank. She had a brush but it was in her saddle pack and that was at the edge of the small clearing where the firelight did not reach. She was not going over there for anything.

"How long 'til daylight, I wonder?" Not that it would be such a relief since she would then be required to get back in the saddle. A whole new collection of aches and pains would cramp her muscles and make her bones hurt.

"Four hours," he said, seeming certain about that even though there was no watchman calling out the hour to the pilot.

"I'm sorry for sounding sharp." He got up from his side of the fire and came to hers. He sat down a friendly distance away.

Funny how she wished he'd move even closer. He was large enough to give off a wave of warmth.

"After a while, you'll get used to this." He indicated the dark beyond the fire's reach.

"If that's so, why'd you bring your gun over here?"

"It's for the two-legged varmints."

"Folks?"

"Ivy, haven't you ever run across someone who wanted to harm you?"

"Reckon I might have, but my uncle and the roustabouts were always nearby."

He set the gun down between them. Maybe he figured if a two-legged marauder did invade their camp, she would help by picking up the side arm and dispatching the troublemaker in a single shot. He would not be reassured to know that Uncle Patrick did not hold with guns aboard the *Queen*. She was as likely to shoot Travis as the invader.

Since she felt as helpless in her new world as a bald baby, she didn't tell him this.

"I've been wondering," Travis said, sounding conversational.

If conversation would keep him awake and on her side of the fire she'd speak everything that came across her mind.

Beginning with, "So have I. Will my…that is, well,

my husband…will he mind sharing his home with Little Mouse?" Not that it mattered in the end. She had kept her existence a secret from Uncle Patrick; she could as easily keep her a secret from…what was his name? Waldo, Wilfred? Winston? Gosh almighty! She'd been so caught up in everything she'd plum forgot her intended's name.

"What made you decide to come with me? To take on all this?" Travis asked, ignoring the interruption of her nonsense question. "You might have refused…left us to deal with things on our own?"

"Uncle Patrick sold the boat. I no longer had a home."

"That wasn't all of it." He looked at her, clearly searching behind her eyes for the true answer.

"Agatha, of course." She was the one and only reason.

At the end of all this was the person she had been longing for all her life. The one she had thought was a dream, an imaginary friend. No longer a hazy desire. Agatha was a flesh-and-bone sister. She had stepped out of the mist and become family.

And with the new bond Ivy would find—or rediscover maybe—love. The fact that she had no solid memories of Agatha did not take away from the new emotion Ivy felt for her.

"No one else would have been able to make me leave my uncle, no matter how much a landlubber he becomes after the *Queen*."

"All of us on the Lucky Clover are beholden to you."

"I don't mean to sound ungrateful, but I reckon if it weren't for my sister I wouldn't be here." Gull-durn it, she did sound ungrateful. Mighty ungrateful when he'd offered her something that most women never even dreamed of. "I'll do my best not to let you down."

"I don't see how you could," he said.

"I could take one look at my groom and run like a Sunday Chicken."

"William English is a handsome man."

William…she'd do her durndest to remember it next time.

"I don't know a thing about running a ranch."

"You won't need to. That's my job."

"But I want to. If it's really mine, I won't sit about as useless as a feathered hat."

"You don't like pretty feathered hats? Most ladies do."

"Why I'd feel sorry for the bird those feathers first belonged to every time I put it on. Besides, they'd tickle my neck. I tell you, Travis, when it comes to their appearance, ladies can be as foolish as peacocks. Struttin' around in their finery with nary a care for comfort. Downright traps is what those feathers and lace are."

Travis made a noise under his breath. Sure wasn't a happy sound. More like a curse but without the word formed.

He crawled back to his side of the fire, stretched out then covered his face with his hat.

"Don't know why you're so prickly, Travis Murphy. You don't have to wear them."

He grunted again, then pretended to be asleep.

She was not mistaken that the wolf pack—and she was gull-durned certain they were not coyotes—had come closer. Since Travis had taken his gun and stored it under his saddle, she hoped he was right about the fire keeping them away.

"Sure do hope this ranch house you're taking me to has four solid walls," she grumbled.

For some reason, that made Travis chuckle in his false sleep. She was relieved to hear the sound.

* * *

Travis knelt beside the kindling he had stacked for the night's campfire. He paused in igniting the match to watch Ivy wading in the knee-deep stream.

Her pant legs were rolled up to her thighs. Her braid dangled over her shoulder as she bent at the waist, peering into the water. Little Mouse clung to the collar of her shirt, peering at the water as intently as Ivy was.

She had promised fresh fish for supper. Without fishing gear he couldn't figure how she'd manage it.

No doubt they would end up eating jerky and hardtack again tonight. But for now he was enjoying watching her try to catch a fish. She moved gracefully through the rushing stream, sometimes standing as still as an egret before she glided a few more steps.

Behind her, the land rolled away to the horizon where the setting sun streaked the clouds in brilliant orange. He'd rarely seen a prettier, more dramatic vista.

This incredible, once-a-year sunset was the perfect backdrop for a once-in-a-lifetime woman.

The scene before him was one that he would always cherish, no matter where his life took him…or hers took her.

Once in a while there were moments out of time that one could only embrace.

But a second later, the thought of where Ivy's life was about to take her suddenly turned his stomach sour.

In the beginning, when he had begun his search for Eleanor, he'd given her future no more than a passing concern. Any woman would certainly want what he was offering: land, wealth and a prominent husband.

Women all over the state would envy Ivy.

All of a sudden he could not look at her. He lit the

kindling and added three small logs, watching while the sparks caught and the tiny flames reached for wood.

He was beginning to fear that she was the one woman who would not want what he offered.

She wanted her sister, yes. But the rest?

Hearing water splash and Ivy laugh, he looked up.

"Got us a big fat one, Travis!" She held up her catch, waving it victoriously in her fists. Little Mouse slipped but caught Ivy's shirt with four pink paws and scrambled inside her breast pocket. "Want one more?"

"That one's big enough for three!" he called back.

For a moment, he tried to picture her in a frilly dress nipped tight at the waist like the ladies wore them. She would look lovely. There was no denying it. But would it make her happy?

From what she'd had to say about fashion so far, he doubted it.

All he could hope for was that she would learn to be comfortable with it. The future of everyone at the Lucky Clover depended upon her being willing to become elegant.

"Heat up the pan while I gut this critter," she said, standing beside him now, her calves and ankles spotted with water that sparkled on her skin with the final rays of the setting sun.

He glanced up at her; the satisfaction of catching dinner bare-handed made her blue eyes light up with pleasure. The mouse crept out of her pocket then crawled up her shirt to sit on her shoulder.

Was it even possible for Ivy to become elegant? Would she end up with a crushed spirit, the same as had happened to her mother?

There would be no divorce for Ivy, though. No second chance at life. William English was not a cruel man, but he was ambitious. His wife would be a reflection of him. Perfection would be required of her.

Given who he was, William would be a perfect husband, a match to his perfect wife, at least in the public eye.

If that did not turn out to be the case privately, William would never allow divorce to ruin the ideal image.

"Better get that pan going!" This time Ivy's voice came from beside the stream. "I'm so hungry I'd fight a bear for this fish!"

He watched her while he fetched the pan from his saddle pack.

Kneeling beside the water, she sliced the fish down the middle. Scooping out the innards, she tossed them into the stream.

They had spent thirteen nights on the road to Cheyenne. The first three had been sleepless misery, but not the last ten. In fact, night before last she had only woken him once, fearing that she heard a bear rustling in the shrubbery.

Which, she had. But the small brown critter had fled when Travis banged the fry pan and the kettle against each other.

"Gosh almighty, you're brave!" she'd declared, grinning at him in clear admiration.

Then she'd slept on his side of the fire the rest of the night without waking. But last night she'd slept on her own side of the fire.

Funny how he'd been the one to wake up, hoping the sounds in the night would be Ivy Magee coming to lie beside him again.

As much as he knew it was wrong to want that, he'd continued to toss about, seeing images of her in his mind and wondering if…wondering nothing. Unrestricted wondering would be a big mistake.

Watching her now while the pan heated, smiling with pride at her filleted fish, he knew it was a damn good thing that they would reach Cheyenne in two days.

That was when he would need to begin making a lady out of Miss Eleanor Ivy Magee. She wouldn't feel so friendly toward him then, and he might find it easier to resist her earthy charm.

There was no doubt that she was going to resist the restrictions on her dress and behavior. Looked at fairly, who was he to force them upon her?

Only the man fighting for the survival of the Lucky Clover and everyone on it.

He could only hope that after a time, she would come to see that this new life was for the best.

Given time, she would forget the ways of the river and embrace being a fine lady.

Curse it, that thought ought to put him at ease. All it did was turn his belly sour, keeping him from anticipating eating his share of that hand-caught fish.

Chapter Five

There were some things Ivy had gotten used to, even come to enjoy.

One thing was the sway of the horse's gait beneath her was no longer frightening. So far, she hadn't tumbled out of the saddle. She reckoned she wouldn't, now that she was better used to things. Besides, it really wasn't that far to the ground.

Another was—and this did surprise her—as long as Travis was close by, she was able to fall asleep beside the campfire. It didn't appear, after all, that she was going to be eaten by a wolf or torn to pieces by a marauding bear.

Also, the folks they had met along the way were as friendly as pie.

But gosh almighty, just when she'd begun to think she might get by living away from the wide and wonderful Missouri River, she'd set eyes on the South Platte.

"This ain't no river, Travis!" She'd stood at the bank, staring in dismay at the ribbon of brown cutting the land. "Why, a body couldn't even paddle a canoe down the middle of this mud puddle."

In her mind, a respectable river ought to gurgle and

ripple. It ought to be overhung with trees. For as far as she could see, those green beauties were scarce.

Land stretched out forever, unbroken by anything but the skyline of Cheyenne, which Travis had called the Magic City.

It was their destination today and even though they were still a couple of hours away, she could see tall buildings against the bright blue sky.

"This river is the life blood of your ranch," he explained. "It's what keeps your cattle watered."

He looked nervous. Could be he thought she might hightail and run, given how ugly things were compared to where she had come from.

Here she was, though, and she would have to make the best of things. In the end, it was her sister she'd come to be with and the sad state of the water didn't count for much by comparison.

Maybe she'd get used to looking up and seeing an ocean of rolling hills instead of a mountain range. As long as she had Agatha, she'd be happy enough.

But that was some miserable looking water.

"How's a body to swim in the natural?" She wagged her finger at the sluggishly flowing water.

Travis Murphy's jaw sagged. "Life is different now, Ivy. You just can't go freely around like you did before."

"I reckon I can if there's miles of land that's mine. I suppose I can do what I want to on it."

"Maybe." His frown set deep in his brow. "I guess I can send one of the help with you if you've got your heart set on bathing in the Platte."

"Help?" Her heart flipped over on itself.

"Hired women? Ladies who work in the house?"

"I hope I'm not supposed to be in charge of them." She'd never been in charge of anyone but Ivy Magee. "I wouldn't know the first thing about that. I reckon they know what to do fine all on their own."

"They do." Poor Travis looked more worried by the minute. "But they might need your opinion, or advice once in a while."

"Don't know that I can advise anyone who already knows what they're doing better than I do." This whole business troubled the daylights out of her.

Travis walked to the shoreline. He stood shoulder to shoulder with her, staring at the water slogging slowly past.

"I reckon you wish someone else was the heir." It bothered her to think that he did, but she couldn't blame him for it. "I'll do my best not to shame you."

"Shame? I'm so damn grateful for you, Ivy."

He turned to face her. Those lush green eyes all but made her weak in the knees. They reminded her of home...of the river and the trees. He tugged gently on her braid then let go so quickly that it was as if her hair had burned him.

"I'll teach you everything you need to know," he said.

"I'm plum obliged." She went up on her toes and kissed his cheek. "I reckon I never had a better friend."

Ivy had kissed his cheek at noon. Here it was three o'clock on a hustle-bustle street in Cheyenne and he still imagined the warm impression on his face.

If she considered him a good friend, she would not for much longer.

Life as she knew it was about to end and he was the one who was going to snuff it out.

"There's not a false storefront on the whole block." Ivy remarked about the city of Cheyenne, as they walked from the livery to the hotel. She looked like a little girl on her first visit to a candy store. Somehow he could not look away from the wonder quickening her expression. "It's like every one of these buildings is a palace."

It was clear why she might think so. Cheyenne was among the richest cities in the nation. Some were wealthy cattlemen, some were even titled Englishmen who spent summers in Wyoming and winters on their estates in England.

"You see that building up the street?"

Ivy nodded, her eyes round as full moons.

"That's the famous Cheyenne Club."

"I'll be snakebit! I might know a few of those gents from the *Queen*. Some of them come to gamble regularly." She started toward the building. "Let's stop in and say howdy-do."

He caught her arm, halting her step. She turned, her eyebrows arched, an inquisitive smile curving her lips— her very pretty lips, he was beginning to notice more and more.

"The wind's beginning to blow. I think we ought to get to the hotel." The last thing he wanted was for William English to encounter Ivy before she was ready.

"Maybe in these parts a breeze counts for wind." She snickered.

"It'll get worse."

A train whistle sounded in the distance. She clapped him on the shoulder. "Say! I've never seen a train before. Sure would like to."

Since the train station was in the opposite direction of the social club, he agreed. There was no point in not making her happy in as far as he could.

The trouble was, the closer they got to the train station the more people there were out strolling…and staring.

A woman who dressed as though she obeyed every

whim of fashion passed them by, clutching the arm of her rich gentleman.

The woman stopped, gawked openly at Ivy.

"Howdy-doo," Ivy greeted.

The woman gasped, swished her fancy skirt and hurried on her way.

"Must have got pinched by her corset." Ivy shrugged, not seeming to recognize the affront the "fine lady" had suffered at her greeting.

Anger frizzled up his spine. He tamped it down, reminding himself that one day soon, Ivy would be the envy of them all.

"You're right about the wind, Travis." She clamped her hat to her head. "Good thing Little Mouse is safe in her pouch, otherwise she might blow clean away."

The train whistle blew again when it pulled into the station. Big wheels screeched on iron rails. A cloud of steam blew away in the wind.

"That's a thing to behold," Ivy stated, the reverence in her tone speaking her awe. "Sure would like to ride it one day."

"From what I've heard, by August, the rails will go all the way to Coulson."

"Might be an easier way to visit Uncle Patrick."

A woman got off the train just then, her arms laden with baggage. A big gush of wind whooshed along the platform and she lost her balance.

Ivy, being only a couple of steps away, put a hand under her elbow, steadying her.

"Thank you, sir," the lady said, then hurried on her way.

"Sir?" Ivy laughed, slapped her knee. All at once her smile vanished. "Say…come to think of it, that ain't so funny."

She glanced down at her flannel shirt, her worn denims. Her dismay kicked him in the heart.

"You are a lovely woman, Ivy...never think otherwise." He meant that. The angst he felt for Ivy at the woman's comment cut him to the quick. "Women dress a bit different here in Cheyenne, that's all."

Another gust whipped the hat from Ivy's head, spun it end over end down the platform.

"Little Mouse!" Ivy cried.

Travis chased the hat down the platform, fearful that the tiny critter would not survive the jouncing.

He knew he wouldn't be in time to save it from falling over the edge. Only a foot from the drop to tragedy, a hand reached out and caught the tattered hat brim.

"Lose something, Murphy?" William English handed the hat to him, his smile polished but sincere. "Not your usual style."

"It belongs to a friend." His nod toward Ivy was brief. In fact, it could have been directed at any one of a dozen people.

"Good to see you back in town." William's glance passed over Ivy without really taking note of her. Funny how Travis felt insulted and relieved at the same time. "Did you find our heir?"

"I found her." Hopefully she was not walking this way.

He glanced back again to be sure. Another fashionable woman was staring rudely at Ivy. This time Ivy was frowning back.

"I'm anxious to meet her."

"Let's let her settle in a bit." Another glance over his shoulder verified that Ivy was coming his way. "We'll meet up later."

He hurried back with the hat, nudging the pouch and hoping to feel movement.

"I think she survived," he said.

"She's an agile little girl." Ivy opened the pouch. A white nose emerged, sniffing the air. "Who was the handsome fellow who saved her?"

"Me?"

"You're as handsome a hero as ever was, but who was it who grabbed the hat?"

"William English."

"*My* William English?"

"Same one."

"Blazin' day! Why didn't you say so? Let's go get acquainted." She turned to hurry after him, but Travis snagged her by her red-flowered belt.

"Not yet… I mean, it's getting windy and he's late for an appointment."

"Well, I wouldn't want him to miss it."

With wind now gusting through town like an insane banshee, folks were beginning to take shelter.

He got Ivy to the hotel with only a single rude stare cast at her—this one from a polished and well-buffed gentleman.

Only the fact that Ivy hadn't noticed kept him from punching the fellow's arrogant face.

Here in her grand hotel room, Ivy was passing the time more regally than the queen of England. Of that she hadn't a single doubt. Funny that Travis would spend so much money on the room when the ranch was in a bad way. Then again, it seemed her father had been all about impressing folks. Travis must be trying to hold the image together.

She wouldn't mind opening the window to gaze down

at the business going on down below. It would remind her of leaning on the rail of the *River Queen* and seeing life unfold.

The trouble was, there was not much business going on beneath her window. Travis had been right about the wind getting worse. She'd never seen such a blower.

Travis had the room next to hers. There was even a connecting door. That was a comfort since he was the only friend she had within four hundred miles.

For propriety's sake the door would remain locked, Travis had explained, but if she needed him she only had to knock three times and they could meet in the hall.

That all seemed a bunch of nonsense since they had slept by the same campfire for more than a week with the only wall between them a curtain of flames.

Sometimes, she thought, while fingering the lace curtain at the window, social rules made no sense. Not when it came to travel or to the manner in which a woman was required to dress.

Earlier today, those fancy ladies who had looked down upon her for her clothing had no idea that she enjoyed a kind of freedom they could not understand.

Outside, sand pelted the window. It had to be near sundown, but she couldn't tell for sure with the horizon being obscured.

She figured she still had an hour before dinner at the elegant place that Travis frequented.

"Little Mouse?" she called. "Where'd you get off to?"

The rodent's sweet white face poked out from under an embroidered pillow on the huge four-poster bed.

Ivy hopped up onto the mattress and held out her palm. "How's your little leg tonight?" The mouse crawled onto her hand. "That tumbling must have hurt something fierce."

Little Mouse had been injured when she was attacked by an owl a few months back. Ivy's makeshift splint had done the job, even though Ivy's only medical training had come from the books that Uncle Patrick kept in his office, but she did what she could, even when it was on a small scale.

Aboard the *Queen*, she had come to be known as the healer. She wasn't really, but when one of the crew needed patching up, they came to her. Anything beyond cuts, bruises and bumps, they would call on the nearest doctor.

"Well, my small friend, you seem to be exploring without a problem." Ivy set a square piece of cloth on the floor. "Don't forget to do your business here."

Ivy walked across the rug barefoot. Plush strands of wool tickled her toes.

"I reckon since dinner is at a high-class place, I should dress high-class. Sure did get a lot of funny looks this afternoon. Ladies would have been fainting all over the boardwalk if they knew you were riding in my hat."

She sat down at the desk where there was paper, pen and ink.

"It's a funny picture to imagine. Say...I ought to write to Uncle Patrick, let him know I got here fine and dandy. And that my intended is quite a handsome fellow. It ought to make him feel comforted since I reckon he's worried."

She began to scratch some words on the paper, but then remembered that she did not know where to send the letter. Her uncle did not know where he would be settling when they had bid each other goodbye.

She should not have left without knowing. Without her being aware that they had begun, tears dripped on the sheet of paper. How would she find him when she wanted to?

Little Mouse hopped onto the desk, lifted up on her hind feet and pawed the air, as if to dry Ivy's tears.

Scooping the mouse up, she pressed the warm furry body to her cheek.

"Only one way to see him again," she said to the mouse as though the critter understood. "…and that is to stay at the Lucky Clover where he knows I am at."

And to make the best of things while she did.

Dinner was in an hour. She would make sure and enjoy every bite.

She swiped her sleeve across her eyes, carried Little Mouse to her wood-and-wire cage, then she crossed the room to the huge and ornate wardrobe. Opening the grand doors, she lifted out her saddle pack.

"Suede pants…yellow shirt with a ruffle at the neck?" The ruffle was small, but it would itch.

Still, if she did not want to shame Travis in front of his friends, she would put on her finest clothes along with a smile.

She stood before a mirror that was taller than she was while she pulled on the pants, buttoned the shirt, then tugged on her boots.

"Something is missing." She tapped her finger on her lip, thinking. "That's it! When a lady is wearing a ruffle, a braid just won't do. She ought to let her hair fall free."

From the bottom of the saddle pack, she withdrew her hairbrush. "Now where's that fool ribbon?"

It was here when she'd packed all her worldly belongings. The satin strip was yellow, a near match in color to her shirt.

There it was! She drew it out, relieved that it was not too wrinkled.

She brushed her hair, watching in the mirror until it changed from dull to shining. At last, it caught the lamplight with a pretty glow, so she fastened it in the ribbon and made a bow of loops and whirls.

With her hands on her hips, she turned front to back, then back to front. She grinned at her reflection.

"No one will mistake me for a boy tonight."

There was a knock on her door.

She opened to Travis, spun about for his approval.

He held a large box in his arms, looking as nervous as a fellow raiding a beehive.

"What'd you bring me, a rattler?"

"Just something to wear to dinner."

Must not have noticed that she'd already put on her respectable best.

He set the box on the bed so gently that she wondered if he thought dynamite was inside.

"Go ahead." He pointed at the box. "Open your gift."

It did have a right pretty bow on it so she reckoned it was not going to bite or explode.

She lifted the lid.

Frilly tissue hid what the box contained. When she lifted it off, a pink gown winked up at her, the bodice covered in sparkly geegaws.

"I'll go to my room and wait while you put it on."

She poked at the two-inch lace trimming the collar. Did he want her to strangle?

"You'll be waiting a mighty long time, Travis Murphy." She crossed her arms over her chest. "As you can see, I'm already dressed for dinner in proper company."

"But Ivy, you can't wear pants. And your hair needs to be worn up. Haven't you ever eaten in an elegant dining room?"

"The *Queen* was gull-durned elegant. Fancy folks

dressed in all kinds of foolish finery just to dine. I had the good sense to eat with Tom."

"This is a high-class place. Please…put on the dress."

"If you're ashamed of how I look I'll go to dinner without you."

When he stared at her, lips drawn tight in silence, she crossed the room making her strides long and quick so that he would know she was hopping mad.

She flung the door open and walked into the hall.

A moment later she heard his boot steps coming behind her, as she'd hoped she would.

She knew enough about men to understand they were uncomfortable hurting a female's feelings. She reckoned Travis would do most anything to set things right.

"I'm sorry, Ivy, but…as lovely as I think you look, folks in Cheyenne won't think so."

"I don't reckon I'll like living among narrow-minded fools."

"They aren't narrow-minded. Did you know that women in Wyoming already have the right to vote?"

"What good is that when they don't have the right to dress sensible?"

"Ivy." He touched her elbow, stroked her upper arm with his thumb and sent strange tingles up it. "You've got to start looking like a lady if things are going to work out."

"You go put on that pink dress. I'll wager you can't eat without getting a bellyache."

He dropped his hand, shook his head.

"You're hungry, I'm hungry. I suppose we're both peevish. Let's have dinner."

"Don't worry, Travis." She walked beside him down the stairs. Good thing she wasn't wearing that dress or he'd be picking her up off the floor below. "Folks will come around. Why, I reckon someday ladies will get smart and wear pants in public every day. After a while, nobody will give a wink about it."

"Sure do wish someday was now," Travis mumbled under his breath as he led her outside.

Positioning his big muscular body just so, he shielded her from most of the dust and grit pelting them.

After hurrying the distance of one block, Travis opened the door of Porter's Steak House. When he closed the door, the howl of the wind was replaced with the sweet strains of a violin.

Gosh almighty, the hotel was elegant, but Porter's Steak House was exquisite. A crystal chandelier hung smack over her head. It cast delicate, fairylike lights on the ceiling and walls.

The polite murmur of diners filtered from the next room. She couldn't see them in all their fanciness past the wall blocking the dining room.

If the chandelier was something to gawk at, the wall was even more so. The whole thing was made of polished wood carved with a floor-to-ceiling depiction of a herd of cattle grazing on the plain.

"Good evening, Charles. Table for two, if you please," she heard Travis say while she watched a calf on the wall bawling for its mother. The image was so vivid she nearly heard the forlorn wail.

"Good evening, Mr. Murphy. It's good to see you back in town."

Ivy turned her attention to the man speaking, ready to give him a cordial greeting. Making friends in her new hometown was important.

It would please Travis to see her doing so.

Blazin' day! The fellow was frowning at her for no reason whatsoever.

"I'd like to, but we do have our standards." The man's gaze slid over her, smirking, finding her lacking from head to toe. Maybe she ought to have spit shined her boots.

"The lady and I will sit at my usual table." Travis said as if the snobbish Charles had not spoken.

"When you are with a lady, I will happily seat you."

Ivy's cheeks flamed. She pressed her fingers to them to see if they were actually burning.

"Come, miss. I'll escort you outside so that the gentleman can enjoy his meal."

Charles grasped her elbow. Roughly, he propelled her toward the door.

Travis's arm shot out. He clamped Charles on the shoulder, spun him about then punched him in the face.

The doorman crumpled to the floor. Blood spurted from his nose.

"I think you broke it. Looks a mite crooked." Ivy knelt beside the unconscious man.

"Let's go," Travis said, his voice sharp. He sure didn't sound like her congenial traveling partner.

"I'll just…" She felt the bridge of Charles's nose. A tweak would set it straight again. "There, good as new. He'll never know what happened."

With a hand under her elbow, Travis lifted her from the doorman's side. His touch was gentler than his tone.

"If he doesn't, I'll damn remind him."

He hurried her outside, once again protecting her from the sandstorm with his body.

Chapter Six

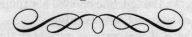

An hour later Ivy sat smack in the middle of the huge bed feeling an overwhelming urge to weep.

It took some time to understand why. She'd had to sift through so many emotions to get to the reason. Home-sickness for one, then add to that the shame of being treated so rudely.

The revulsion of a stranger forcing his hand upon her, trying to make her go somewhere against her will—that was what constricted her throat and made tears press against her eyes.

All of those emotions spun her about. But she could not deny an overwhelming gratitude to Travis for being there to defend her.

And after she had been so stubborn! So foolish! He had been so right about what she ought to have worn and she had been so wrong.

Even given her mistaken judgment of how things were, Travis had defended her. Funny how that made her heart feel all fluttery.

It was for his sake that she had taken a moment to set Charles's nose. She didn't know if there would be re-percussions from what had happened, but at least folks would not be constantly reminded about it by the doorman's disfigurement.

A knock tapped on her door. She opened to Travis.

"You as hungry as I am?" he asked, coming in and closing the door behind him.

He crossed the room and set a tray on the bed.

She swallowed her bout of self-pity and discovered that, "I could eat a cow."

"Good thing there's plenty of steak in these parts."

"You went back there to get dinner?" She hoped not, if only for no more reason than the wind had grown fiercer in the last half hour.

"The hotel's got a kitchen. The food is decent, if not as fancy as Porter's."

"I reckon I don't have a fancy for fancy."

"I'm sorry for what happened, Ivy. Charles has always been a snob, seeing himself better than he is."

"It's my own fault…thinking everyone should fall into line with what I want." The pink dress, spread across a chair in the corner of the room glared at her in accusation. "Or don't want."

She thought that Travis was going to uncover the food, but instead, he reached over the tray to put his arms about her.

"None of this is your fault, honey." She felt his beard stubble against her cheek, felt one big hand cup the back of her head. "Not a bit of it."

He pulled away, but the scent of his skin lingered on her face. She inhaled deeply.

"I should have listened to you, Travis. I worry about what will happen once that man spreads his story."

"A punch in the nose in defense of a lady is acceptable. The shame is on him. It's unlikely that he'll talk much about it."

"That is a relief." It was but…did he really think—
"Do you think I'm a lady?"

"A fine lady, Ivy. Don't let anyone make you believe otherwise."

"That woman at the station thought I was a man."

"If you'll allow me to help, I promise that will not happen again."

Help by stuffing her in gowns, did he mean? She stared at him silently for a time.

Briefly, he squeezed her hand.

"Eat up, we've got steak, mashed potatoes, some kind of fancy bread. And…that?" he said.

She shook her head. "That" was something bluish in color, with veins in it, drowning in an orange sort of sauce. She'd never seen the like before.

"I don't know what it is…don't know what a lot of things are."

"What is it you need to know?"

"I understand that I've got to marry the neighbor, save the ranch and everyone on it. But what I don't know is what's wrong with the place that it's in such a scrape?" She stabbed a piece of beef with her knife then pointed it at him. "How can a simple river gal possibly bring Mr. English?"

"I reckon you should have known it all from the beginning, before you made your choice." He set the piece of bread that he had been about to take a big bite of back on his plate.

Wind rattled the windows, sand pinged against them. He jerked his hand through his hair, stared at the floor then at her.

"I didn't tell you the whole of it because I thought if you knew, you wouldn't come."

"What is the whole of it?" As hungry as she was, she

set her plate aside. "Gosh almighty, Travis, did you think I'd abandon Agatha?"

"I know now you wouldn't have." He picked up her hand, rubbed his fingers across her knuckles. "The reason the ranch is in trouble is that your father took out a note on it. There was a drought a couple of summers ago. We lost a lot of cattle. Restocking cost more money than he had. So he borrowed from the bank and bought a bunch of the sweetest cows around.

"The trouble was, the following winter was a hard one. We lost most of the herd. Now, without them, we don't have the money to repay the loan. Your father thought a marriage to William would get us past that debt. When William agreed, your father changed his will, leaving Agatha out and giving it all to you."

"Seems a cold thing to do to her. She's been his daughter all along. He never knew me."

"It might seem a cold thing. I thought so too at first, but really, it was the only way he could see to protect Agatha."

That made as much sense as a fish walking on land.

"So, the ranch has an heir, William English will have a bride, but what I can't figure is why he wants me. What do I have to offer him?"

"Respect."

"You funnin' me, Travis?" She grabbed the bread off her plate and bit off a hunk. "I'm a mite shy of being respectable by this town's standards."

"I told you he wants to be elected to the territorial legislature, but that's not all. He's got his eye on being governor of Wyoming once we become a state. That's a long time off, but English is an ambitious man. He figures if he doesn't set his course early on, he won't get where he wants to go.

"While he's got money, he's also fairly new to Cheyenne. If he wants votes he's got to win over the folks who have been here all their lives. The Lucky Clover is an old established ranch—it's got a lot of prestige. Like I told you back on the *River Queen*, the ranch is one of the biggest in Laramie County. If he's got the Magee name behind him, it will guarantee votes."

"Why didn't he just marry Agatha? Would have made things simpler."

"Your sister isn't fit for the life he's aiming for. All that rigorous socializing would be too much for her. Hilda Brunne believes it's risky for her to go outside, or even leave her room."

A finger of heat nipped at Ivy's temper. Any fool knew that the great outdoors was good for the constitution.

"We'll see about that," she muttered but with bread in her mouth so she was pretty sure the statement had been garbled beyond recognition. She swallowed. "How much authority as heir do I have?"

"It's your ranch. You make all the decisions."

"Gosh almighty, I don't know a thing about ranching. You won't quit on me, will you? I just want the say-so when it comes to Agatha."

"I won't leave you, honey. Besides, the Lucky Clover is the blood in my veins. Couldn't ride away from it even if I wanted to."

As much as she disliked what she was coming to understand, she could not run from the fact that the life she had known was about to fold up on her.

When it came down to things, Ivy would do anything for Agatha. If she could pilot a steamboat, she sure as shootin' could navigate the baffling waters of high society, could become the well-mannered wife that the governor of Wyoming would require.

"All right then, Travis, teach me how to be a lady."

"Gull-durned bunch of pink trouble!"

Ivy glared at the mess of rose-petal-hued petticoats she had tossed on the floor. She'd stomp on the stiff, lacy snake but she figured Travis had spent a lot of money on it.

For the life of her she couldn't figure out how to get it on. Over the head? Step into it? There were so many ribbons and ties, how was she to know which matched up with which?

If there was only one of them fluffy demons, she might have figured it out, but there were three of the blasted things. She'd need a book to know what went where.

Steady rain tapped on her window. No sun this morning, and no breakfast either. If she didn't get some vittles soon, she'd waste away.

She glanced in the mirror, relieved that she was not completely ignorant of women's things. At least she'd figured out that the chemise went on first and the bloomers went over her legs.

Too bad she couldn't just go around in bloomers. Those were just like fancy trousers.

She snatched the corset off the bed, stared at it in confusion. It laced up, but did the laces go in front, back, or side? The wicked garment should have come with instructions.

The sooner she figured it out, the sooner she would be able to put on the dress—without all the petticoats— and go find a bite of breakfast from the kitchen Travis had mentioned.

She stood in front of the big mirror frowning and dangling the corset this way and that.

Then, all of sudden, she stopped, stared in surprise. She did look rather fetching in the soft underclothes. The lace tickling her flesh a full inch below the upper swell of her breasts was not annoying like she figured it would be.

The odd sight made her feel feminine in a way she never had. She fluffed her hair about her shoulders, turned this way and back.

If this was all she was required to wear, life would be fine. Sadly, there was still the mystery of the corset to be solved.

She stared at it, gripped the edges and spread it out. Clearly, the miserable thing was intended to go over the chemise and choke the breath out of her.

But how?

The strings had to go in the front, otherwise how was one to pull them taut?

"Count your blessings that you were born a rodent!" she called over her shoulder.

She wrapped the pesky underthing around her back. It was two inches shy of coming together over her ribs and waist! Must have been made for a child.

Cursing like a roustabout lifting a heavy load, she yanked the stubborn thing left, then right…squeezed both ends together. Blame it! She'd bet a dollar the corset wasn't even meant to close.

A knock wrapped on the door.

"Come on in," she growled, looking down in concentration at what she was trying to do. "I reckon you know more about this contraption than I do, Travis Murphy."

"Mon Dieu!" a woman's voice scolded loudly.

* * *

Ivy was wrong. He did not know all that much about ladies' undergarments.

But he did know enough to see that she was trying to put the corset on backward. And that even cursing and glaring, she was the loveliest woman he had ever seen.

From the looks of things, he'd sure as shootin' made the right decision in hiring a woman to help Ivy learn about dressing and manners.

"Ivy, this is Antoinette du Mer. She's to be your instructor in…" Everything. "Dressing and…and such."

Antoinette du Mer dropped her satchel. She clucked her tongue, making the odd noise sound reproachful.

Then she circled Ivy, her black skirt making the stiff, scratching sound that came from using excessive starch.

Madame du Mer frowned as though she were studying a specimen in a jar.

"I'm mighty grateful, ma'am." Ivy shoved the corset at Madame du Mer. "Can't tell heads from tails of this thing."

All of a sudden, Madame du Mer spun about to cast Travis an incensed glare.

"Monsieur, you will take your hungry eyes off this young lady and leave the room at once!"

"No need to get riled, ma'am. Travis here is like a brother to me." She looked at him and winked. "Besides, he's already seen me naked. I'm a good bit more covered now than I was then."

Like a brother? He couldn't say why that pronouncement bothered him, but it did. Something, a feeling he should not have for Ivy, was beginning to take root in his heart.

He needed to weed it out. Ivy was never intended for him. She was meant for William English. If he did anything to interfere with that, the ranch and everyone depending upon it would be ruined.

"This is true?" Madame du Mer narrowed her eyes at him. The instructor tried to block his view of Ivy by standing in front of her with arms spread wide. The teacher was tiny, so he was able to look at Ivy, savor every pretty curve, mistake though it was.

"Yes, but it was by accident," he declared.

"Turned out to be fair in the end," Ivy reassured Madame du Mer who looked anything but reassured. "I got to see Travis in the naked too, and not by accident. Reckon I've got one up on him."

Ivy slapped her knee and laughed. Her eyes twinkled at him, blue and pretty. It was good to know that she held the memory of their first meeting with the same fondness as he did.

"This, I will not have!" Madame picked up her satchel, looking as though she were about to storm in outrage from the room. "You assured me my student was pure."

"Gosh almighty! I'm as virgin as the day I was born!" Ivy's cheeks blushed pinker than the petticoats mounded on the floor.

"A word, Monsieur." The small, dark-haired woman crooked her finger at him. He followed her to the far corner of the room.

"I have been around young ladies and their gentlemen for a very long time. I know what is in a young man's heart. It is clear to me that you do not share Miss Magee's feeling of sibling fondness," she murmured, her intent dark eyes commanding his attention. "If I am to prepare her for Monsieur English, I will not have you mooning over her. This will make things difficult, you understand? I will not deceive the gentleman by giving him someone who is not pure."

"There's one thing you'll learn, just as I have, ma'am. Ivy Magee is the purest soul you will ever meet."

"Perhaps that is true." She cast a quick glance at Ivy then back at him. "She is quite forthcoming."

"Travis," Ivy called from where she had gone to sit on the tall bed. Her bare feet dangled over the edge, swinging. "Learning to dress is taking a mite longer than I imagined. I'll need something to eat before I begin gnawing on the furniture."

Madame du Mer sighed deeply. "I will need more money. And I will sleep on a cot in front of that door. But, I will teach the child to be a woman of impeccable manners."

Travis reckoned he saw Ivy a bit differently than Madame du Mer did.

Where she saw a child, he saw a woman. A woman whose breasts undulated beneath her chemise with the swinging of her feet.

He might never feel brotherly toward Ivy, but he would do everything in his power to try.

"The first thing an unmarried lady must learn is to never be alone in a room with a gentleman."

Madame du Mer placed the corset at Ivy's waist. Ah…the pesky strings went in the back! Mighty poor design in Ivy's opinion. How was a body supposed to dress herself of a morning?

Watching the mirror, she could see her instructor pulling at the laces with single-minded purpose. If the woman tugged much harder Ivy was going to suffocate.

"And the next is, never ever, allow a man to see you

naked. We must avoid such accidents at all costs, *ma chère.*"

All of a sudden Madame du Mer wrenched the corset strings, anchored them in a knot at the small of Ivy's back.

She would have gasped had she enough air in her lungs. Gosh almighty! How did such slender arms as Madame's have so much strength?

"I…can't…breathe." Couldn't hardly sputter words either.

"Oh, but look at how lovely you look!" Madame clapped her hands, her smile wide and pleased looking. "Such a tiny waist. Any man would be proud."

"Only until he sees me naked, then he'll know the truth of what I look like. Please, let me out of this female trap!"

"When your husband sees you naked, he will not be thinking of your waist. The deception we play on *les hommes* is for their benefit. They do not mind in the least."

Ivy looked at her reflection in the mirror. Her waist was unnaturally small, her face pale as cold milk…but she did look fashionable. She also looked like she was going to pass out.

"Still can't breathe. Madame du Mer, have mercy on me."

"You will grow accustomed to the feeling. And if you do faint on occasion, it gives the gentlemen great pleasure to come to your aid. We grant them a moment to be our heroes."

If Ivy had ever heard of anything more foolish she could not recall it. If a woman's self-inflicted distress caused a man's false heroics, why was anyone pleased about it?

"That's the most foolish thing I ever heard of," she groaned. "Don't care how short of breath I get, I ain't going to faint to make some male feel good about himself."

"After you become accustomed to breathing shallowly, we will develop your speech."

"I'd argue 'til I'm blue, but I'm already blue."

"This only makes you look delicate. Your husband will be pleased."

"Devil take him if that's what pleases him. I ain't never been delicate and I won't ever be."

Madame du Mer pulled a stool before the mirror, indicated that she should sit. Blast if sitting didn't push the little bit of air she had in her lungs clean out.

"And here, *ma chère*, is the secret that we women keep." Madame took a brush to Ivy's hair. With a loop here and a whirl there, somehow Ivy's hair got piled on top of her head. Madame smiled down at it in apparent approval. At least there was something about Ivy that pleased her keeper. "We look delicate to make *les hommes* protect us…but in truth we are the strong ones."

"Reckon I don't want a man who wants me weak."

"He will know you are not. It's just the illusion that we cling to."

"Madame du Mer…I don't mind admitting that I'm right puzzled."

"Of, course, *ma chère*. That is why I am here." She squeezed Ivy's shoulders with deceptively delicate-looking hands. "All will be well. And now you will call me by my name."

"Miss Antoinette?"

"*Oui*, for some. But you, you will call me Antie."

This was a form of endearment, Ivy was certain, but if Antie felt kindly toward her… "Set me free, Antie."

"I will be strict...you have grown up wild as a weed. But in time you will see that what I am giving you is freedom."

Ivy covered her face with her hands, wanting to weep but refusing to.

Antie's starched skirt crackled when she knelt on the floor in front of the stool. She drew Ivy's hands away from her face.

"You are strong, *ma petite*. This will not change. All will be well in time."

There was a soft knock on that adjoining door to Travis's room.

"I've brought breakfast," he announced, his voice muffled by the wood.

A hope flared inside her that he would come in and rescue her. That he would rush in, sword drawn like a knight of old, and cut her out of the corset.

That was a false hope, since curse it, he was the one who had put her in it.

"You will wait. I will tell you when our lady is properly dressed."

"Hope this dressing business doesn't take long, Antie. I could eat a horse." Her stomach would be growling in agreement if it had the room to. But unless she missed her guess, that hungry organ was squeezed to the size of a needle.

"In private, you may eat a horse; in public, you will eat a bird."

"An ostrich?"

Antie pursed her lips, shook her head.

"A sparrow."

Travis nearly dropped the breakfast tray. He was damn sure that his heart had rolled over on itself.

Ivy stood beside the window gazing out at the morning rain. In profile he saw that her lips were pursed, her brows creased in a frown, but in the forty-five minutes he had been gone fetching breakfast, she had been transformed—at least on the outside.

For as miserable as the Lucky Clover's heir looked, Madame du Mer was beaming.

"Is she not a delight, *monsieur*?"

The instructor touched Ivy's elbow, turning her from the window to face him.

No, not exactly a delight. A delightful woman would be smiling.

But she did rob him of breath. With her blond hair curled and tumbling from the crown of her head past her shoulders, she resembled a porcelain doll.

Madame touched Ivy's waist, indicating the cinched curve, the flare of her hips under the pink skirt. Very clearly the petticoats she scorned were underneath.

No, he was wrong about the doll. With her blue eyes, pink cheeks and sunshine colored hair, she was nothing short of an angel touching her toes to earth.

"I blame you for this, Travis Murphy!" Ah! Her voice was less than angelic. "I feel like an extra pea in a pod."

"Your sister dresses like this every day," he answered because he didn't know what else to say.

"No wonder she's sickly." Ivy charged away from the window, stabbed him in the chest with her finger. "If she's eating sparrows, I'll have something to say about that!"

"Eating spar—"

"We waste time!" Madame declared. "As you can see, *monsieur*, we have much work to do."

"Sure do hope it involves eating," Ivy grumbled then

stalked across the room, kicking and batting her skirt aside as she passed him. "Gull-durned blasted thing."

She thumped down in a chair, plopped her chin in her hands.

"All will be well," Madame assured him in a whisper.

He couldn't rightly figure out how. Seemed that taming Ivy was like taming a wildcat…and he rather liked the wild cat.

"What's covered up under that tray?" Ivy sniffed when he set it on the table in front of her.

"Ham, fried potatoes, some fancy pastry."

Madame du Mer set utensils beside the tray, then lifted off the napkin.

"This," Madame instructed, "lies across your lap. When you feel the need, every second bite or so, gently dap the corners of your mouth."

Ivy picked up the cloth, demonstrating by a light touch to one corner of her mouth.

"Lovely—perfect, *ma chère*! Now you may eat."

Ivy cut a piece of the ham, her elbows pumping.

Madame's brows plunged.

"Smells mighty fine." Ivy jabbed the point of her knife into the piece of ham.

She nearly had it to her lips when Madame du Mer shouted.

"Non!"

"Can't rightly eat unless I put the food in my mouth."

"There is a proper way, and there is a heathen way."

Ivy's frown matched her mentor's.

Madame eased gracefully into the chair across from Ivy. "This is the way a lady eats."

Travis stood quietly to the side, his heart heavy. For some reason, he felt like he had captured a beautiful meadowlark and locked her in a cage.

He looked away from the glares the ladies were casting each other to stare at the rain dripping down the window.

All of a sudden he didn't think much of himself. Ivy had been happy with her life—lovely and free of spirit. Who was he to capture her, to cage her?

No one...except a man who would do anything to protect those who depended upon him.

And to be fair, a capture was not what had happened. Ivy had made this choice of her own free will. His duty was to help her have the happy future in store for her.

Yes, and for everyone else, as well. He could not deny that part of it.

"Yes, much better," Madame commented. "Little birdlike nibbles with the proper fork."

He looked back. Madame du Mer was no longer frowning, but she was still not as pleased looking as she had been with the napkin dabbing.

"A nibble's all that's going to make it past the corset and into my belly, anyway."

"A lady does not use the word *belly*, but that is a lesson for another time."

"It seemed better than saying *gut*," Ivy replied and shoved the little bite past her lips.

"Or *craw*," Travis added, feeling a need to come to Ivy's defense.

"You do not help our cause, *monsieur*." After casting him a scowl, she turned her attention back to her reluctant student. "A lady does not discuss body parts in the presence of a gentleman."

Ivy swallowed her bite of ham, dabbed the napkin to one corner of her mouth, then set it aside.

"I'm worried, Travis." She indicated with a sweep of her hand that he should sit at the third place at the table.

"What is it?" he sat down and would have picked up Ivy's hand but Madame would not approve.

"How am I going to learn everything? I'm bound to eat wrong, speak wrong, be a disappointment to Mr. English. Maybe even an embarrassment."

In his opinion, William was one lucky fellow who had better appreciate the woman Ivy was.

"No, no, *ma petite*, this will not happen." Madame placed a fork in Ivy's hand, positioned it just so. "I am here."

Ivy did know how to use a fork, he'd seen her use one, but Madame du Mer insisted on the fingers being poised just so. Even he had never noticed that there was such intricacy to proper manners.

"Très bien!" Madame touched Ivy's shoulder. "You have done well. *Monsieur* will go back to his room now."

"Monsieur would like to visit his friend."

Madame lifted one eyebrow at him. The canny woman understood that his feelings for Ivy, while friendly, were beginning to change in a way that would not be good for anyone.

"There is much to be done. A wardrobe to be purchased, *oui*?"

"I reckon, but—"

"Our mademoiselle has been through much change today. She will now take off her restrictive clothing and eat the breakfast you have brought her."

Ivy leapt from her chair and bent to hug her teacher.

"Gosh almighty, Antie! Thank you."

"Away with you Travis Murphy. We will meet again this afternoon."

As much as he didn't want to go, it was the right thing to do. Ivy did need to eat.

And he should not be alone with her. He couldn't say it didn't rankle though.

They had spent over a week together with no one else around and it had never felt improper.

But now there was William English to be considered, and his ambition to be elected to the territorial legislature this fall. His wife would need to be of impeccable manners, virtuous in every way.

That rankled, too. Eleanor Ivy Magee was the most virtuous person he had ever met. She was generous, she laughed heartily, and had a loving spirit.

A man who wanted more was no man at all. He only hoped that English would recognize the prize he was getting.

Chapter Seven

Ivy sat on the floor, her back against the door that connected to Travis's room with her breakfast tray on her lap.

Praise the good Lord that, with the fancy duds now heaped on the chair and not on her, she could breathe again.

"Are you in there, Travis?"

She heard the creak of bedsprings, then the tap of boots crossing the floor.

"I'm here. What are you doing?"

"Practicing the use of this here fork." She turned it in her hand, trying to remember the exact way Antie had showed her to hold it. "I'm powerful hungry, though. I might just stuff the food in my mouth all at once."

"Take care not to choke on a pig."

"Don't make me laugh and I won't."

There, that was it. With her pinkie finger poised just so, she gently poked the tines into the ham. "Wish you were on this side of the door."

She heard the door creak as he slid down his side of it. He would be sitting back-to-back with her.

"It seems funny not to be able to talk with you face-to-face," she said.

"When we get to the Lucky Clover things will be more relaxed."

"Sure do hope it's soon."

"That depends on you more than anyone." She heard him sigh, rap the floor with his knuckles. "The sooner you learn the ways of a proper lady the sooner we'll go home."

"I reckon you miss the ranch the same as I miss the *Queen*."

"Honey, I miss it like I would a living, breathing person." He was silent for a long time, but she heard his exhalation through the door. "I'm sorry this all led to you losing your home. I can't lie—it did help me, but I wish things could have been different."

"I like you, Travis. For you and for Agatha, I'll do my durndest to make sure you don't lose your ranch."

"I need some fresh air. Let's get out of here."

"Antie won't like it." In fact, her poor instructor might turn purple over it. "I'll beat you to the hallway."

She gobbled a bite of pastry on the run.

Out in the hall, she nearly ran headlong into Travis.

"We'll need to be quick—Antie's planning on being gone a few hours, but plans change."

"Let's go!" He scooped up her hand then led her on a fast pace down the hallway.

Once outside, Travis took off his jacket and placed it over her head to shield her from the rain.

She wasn't sure if he was trying to hide her or keep her dry. He wouldn't know that she didn't mind getting soaked in a storm.

Drops pelted the leather on her head. At the end of the boardwalk, Travis leapt off then lifted her down.

Their running footsteps squelched in the mud.

She had no idea where he was leading her. With the jacket over her head, all she could see was rain hitting the dirt.

It was funny, but even at the fast pace he set, she trusted him not to let her fall.

"Not much farther." His breath came quick with the exertion of running.

After a turn and a short sprint they came to a shelter. The tap of rain changed from hitting leather to tapping a roof.

She drew the jacket off her head and handed it back to him.

"Where are we?" Not indoors, she saw, but under the overhang of a porch.

"A storage building that belonged to the railroad— they no longer use it. Figured you might like to see the train come in."

"You figured right."

He was still holding her hand when they sat down on the bench facing the track. Interestingly, she had no mind to bring this lack of manners to his attention.

She'd never sat and just held a man's hand. It was a right pleasant thing to do. His big calloused palm made her hand feel delicate.

It was odd that she didn't mind feeling delicate in this way.

Looking down the tracks, she didn't see any sign of the train spewing smoke. That was fine; she was in no hurry to go back to the hotel.

Rain rolled off the overhang and splattered the mud a few feet away. It smelled fresh. She closed her eyes. If she imagined things just right she could pretend she was on the banks of the Missouri.

"What are you thinking about, Ivy? You seem miles away."

Opening her eyes she smiled at him, felt his hand squeeze hers. It was a right friendly gesture, one she hoped her future intended would not object to. She had yet to even meet the man so she could hardly be held accountable for an innocent hand-holding.

"I suppose I was. I was thinking how the rain and the mud smell like home."

Travis stared out at the wet afternoon, rubbing his thumb across her knuckles while he did. Seemed like he was the one deep in thought now.

"Do you think once I'm married, my husband will take me home for a visit?"

"Could be, after some time. Right now all his attention is on the election in November."

"Must mean he'll want a quick wedding, then. I won't mind something simple."

"William English won't want simple, honey. He'll make a social event of the wedding. Because appearances are everything to him, he'll be showing you off, hoping folks will vote for him because of his beautiful wife. A wife who just happens to be the heir to one of the most well-respected ranches in the state."

Travis thought she was beautiful?

That couldn't be true. But if it was, if he did—

No! Ivy Magee was a river rat. Appearances meant nothing to her—except that maybe when Travis thought she was beautiful, they did mean something.

Why else would his words go and make her belly shiver? Or more properly, her middle?

Words were tricky critters, but wasn't she allowed to say what she wanted to in the privacy of her own mind?

Gull-durn it, she was going to since there was no one to know the difference.

"Tell me more about William English," she said, to distract herself from the strange flutter going on low down in her belly. "I know what he wants but who is he? Besides handsome. I saw that. But good looks don't mean an upstanding fellow on the inside. They say Lucifer was something to look at."

"He's no Lucifer. He's friendly, charismatic. And he's got a way of making folks feel special. He'd give you the shirt off his back if you needed it. Partly to get your vote, but also because he's got lots of shirts.

"I like him. I wouldn't send you to a man I didn't like and trust. Not even for the sake of the Lucky Clover."

He wouldn't? Just when the stirrings within her middle started to ease, her heart softened...simmered inside her like warm honey being poured over biscuits.

"The thing to remember about William is that he's ambitious—nothing means quite as much to him as winning this election."

"Must be true if he's willing to marry a stranger."

"He won't be unkind to you."

"Most people do treat their prize horseflesh well."

"If you ever have a concern, about anything, I'll be there."

"How far is the English spread from the Lucky Clover?"

"A day's ride, but William plans to make his home on the Lucky Clover."

This was good news! Somehow this made her feel better about things. There was something about the ranch, the idea of it being hers, that gave her comfort, a sense of home and stability.

That made as much sense as a fly sucking vinegar,

given that she hadn't set eyes on the place since she was a tot.

But William would be in charge. "Will that change things for you...for everyone else?"

Especially Agatha?

"I'll be in charge of running the ranch. The only interest English has as far as the Lucky Clover goes is that it continues to be well respected. It's why he's willing to cover the mortgage note."

"I reckon that's a fine thing, then. Not much will change."

Except for her. She would change into a person she would have ridiculed only weeks ago. She would be stuffed into a woman's traps, using refined words and keeping her clothes on, even near water. Not that the water in these parts looked refreshing or private enough to indulge in a midnight swim.

"Who will I be?" she murmured under her breath.

Travis lifted her fingers to his mouth, kissed them. He slipped his arm about her shoulder and drew her close to his side.

She hadn't meant to say that out loud. She reckoned that's what happened when one had a strong friendship with someone. You spoke from your heart. Trusted them to understand.

She'd never felt this companionship with anyone but Uncle Patrick. But gosh almighty, this was something different than she felt for her uncle.

She leaned her head into the crook of Travis's neck. Sighed and snuggled against him. In a world gone out of her control, his presence was a sanctuary.

Chances were, English wouldn't like seeing her cozied up to Travis this way, but she had yet to even meet the man who was appointed to be her husband.

Travis' nose touched her hair. His warm breath stirred it.

"You smell like the Missouri," he whispered.

"You smell like the plains."

"Cow dung and horse sweat?"

His laugh rumbled through her, made her insides ache.

"Acres of grass with a warm wind blowing across it."

He kissed the top of her head. Why was it that the warmth of his lips on her hair made her heart constrict? Uncle Patrick had kissed her head but it had never made her insides shiver.

"I'm glad that I'll be living at the Lucky Clover. I'd miss you something terrible if I had to ride a whole day to see you," she admitted.

"I'd miss you too, honey." He slid away, but only enough to pivot toward her, to take her face in his hands. "You are a special woman, Ivy." His breath fanned her face. She watched his lips move. "You wonder who you will be? Amazing, generous, wonderful. You won't quit being who you are."

"I like you, Travis," she whispered. "You are a dear friend."

"A friend," he agreed, but his lips moved closer to hers.

"A dear friend."

"Yes."

Then his lips touched hers so lightly that the pressure might have been the whisk of a bird's wing against her mouth.

Far in the distance, the train's whistle echoed across the land.

She scooted away from Travis at the same time he scooted away from her.

But it didn't matter how far away he scooted. He could slide to Texas and she would still feel the warmth of his lips, smell the scent of his skin on her face.

She licked her lips, trying to wash the feel of him away but it only made things worse because she tasted him again.

She squeezed her eyes shut against the emotion she saw in Travis's eyes, rejected the yearning in her chest. There was only one man she was meant to taste in her life and it was the one sitting in front of her.

Two days.

Almost exactly forty-eight hours since Travis had done the unforgiveable and kissed Ivy.

He'd always heard that forbidden fruit was sweet. Now he knew it to be fact. Nothing had ever been quite so wonderful as kissing William's future intended.

At the same time, nothing had ever felt worse. For a moment's pleasure…no, not mere pleasure, for an instant of giving in to intimate yearnings for Ivy, he had threatened everything. Betrayed everyone.

Now it had been two days since he'd seen her. He'd spent time meeting with cattle buyers. He'd caught up on town news and purchased supplies for the ranch. Still, he'd ended up with too much free time on his hands.

He'd spent those long hours in a chair at the Cheyenne Club, brooding, wounded. Being a fool.

Yes, he was attracted to Ivy, cared for her deeply, but that did not give him the right to risk the futures of everyone at the Lucky Clover.

Ivy claimed to be his friend. He only hoped he hadn't ruined the relationship that was permitted to them by an inappropriate kiss.

He cast a frown at the mirror, yanked the lapels of

his coat into place. He could not run from his mistake forever.

He glanced at the door that connected their rooms, shook his head. Might be a good idea to nail the door closed.

Going into the hall, he pivoted right then rapped on Ivy's door.

"Enter!" Madame's voice called.

He walked into the room to find Ivy standing on a short stool wearing a yellow gown with yards of fabric draped this way and that. The bustle area stuck out so far that a dinner tray could be placed there.

Madame du Mer knelt on the floor with pins stuck in her sleeve while she tucked up the hem of the skirt.

"Howdy-do, Travis!" Ivy's grin at him was wide and welcoming. Relief rushed through him. She still considered him a friend. "Don't I look like the Queen of Sheba?"

"Non!" From her place on the floor, Madame clapped her hands. "How does a lady greet a gentleman?"

Ivy blushed becomingly. He doubted that was a part of Madame's teaching.

"Antie and I have spent the livelong day learning the proper way to speak so—Good afternoon, Mr. Murphy." Ivy nodded her head once.

"Much better, *ma chère*. Now give our gentleman the *petite* smile with your lips closed."

Ivy smiled at him as instructed but the gesture did not look natural.

That stilted greeting ought to do fine in the social circle she was about to enter. Those polished women smiled falsely in the face of adversity every day.

"Help the lady down," Madame said, standing with more agility than most women her age.

He crossed the room, politely offered his hand. Ivy took it, shot him a grin when Madame briefly glanced the other way.

"Now we will see how you walk in your pretty new slippers."

Ivy lifted her skirt to her shin. "You paid a pretty penny for theses pinchers, Travis."

"A lady's skirt must go no higher than her ankles."

"Blamed if I won't have to walk around reading a rule book." Ivy dropped the skirt but pointed the narrow toe of the shoe at him, turning it this way and that.

As much as she complained, he hoped she was at least a little bit pleased with the elegant clothing.

"Now, *chère*, go to the window, turn and come back. Greet Monsieur Murphy as though he were Mr. English come to call."

Mr. English coming to call was something he was going to have to get used to, but right now the idea made him feel like he had ants crawling under his skin.

Ivy wobbled across the room, grasped the windowsill.

"Sure would like to take a switch to whoever decided women needed to walk around with their feet off the floor," she grumbled, stomped the heel of her shoe on the rug. "Feels like I'm going to fall nose down on the carpet."

"Wasn't me," he said. "I'm just standing here pretending to be your intended."

"It's but two inches. The elevation will become as natural to you as going barefoot," Madame explained, but Ivy did not look half-convinced. "Come now, greet your gentleman."

"I reckon a gentleman wouldn't torture a lady."

If Ivy was his wife, her pants and shirt would suit

fine. As the owner of the Lucky Clover, her clothing would be practical.

But she was not going to be his wife, not ever, so the torture would have to continue.

Walking back across the room, she did better, only listing to the left three times.

In the middle of shooting him that tight, closed-mouthed smile, the formal nod of greeting, the heel of her left shoe caught in the carpet. Her arms flailed in open air.

She toppled toward him like a felled tree. Caught off guard, her weight knocked him off balance and he went down, his arms hugging her middle.

Petticoats exploded around his face, buried his chest. Through a clearing in the lace, he spotted the despised slippers kicking madly in the air.

But in the fall, his hand had shifted. His palm was pressing her breast.

"Gull-durned blasted female trap!"

With all the squirming she was doing to get free of the garment, he doubted that she noticed the brief indiscretion.

But if he lived to be ninety-three, he'd never forget how she had felt so full in his hand. In her struggle with the dress, her flesh jiggled against his palm.

The experience lasted only seconds, but the memory would serve a lifetime.

"Tiens!" Madame's patience had to be near an end, but she helped untangle Ivy from him without the censure he had expected. "This is why we practice relentlessly. It would not do for this to happen in a drawing room."

With a lot of tugging, pulling and yanking, Ivy's dress fell away from him.

Sitting across from him on the floor, her legs bent at the knee and more petticoat showing than skirt, she grinned.

Apparently remembering her manners, she covered her mouth with both hands, but her eyes watered as she shook her head.

In the end, she didn't seem able to hold back the laughter. It started as a quiet snicker then built to an outright chuckle that convulsed her shoulders.

Surprisingly, Madame smiled behind her hand.

In his day-to-day life, Travis tended to be serious natured. He had to be since folks depended upon him to be in charge, make the decisions that shaped their lives on the ranch.

But when he was with Ivy, the boy he had once been came out to play.

Restless, Ivy kicked off her blanket.

Back home on the *Queen*, the wee hours would see her on her private swim. She missed floating about, listening to frogs and crickets, watching the stars and just…being.

But here she was in Cheyenne. Wyoming was home now.

She sat up, looked out the window to see the full moon lighting the land.

Just because she could not float about naked, did not mean she could not go outside and enjoy the moon and the stars.

Dressing quickly in her natural clothes and snatching up Little Mouse, she left her room and tiptoed down the back stairs.

It wouldn't do to go far from the hotel. She was well

aware now that she didn't have a boatload of men seeing to her safety.

Only one, and he would not approve of this outing.

Behind the hotel there was a private courtyard with a bench.

Following a short path, she came to an opening in the shrubbery. She sat on the bench, satisfied to see that the bushes grew taller than her head.

If such a sanctuary did not currently exist at the Lucky Clover, it soon would.

Little Mouse wriggled in her hand. Ivy opened her palm. "All right, go have your fun. Just watch out for owls and such."

With her arms braced behind her head, Ivy looked up. Millions of stars speckled the black sky, more stars than she could even see.

As always, she felt small. But somehow, in her smallness, she knew her life mattered. There was a Creator. He had formed her the same as He had the stars.

That meant there must be a purpose for her life taking the turn it had. She might not care for the road she was traveling, but sometimes the hardest roads led to beautiful places.

This one was leading to the sister she had always dreamed of.

Was Agatha looking at the moon right now? Did she have any blurry memories of Ivy? Had she shared the same longings over the years that Ivy did?

Travis had told Agatha that he was leaving the ranch to try and find her. How would she feel about having a secret sister come home?

There was so much that she wondered about when it came to her sister.

Once Ivy got to the ranch she would know firsthand

what was ailing her…figure out what was to be done about it.

All of a sudden, she was impatient to leave Cheyenne, to get to the Lucky Clover.

Truth to tell, she had been resisting becoming cultured because the sooner she became a society belle, the sooner she would be married.

That did frighten her some.

But Agatha was the reason she was doing this. It made no sense to fight the inevitable…the thing she had agreed to do.

The sooner she learned what she needed to, the better.

Come tomorrow, Antie would find a new student waiting for instruction…one who was as willing as it was possible to be.

"Little Mouse," she called, but quietly. "Time to go back inside. We need our rest if we are to become civilized."

It took a moment longer for the mouse to emerge from playing in the shrubbery than it normally did. With relief, Ivy heard the rustle of leaves. Tiny pink feet climbed onto her waiting hand then scurried up her arm.

Passing under Travis's window, she glanced up. During the time she'd been out, he had turned on his lamp. She didn't worry that he was wise to her excursion. If he was, he'd be down here scolding her for being reckless.

No doubt he was wakeful. He must be worried. So far his efforts to help her learn to be a lady were failing. She was a sow's ear and no amount of mending was turning her into a silk purse. If she didn't manage the change, he would lose his home. So would a lot of other folks.

One of them was Agatha.

Stars were made for wishing upon so she picked the brightest one.

"Please make me acceptable for William English," she said, then blew a kiss at the moon for extra insurance.

Above her head, Travis's window slid open. She pressed against a wall where the shadow was deep black.

"Best put your shirt back on, Mr. Murphy," she whispered, her mouth going suddenly dry.

If she had any hope of having an acceptable marriage with William English, she had to forget a few things.

Like how very muscular and attractive Travis's naked buttocks were, like how his hand had felt on her breast, how his fingers had flexed ever so subtly when he and she were hidden in her petticoats. And how his lips made her go soft inside even when they barely brushed hers two nights ago.

Learning to be a lady was going to be a whole lot easier than forgetting how to be a woman.

Chapter Eight

On the Fourth of July, Ivy focused her effort on giving away her independence.

She sat dutifully on a chair while Antie curled her hair with a hot iron. Blond ringlets, stiffened by molasses tumbled from her crown to her shoulders. A twister could spin through the room and she doubted that those pretty springs would sway.

While her teacher worked, she chatted on about Ivy's duties as the wife of a prominent man.

Becoming a lady, she was quickly learning, had much to do with appearing to be dependent on a man. From the way she spoke to the way she moved, it all added up to letting a fellow believe, falsely in her opinion, that a woman needed protecting.

While she would never truly accept this, she would appear to. And she could hardly avoid the fact that she did need William English—or rather, the protection his money offered.

She would do her best to give him what he wanted: a wife whose social skills were the envy of all. In return, he would give her what she needed: the funds to keep the Lucky Clover solvent and those who lived there secure.

But gosh almighty, it wasn't easy.

She'd nearly worn the rug bare getting used to those narrow-toed, block-heeled shoes. After a day spent walking around and around in heavy fabric that bulged over her backside in a ridiculous way, she felt equal parts confident and worried.

The most amazing thing she had learned today was a new respect for the ladies she had maligned over the years. The more delicate gender had overcome some serious challenges just to maneuver safely about.

She could nearly eat and breathe wearing the dadgum—the prettily decorated corset, that is.

Turns out she wasn't a whole lot different than a pony being broke to the saddle.

The biggest challenge that Antie now faced in training Ivy, was teaching her to speak properly. Not just with appropriate words, but with those words delivered in the proper tone and at the appropriate time.

Gosh almighty she was having a hard time taming her tongue. My word, mercy me, yes she was.

Not having had a woman's influence growing up, she naturally learned language from firemen, deckhands and roustabouts.

She'd never really paid attention to the fact that they were not the most cultured of souls. That she, a girl, had grown to be like them.

In her opinion, it was not a horrible thing.

But now it was time to live in the real world, to leave behind the carefree youngster and become a woman, a woman of impeccable social manners.

Gosh almighty—drat it—mercy me, she hoped she could do it.

"One week, *ma chère*." With a frown of concentration, Antie formed curls and placed them just so. The woman sure was dedicated to making Ivy's hair behave.

Like the troublesome bustle anchored at her back, her hairstyle had to be of the latest fashion. "We dine at Porter's. You will steal everyone's heart."

"Last time I tried to eat there, a fellow ended up with a broken nose."

"That pompous Charles! This time he— Ohhh!" Antie dropped the iron.

Ivy shot up from the stool and cupped Antie's hand. A red welt crossed her palm. Time was important when it came to burns.

Ivy dashed across the room and snatched up the pitcher of water.

"Soak your hand. The water's cold—it will help."

"You ran in your dress and shoes," Clearly, Antie was trying not to admit to the pain. "Well done, *ma chère*."

"I've got some aloe salve in my saddle pack."

If she ran once, she could do it again. Hopefully she would not have to splint her own leg.

Dashing across the large room, she pounded on Travis's door. "Come quick!" she called.

No sooner had she lifted her knuckles from the wood, than the door swung open.

"Madame burned herself. Go fetch some clean bandages from the mercantile."

"I hope it's still open. The fireworks are starting soon. The store might be closed."

"We'd be ever so grateful for your help," she said, smiling sweetly, experimenting with seeming helpless.

It was irksome to know that if she wasn't wearing this restrictive dress she could be back from the store in a blink, and all on her own.

In the end, she had agreed to wear the frilly trap of her own free will so she blinked and smiled at Travis.

He looked at her in confusion for a second, but quickly gathered himself and hurried out of the room.

A few moments after she'd spread the aloe salve on Antie's hand, Travis ran back into the room, hands gripping a variety of bandages.

"Thank you, *ma chère*. It feels much better already."

"It'll smart for a while," Ivy said, selecting one of the bandages Travis held. "But it doesn't look like you'll need to see a doctor."

"Travis, *mon cher*, you will deliver dinner to my room?"

"It would be my pleasure," he replied.

"You may dine here with our Ivy and practice mealtime manners."

She watched while Travis led the instructor from the room, so full of manly concern.

Ivy was certain that Madame had not burned her hand on purpose, but she had delivered a lesson with the experience.

Sure as shootin', she'd used the situation to illustrate that by seeming in need—by making a man feel important—he would do whatever a lady asked of him.

Blazin' day! Ivy had been sweet as pie asking Travis to get the bandages and he'd been back in a heartbeat.

Somehow, she didn't like thinking that she could manipulate him in that way.

But maybe she hadn't. From all she knew of him, he was kind, dedicated to doing the right thing, even without female trickery.

Going to the window, she watched folks walking toward the east end of town. That must be where the fireworks were going to be shot off.

She always enjoyed a good Independence Day show.

Below, a woman passed by, her gloved hand in the crook of a gentleman's elbow. She glanced up at his face, her laugh light and twittering. The man seemed pleased and patted her hand.

Antie hadn't delivered a lesson on the proper way to twitter yet. Now, watching the woman's bustle sway away, she knew it was coming.

"Sure hope she doesn't make me learn to sway like a flag in a breeze."

"You're pretty enough—you won't need to sway to get England's attention."

She turned, surprised that she hadn't heard Travis enter.

"Howdy-do—gull-durn it—good evening, Mr. Murphy. It's a lovely evening for a fireworks display. Would you care to join me in watching the show?"

"It's just me, honey." For all the loveliness she was hurling at him, it left him frowning. According to Madame, that was not how it was supposed to work. "You don't need to put on airs."

"In that case fetch us over a couple of chairs. I'll end up sprawled all over you again if I try and haul them over in this getup."

A slow smile curled his lips. His eyebrows lifted. It was clear as a starry night that he remembered how he had touched her when she fell…and that it had only begun as an accident.

His heated expression sent an odd shiver over her skin.

A pleasant twisting sensation settled in the mysterious core of her.

A boom exploded in the sky beyond the window.

"What was that?" she asked without turning to look.

"The beginning of the fireworks, I reckon," he answered, but he was not looking out the window either.

Ivy looked elegant. From her posture to her practiced smile she could not have appeared more of a lady.

And not just a common lady, but a beautiful one. With her blue eyes scanning the foyer of Porter's Steak House, so full of humor and curiosity, with her tiny waist and the golden curls cascading down her fair neck, she was exquisite.

If she was nervous about passing her first test in polite society, she didn't show it.

Her emotions seemed as tucked away as any seasoned socialite's would be.

When Charles's head popped up from whatever he was doing behind the counter, Ivy's only reaction was to clench her fingers on Travis's sleeve. In spite of the fact that she must be wondering if the pompous fool was going to call her out as a fraud, her smile did not waver.

Splintered light from the chandelier winked upon her, but in Travis's opinion, the sparkle came from within Ivy.

He had every confidence she was going to charm everyone she met. He'd bet a month's wages that the folks in the dining room would flock to meet Cheyenne's newest landowner.

"*Allons, ma petite,*" Madame du Mer murmured. "Let us slay the dragons."

Charles, the first of her challenges, brushed a bit of dust from the lapels of his coat and shot Travis a tight smile.

As far as greetings went, this one had to be as insincere as they came. A man just didn't forget someone busting his nose any more than Travis forgot the reason for it.

"Good evening, Charles," he stated coolly. "My usual table."

Charles gave a curt half bow then came out from behind the desk.

"This way, Mr. Murphy, ladies."

He walked before them, his posture straight as a nail. No doubt he considered himself king of the steak house.

Travis sure wouldn't mind knocking him down a peg or two. But this was Ivy's moment to practice all she had learned. He would not make it more difficult by giving the fellow his due...again.

"Charles?" Ivy called, her tone sweet as a summer melon. "Haven't we met before?"

Charles turned, his brows raised. "I don't believe so, miss."

"Odd. You do look familiar to me."

Madame du Mer deserved more than he was paying her. Ivy's smile appeared nothing if not sincere, which he guessed was far from the truth. And the way she spoke with such refinement?

If he didn't know who she was, he would not know who she was.

"I have an excellent memory for faces. I would not forget yours." Charles, clearly putting the subject behind him, turned and led the way to the table.

With a bit of flair, Charles pulled out Ivy's chair for her. She glided onto it lithely.

Madame's smile beamed. Travis felt a good bit of pride in Ivy, too.

She had worked hard, learned what she did not want to learn. In the moment, she left Travis breathless... and grateful.

"That's it. Your face." Ivy folded her hands demurely in her lap. "You have a distinctive nose, but it wasn't purple when we met before. You poor man, I hope the break was not too painful."

"I do appreciate your concern, miss. It wasn't a break, though. I simply got hit by a swinging door."

"My word, something so simple to leave such a mark." Ivy sighed, blinked her eyes once.

With a half bow, Charles pivoted then strode back to his station in the foyer.

"Gull-durned worm didn't even know who I was!" Ivy half whispered. She started to grin, glanced about then narrowed her mouth in favor of a ladylike smile. "Reckon that's a good thing."

"That is a marvelous thing, *ma chère*." Madame patted her hand. "You have done well."

She had done more than well. Only weeks ago he had despaired of her being willing to make the change and now, as far as appearances went, she was a proper lady.

The problem was, he liked the outspoken Ivy. The one who said what she meant and lived who she was.

He liked her more than he ought to.

"I believe," Madame said, her voice low so as not to be heard at nearby tables. "That after a successful visit to the dressmaker and one to the mercantile, your testing will be concluded. You may take your heir home, Travis."

"We're going home tomorrow, Little Mouse."

Ivy sat beside her open bedroom window naked. It was after midnight and while a body couldn't swim in moonlight, she could let the pure white light bathe her skin.

She'd been tied up in clothing and fancy manners for

too long. For just an hour, she wanted to breathe deeply and allow air to touch her instead of stiff underclothes.

"Not home to the *River Queen*, I don't mean that. I reckon she's gone by now. But to hear Travis talk, the ranch is a step shy of paradise. Might be it could come to be home."

A breeze slid in through the window, drying the sweat that the hot July night had slathered her in.

"I'm nervous, but reckon I'm ready to go. Didn't do half bad on my lessons, I'm proud to say. I only tripped on my dress and cursed the one time. Even a born and bred lady would cuss if she found herself suddenly neck-deep in a smelly horse trough."

And it was a shame about the gown. Antie hadn't raised much of a fuss about it though. Travis had even laughed.

"Felt like there was pond scum all over my skin. I can't say I minded using that lavender soap for my bath. Can you smell it still?"

She lifted her hand to Little Mouse who was exploring the windowsill. The mouse sniffed then sat and cleaned herself.

"I do like fancy soap. Makes me smell like a flower. Say, you look a mite pudgy around the middle. Too much bread I reckon. Once we get to the ranch it's seeds and fruit for you."

Ivy rested her arms on the sill then cradled her chin on them.

"Just look at all those stars…and the moon so round and bright. You reckon Agatha is watching them right now, too?"

Finished with her cleansing, Little Mouse hopped off the windowsill then hurried across the floor. Ivy turned on her stool to watch her scramble up the quilt and into her small house.

"What are you doing up there, Ivy?"

Pivoting about on her stool, she saw Travis standing below her window two stories down. Sitting as low as she was she would be properly concealed.

Lucky thing for her that Travis was standing in the open. There wasn't a thing he could do to hide his bare chest…or the dusting of hair that arrowed away beneath his low-hung trousers.

"I'm moon bathing. What are you doing?"

"Hunting up a breath of cool air."

"You find any?"

"Only that breeze that came up just now."

"Sure do hope it's cooler at the ranch."

"We'll find out soon enough. Ivy, honey, I just want to say how proud of you I am. No, more than that. I'm damned grateful. Thank you, from me and everyone at the ranch."

"I'm grateful to you, too. For Agatha. I might have gone my whole life and never known I had a sister."

"I only hope you'll be happy." While he spoke, he shoved his arms through his shirtsleeves but left the shirt hanging open. "I know you never wanted any of this."

"I did want some of it, Travis. I wanted my sister." Ivy shrugged, rested her chin in her palms then glanced down to double-check nothing showed above the sill that ought not to show.

"I just hope you won't be unhappy."

"I'm not unhappy with lavender soap. I even like the pretty colors of the dresses you bought me. Don't like the way they tend to trip a woman up unawares, though."

"Well, I reckon we ought to get some sleep since we're leaving at dawn."

"I reckon so. Good night, Travis."

"Good night, Ivy." He lifted his hand in farewell then turned to walk away.

He sure did have a manly gait, so surefooted and bold.

All at once he pivoted. His shirt flared wide, giving her one last glimpse of his chest.

"I like you, Ivy."

Her belly tingled, as though he had run his fingers over her hot skin.

"I like you, too."

She only hoped she would like William English half as much.

Chapter Nine

One week and one day later

Hills of golden grass rolled away in every direction for as far as Ivy could see. A breeze that had been with them all day, along with a shot of afternoon sunshine, gave the earth a warm shimmer.

"I'd like to know how a place that's the same for miles on end can be so ever-changing," she said.

"Where is this change, *ma chère*?" Madame asked. "It has looked the same all week long."

"Ivy's right. Things change by the moment, become dangerous even. It might seem predictable, but if a cowboy isn't watchful he might not make it home."

Was a cowboy so different from a river pilot in that? The thought lifted her spirits, helped make up for the fact that she was stuffed into a fluffy yellow dress.

This land was a mystery, whose ways she was determined to learn.

To begin, she studied the grass. If the wind blew it one way it looked golden, if it blew another it looked brown. Sometimes, a hill looked sky-high until you came upon it and found it to be no more than a gentle slope. Then riding over a hill that seemed a tame little thing, one would get caught by surprise because it had a downward slope that had Travis struggling to control the wagon.

Gosh almighty, when she thought about it, the Lucky Clover wasn't so different than the Missouri in its changeability.

If she put her mind to it, maybe she'd learn to pilot the land the way she'd wanted to do with the river. There was plenty of rocking going on, be it steamer, wagon or horseback.

One thing was for sure, the earth always stretched on. Like the river it seemed to roll along forever.

They had crossed the border of the ranch last night and still the house was nowhere in sight.

Travis said it was a two-day ride from the eastern border of the Lucky Clover to the western border, and that was during fair weather. Going north and south took even longer.

With the ranch house on the eastern portion of the ranch, the trip from Cheyenne took only twelve hours.

As far as Ivy was concerned, that still made for a long wagon ride.

Gosh almighty, she was relieved that she could count on Travis to run this huge ranch. While she knew every board and nail of the *Queen*, she knew nothing about the Lucky Clover and it was vastly bigger than the boat.

"By glory, there's another one of them little houses with a tree growing near it. Sort of small for anyone to live in though."

"Those little houses," Antie corrected.

"Your father didn't mean them for living in. They're for shelter in case of sudden storms. The tree can be seen from a distance so folks know where to hurry to.

There's enough food for a couple of men and horses to last a day or two."

"I reckon my pa cared about his men." That was something good to learn about him.

"He cared deeply for them...for everyone who calls this ranch home."

After a time, the breeze with its constant whisper across the grass, and the regular clop of the team's hooves, made her sleepy.

Just when she was about to nod off in a lovely little doze, the wagon hit a rut and jounced her up from the bench.

Yep, the land was unpredictable.

She clamped her frilly yellow hat to her head before it could take flight and disappear into the grass.

It sure hadn't been her wish to travel in female trappings, but Antie had insisted, saying that folks needed to see their new "mistress" gowned appropriately.

Being someone's "mistress" was an idea that made her stomach churn. But because Antie had agreed to come to the ranch in a bouncing wagon, sleeping under the stars, and with no proper bath at hand, all in order to insure that Ivy did not make a fool of herself in front of Mr. English, she hadn't argued about the dress.

But gosh almighty, that last wagon jarring was bound to leave a bruise where her corset pinched.

Travis was nearly home. All day excitement had been building in him.

He could nearly hear the bawl of newborn calves, the shouts of cowboys in the yard and the laughter of the children who would be free of the schoolroom by now.

Yes, just there, if he strained his ears, he heard the school bell ringing out the time, four o'clock.

At this distance he could only pretend to smell what Señora Morgan was preparing for dinner.

Gazing down from the hill where he had drawn the team to a halt, his heart swelled. Home was never so precious as it was in this moment.

He was so damn grateful to Ivy for saving it all.

"Is that the house? Gosh almighty it's big!"

"That's the bunkhouse for the single men." And it was big. Large enough to house thirty or more men. "The single ladies have a place attached to the main house."

"Gosh almighty," he heard Ivy whisper under her breath.

He was anxious to see the look on her face when she saw her own home.

"It must be one of them cottages down by the stream, then?"

"Those cottages," Madame said in her teaching voice. "The cottages are for the families."

"I'm feeling a mite like a fish out of water, Travis." She inched closer to him on the wagon bench. Damned if she didn't still smell like the Missouri River—with a dash of flowery soap added in. "There's a lot of people to be responsible for. Can't see how my pa did it."

"He had me to help, and so do you."

From the small settlement below he heard the yip of a cowboy. Seconds later a pair of young cowhands on horseback raced up the hill.

"Mr. Murphy!" A fifteen-year-old boy with hair the color of ripe strawberries drew his pinto pony up sharp only a yard from the wagon. "You're home!"

The other rider circled the wagon on his palomino-colored mount.

"That her?" Jose Morgan, the sixteen-year-old son of

the Lucky Clover's cook, shouted, his blue eyes locked on Ivy in amazement. "You brought her home?"

"Meet your new boss, Miss Magee."

"Pleasure, ma'am!" Mac snatched the Stetson off his head, circled it in the air.

"Yee-haw!" Mac's shout boomed across open land, rolled down the hill. It had to have been heard down below.

"Mighty glad you came, Miss Magee." Jose tipped his hat to Ivy then spun his horse about, racing down the hill after Mac.

"Welcome to the Lucky Clover, Ivy."

All of a sudden he wanted to be home, to the main house. The urge kicked his heart against his ribs.

"Hang on, ladies!"

He urged the team to a gallop.

The wagon jolted downhill, rocking this way and that.

Madame du Mer screeched.

Ivy leaned forward on the bench, the grin on her face wide in exhilaration. Gripping the side of the wagon with one hand, she clamped her hat to her head with the other.

Yellow ribbons from the bonnet streamed out behind her.

"Yee-haw!" she shouted, as gustily as the boys racing ahead of them down the hill were doing.

Warm air rushed past Ivy's face. The scents of grass, cattle and the muddy river a short distance to the west filled her senses.

The young cowboys' shouts of exuberance must have been catchy. She'd even joined in a time or two—much to Antie's disapproval. But the excitement was infectious.

There had to be a couple dozen folks running on foot behind the wagon, shouting and yee-hawing.

Some called out "Lady Boss!" while others called "Señorita Boss!"

Every one of them seemed overjoyed to see Travis.

Dogs of all shapes, colors and sizes barked and raced alongside.

Everyone was in right high spirits.

Travis urged the team past the settlement then around a bend at the foot of the hill where a long shadow announced the coming of evening.

Emerging from the shadow, Ivy spotted what had been hidden by the rise of the hill.

Her voice dried up within her at the first sight of her new home—or, more rightly, palace.

Why the place was nearly as big as the *Queen*!

For all that it was the size of a castle, it wasn't made of stone like she'd read those cold fortresses were.

The Lucky Clover's main house was made of white-washed wood, two stories high and with wide porches, one circling the top floor and one the bottom.

Gosh almighty, it was something like the *Queen* in shape and color. Her heart caught in her throat, thinking that the structures could be sisters, or at least cousins. For some reason that was comforting.

To her great relief, there were trees. She was used to trees, was greatly fond of them. Over the years she had even given names to ones that grew along the shore of the Missouri. Like the river itself, they were a part of home.

This house had a yard full of green, leafy beauties. Many of them grew clear past the roof.

Maybe it was silly to imagine that the leaves, scratching against each other in the afternoon breeze, sang her a welcome song.

Perhaps she had played under them as a baby—she, Agatha and Mama.

In a land where shade was scarce, this was an oasis.

When they were still a hundred yards away, people came out the front door. They dashed down the stairs waving arms and aprons.

Gosh almighty, she didn't think she'd be able to learn all their names, let alone be responsible for keeping roofs over their heads.

But Travis had said he would be there to keep the ranch running.

All she had to do was marry some rich man.

Most of the folks running out of the house were women.

Was one of them Agatha? Would Ivy even recognize her own sister?

But no. From what she understood, her sister would not be running.

Sorrow for the lost years hit her hard. She felt her smile sag; the excitement of seeing her new home for the first time faded.

Until this moment of reunion, she hadn't fully recognized all she had lost when her mother took her from the ranch.

Of course, she'd gained as well. There was Uncle Patrick and all the men on the *Queen* she had come to love…and the river, the dear, beautiful Missouri River.

"You all right, honey?" Travis asked, pulling the wagon to a stop in front of the big white porch.

"A mite overwhelmed, I reckon."

She scanned the faces of the ladies gathering about the buckboard. Some had dark hair and brown eyes, others red hair and green eyes. There were some with golden-blond hair.

Several of them appeared to be Ivy's age.

"Where is Agatha?" she asked over the din of excitement and welcome.

"Your sister will be upstairs in her room. Ever since the fever, her nurse is afraid to let her out among people."

That was gull-durned nonsense. Everyone benefited from fresh air and sunshine.

Ivy scanned the upstairs windows. A curtain moved, the last one on the left.

A young woman gazed down. Her hair was red but Ivy couldn't tell what color her eyes were. All of a sudden a shadow crossed the window. A hand yanked the curtain closed.

Could be the shadow belonged to the nurse who didn't believe in the healing properties of the outdoors.

"Señorita Eleanor!" A woman exclaimed, laying her hand on the side of the wagon, her grin wide. "Welcome home."

Something about the woman's greeting—the welcome home part of it—made Ivy wonder if she knew her from before, from when she was a baby.

"Howdy—" A petite yet sharp elbow jabbed her ribs. The reminder might have been painful had her middle not been protected by corset boning. "It's a pleasure to make your acquaintance, ma'am."

"Please meet Señora Morgan," Travis said. "She's probably the most important person living here, being that she heads up the kitchen."

"Slim!" Travis shouted to a man crossing the yard on horseback.

The fellow reigned in alongside the wagon. "Slim, I reckon you've heard that this is our Miss Magee. Eleanor, this is Mr. Morgan, Maria Morgan's husband. Couldn't do without him either. He's our head cowhand, keeps all the young hotbloods in line."

"Thank you for coming, Miss Magee." The weatherworn cowhand placed his hat over his heart, grinning. His eyes reflected the blue of the late afternoon sky. "Things have been glum for a while, not knowing what was to become of us, but now that you're here… Well, you can see by all the celebration we're back to who we were."

He set his hat back on his head, tipped it to Ivy, then leaned down in the saddle to kiss his wife's cheek.

Mrs. Morgan shoved Mr. Morgan away with a swat and a smile.

"Go tend to your boys before they annoy my girls."

Mr. Morgan winked at Ivy. "Now that my lads know they have a future here, I reckon there will be some courting going on…some weddings too maybe."

"You keep those boys in hand until the vows are said. I won't have my girls forced into marriage."

All of a sudden Señora Morgan covered her mouth, clearly embarrassed to have pointed out Ivy's upcoming obligation.

She felt Travis stiffen beside her then make an effort to let his shoulders relax.

Now she understood his desperation to get her here. The whole time he'd been trying to convince her, he'd been seeing the faces of the people he needed to protect. He knew the names and the dreams of those whose futures depended upon Ivy taking her place.

Until this moment she hadn't felt the full impact of that responsibility. In her mind, it was Agatha she had come for.

"It's all right, Mrs. Morgan," Ivy leaned down to

whisper. "I'm glad I'm here. And I'd be pleased if you, and everyone else, would call me by the name I grew up with. It's Ivy."

And at least, even after her marriage, she would remain here on the Lucky Clover.

In time she hoped to feel about the ranch the way she felt about the *Queen*.

Could be that one day the rolling plains and the muddy Platte would feel like home the same as the steamboat had.

And Travis would be here. She glanced over at him, feeling happy to see the joy on his face at being where he belonged.

At least she would not be separated from him.

Some folks might call her disloyal for feeling that way, given that she was about to become engaged to someone else.

But the fact was, she wasn't engaged yet, hadn't even met the fellow. What harm could it do to have soft-hearted feelings for Travis? They were friends.

No matter what happened with William English, she and Travis would be friends. With some effort, she scrubbed the image of his chest, bared to the summer moonlight, from her mind.

The image was a bit more intimate than it ought to be.

For now, all she wanted was to be reunited with Agatha. She knew for a fact that she loved her sister. This was a family bond. A love that a person was born with and would carry until her last breath.

It didn't matter that she hadn't even known about Agatha until recently. A sister was a sister.

"You ready to go inside? See your new home?"

"Reckon so," she muttered under her breath, but then,

remembering the person she was supposed to be, said more loudly, "Why, yes, I'd be delighted to, Mr. Murphy."

Travis leapt from the wagon, like she wished she could do. But since she was a lady wearing a pretty yellow gown, she offered her gloved hand instead.

She felt Antie's smile more than saw it. This acting a lady business was going to be a challenge, but for the sakes of all these people greeting her and wishing her well, she would smile when she wanted to grin, she would take small steps when she wanted to run.

She would marry William English and forget how good it felt to lay her hand in the crook of Travis's strong arm.

Chapter Ten

The first thing that Ivy noticed when she entered the house was not the foyer's high ceiling or the huge parlor beyond it.

It wasn't even Travis's sigh of relief at being home or Madame's gasp of surprise at the fine surroundings.

While the surroundings were impressive, it was the scent of dinner being prepared that caught Ivy's attention.

An aroma that made her stomach growl drifted from somewhere out of sight. She pressed her belly, hoping no one had heard the inner ruckus. Especially Madame du Mer. No amount of training in ladylike behavior would prevent her body's reaction to good food.

Aboard the *Queen*, a hearty rumble meant a compliment to the cook. She didn't reckon that was the case here at the Lucky Clover.

"Gosh almighty, Travis. This is a big house." She let go of his arm, turning in a circle to take it all in. "A girl could get lost."

"There's always someone about who will point you right. Besides, it's an easy place to figure out."

Travis led her from the foyer to the parlor. While the

room was huge, it did not feel vast. It was decorated to look cozy, just like the saloon aboard the *Queen*.

No wonder William English wanted to live here. A territorial legislator could hold some big soirees in this room.

There were plenty of windows with views to the yard. Late afternoon shadows cast a pattern of twisting leaves and blowing branches across rugs of red and brown.

First thing upon coming into the room, one was greeted by a huge stone fireplace.

She reckoned she'd enjoy sitting beside it on a winter's night. Those soft-looking chairs would make a body feel like she was lounging on a cloud.

There were plenty of other tables and chairs arranged casually about the room. Large and small groups of visitors would feel welcome here.

What she wondered was, did Agatha ever come down? Did she ever get to warm her feet by the fire on chilly nights and watch the pretty glow of the flames?

"Where is my sister's room?"

"Agatha's quarters are right overhead."

"Point me the way up." The need to see her sister was more powerful than seeing another inch of the house.

"Down this hall, there's a staircase. I'll take you—" Travis glanced away from her when a woman carrying a tray of food passed by the parlor. "There's Hilda Brunne, now."

The woman with the tray was dressed in black, her thin graying hair knotted in a bun that looked so tight it had to pinch. She nodded at them then continued on her way.

"Mrs. Brunne!" Travis called after her. "Wait one moment and meet Agatha's sister."

"Why, in my hurry, I nearly didn't see you, Mr. Murphy. It's good to have you home." Mrs. Brunne cast him a warm, twinkling smile.

"Welcome home, Miss Magee!" A cowboy strode into the room, hat in hands and nodded at Ivy. "Mr. Murphy, I hate to trouble you just coming in, but there is a question I have about one of the young hands. If you could speak with me in the hall?"

"I won't be a moment, ladies," he said then walked away with the cowboy.

Ivy walked toward the nurse gracefully, her elegant motion sure to make Antie proud.

"How do you do, Mrs. Brunne?" Ivy nodded her head, the way she had been instructed to do when meeting a member of the staff. She smiled just so. It was important to start things off appropriately with Agatha's nurse. "I'm Ivy Magee."

"Yes, I assumed it must be you, given all the hoopla happening outside." Mrs. Brunne's lips curved, but it was odd. The gesture seemed friendly, but only until Ivy looked deeply into her eyes. What she saw in the depths made her feel ill at ease. Something about the woman seemed a bit off, harsh even in spite of her smile.

"Everyone was most welcoming," she said, puzzled because Travis had never mentioned anything about Mrs. Brunne being thorny.

"No doubt," the nurse said.

"I understand that you've been caring for my sister for some time. I—"

"Since she was born."

Gosh almighty! That would mean she'd cared for Ivy, too.

Ivy's misgivings must be unfounded. Surely her father

would not have put his daughters in the care of anyone who was not of sterling character.

"I'll visit my sister now, if you will kindly lead the way."

"That is quite impossible." Hilda jerked her head. Her black-rimmed glasses inched up her nose, but there was a hump that they were not able to slide past. "It's meal time and then bed. I won't have Agatha's routine upset."

"The sun's still up," Ivy pointed out. In fact, judging by the length of the shadows streaming in the long windows, there was still a half hour of daylight. "I'm certain we have a few moments to get reacquainted."

"Routine is routine. It shall be observed."

Ivy believed a person could not help the way she looked—especially when it made her look like a witch—but she sure could help acting like a one.

Ivy wasn't certain Mrs. Brunne's feet even touched the ground when she walked. She glided down the hallway carrying her tray, stiff as a starched sail.

"Why, she must have been weaned on lemons."

"What makes you say so?" Travis asked, coming back into the parlor. "Agatha is quite attached to her."

"I'm not sure I trust her, Travis. Can't say why, exactly, since I only just met her."

"Maybe it's just that you are tired and hungry. Things will look better after you have eaten and rested."

"I too must be tired and hungry. Not a lady of quality, that one," Antie said. "No matter her low station in life."

"Mrs. Brunne?" came a voice from the foyer. Mrs. Morgan bustled into the room, her apron a bright, happy burst of yellow and orange. "I do wonder myself, lately, Travis. She's always had her times, but since you've been gone…"

Mrs. Morgan shrugged, shook her head.

"And our Agatha has lost weight instead of gaining it. I prepare the best of food and still she is weak." Mrs. Morgan wiped her hands on her apron. "But now you all will eat. Especially you, my sweet *señorita*, you are also too thin."

Ivy would like to argue. She was not too thin. It was only the dad-gummed corset pulled tight that made her look like a wasp.

Since Antie was looking at her with such pride, she held her tongue.

"Dinner would be most welcome," she said instead.

She even said it with a smile so sincere that no one would know what was really paddling about in her mind.

Given that this was her home and she'd been reassured she was in charge of it, she ought to be able to climb the stairs to her sister's room and walk boldly inside.

But she'd only been the "Mistress" for a few minutes and was not comfortable with…well, with anything yet. Most especially asserting authority.

For now she would have dinner—and smile.

Even in the dead of night, finding Agatha's room had been easy. It was on the same floor as Ivy's, but all the way down a long hallway, on the south side of the house instead of the north.

It rankled that she was creeping along unfamiliar passages in the dark of night. This was her home, now. She had no need to sneak about.

But she was sneaking, barefooted and in a sheer gown covered by a ruffled robe. She reckoned the sleeping attire would have looked revealing to anyone she encountered, but the point of making this excursion at this late hour was to make sure she did not encounter anyone.

Wasn't it odd that she felt less exposed while swimming naked in the river than she did tiptoeing about a shadowed house with everything but her feet covered?

Must be because she was among so many strangers.

When it came right down to it, modesty didn't count for much when she wanted to see her sister so badly.

And she wasn't about to give up her nightly hours of freedom from tight clothing just to venture from her bedroom decently dressed.

Now, standing in front of Agatha's door with her hand on the knob, she was nervous. She didn't recall ever feeling nervous on the *Queen*. Must be because on board everything was as familiar as her own face.

Here, not only was she surrounded by the unfamiliar, but she was about to meet a person who should be familiar but was not. Someone she had not seen since babyhood, and yet loved.

No wonder it felt like fish were spawning in her belly.

Since nothing was to be gained by standing here with her fingers sweating on the knob, she turned it.

It was locked. Not so surprising, she reckoned, given the hour. Sure wouldn't do to knock and wake the house, especially Miss Brunne if she was nearby. Ivy would rather see Agatha alone.

It was a lucky thing she was a fair hand at jimmying a window.

Three rooms back down the hallway she'd passed by doors that opened to the upper-story deck.

Walking toward Agatha's windows, Ivy pulled the fabric of her nightclothes away from her skin. The air was muggy enough to mistake for hot tea.

Coming to the first window she peered inside. This was a well-appointed parlor.

On one wall was a fireplace. The wall opposite had

two doors—bedroom suites, she figured. Unless she missed her guess, Hilda had a room in Agatha's suite.

She walked to the other window. Peering in, she saw a slender figure in a bed. Red hair peeped over the coverlet.

Ivy tried the window. To her surprise, it slid open without a whisper.

Something tickled her memory. A picture flashed across her mind so quickly she nearly didn't catch it. She saw a blue blanket, sunshine and a small girl with red hair. Ivy's chubby hand reached for the curls. But then again, maybe it had only been a wish or a dream.

On tiptoe, her breath held, she approached the bed. The swish of fabric about her legs was too loud. She stopped, listened for sounds coming from the sitting room.

Tic, tic, tic, went a clock, but nothing else disturbed the silence.

Agatha slept on her back, her hair flared out on the pillow. She wore a heavy nightgown buttoned to her chin. In this heat her poor sister had to be uncomfortable.

How was a soul to breathe in such constrictive sleep-wear? Ivy touched her own throat, traced her fingers down her chest to the swell of her breasts, more than grateful to be blessedly free of fabric.

Slipping down to her knees, she leaned over the still form in silence. She did not want to speak out loud and wake her suddenly. Surely Agatha would be frightened by the appearance of a stranger in her room in the middle of the night.

Ivy hovered her fingers over the arch of her sister's brow, down the line of her cheek. What should be plump and firm was gaunt, shadowed.

I've come home for you, Ivy thought. She didn't know

she had begun to cry until a drop fell onto Agatha's nightgown.

Ivy swiped at her cheeks with her bare arm.

Close by, a door opened and closed. Hilda coming out of her room!

Ivy went still. She held her breath, listened.

The squeak of springs being compressed told her that Hilda Brunne had settled into a chair. Lamplight suddenly flared under the doorway.

While the sitting room had appeared stylishly decorated, she could now see enough to know that Agatha's room was sparse. Not even an interesting picture decorated the walls. The only items in here were a bed, a wicker wheelchair and a bedside table with a book on it. A book, well, that was something, at least.

With the added light, she could see how pale Agatha's skin really was. Any whiter and she'd look like a mound of snow.

Ivy stroked her sister's thin hand where it lay across her chest. That ought to have made her stir, but did not.

Probably because she was prostrate from the heat in that absurdly wrong nightgown.

"Let's cool you off." Ivy said moving her lips but uttering no sound.

She unbuttoned the gown from throat to chest, fanned the lapels to cool the sweat on her skin. Agatha's chest lifted in a deep sigh that Ivy took as relief.

She oughtn't to be skinny, not with the rich food Mrs. Morgan prepared.

Ivy was sure she'd gained a full inch around the waist after a single meal. Come morning, Antie was going to have the devil of a time harnessing her into her clothes.

The springs of the chair squeaked again, this time in a rhythmic way. It seemed that Hilda Brunne was rocking back and forth. She mumbled something in a tender voice but Ivy could not understand it. Then she began to sing a child's lullaby…but at the same time, it sounded like she was weeping.

"Things are going to change, sister. I'm here now. Don't you worry."

Many things were going to change, she vowed while backing toward the window. This oppressive room being one of them.

Even after midnight, a band of sweat dampened Travis's collar.

Sitting at his desk and staring down at the account books, he opened his shirt then yanked it out of his britches.

Familiar sounds drifted in through the open window. The summer song of crickets, the twitter of night birds and a breeze rustling the leaves outside made him roll his head back on his neck and sigh.

It was good to be home.

Picking up a pen he returned his attention to several weeks of neglected work piled beside his elbow. With a long, loud yawn, he scraped his palm over his face.

As sleepy as he was, he needed to spend a few hours in his office, setting things to order.

Dipping his pen into the ink bottle, he continued entering invoices and receipts into the ledger.

One invoice was from the new schoolteacher he had hired. The fellow came at a high price, but it seemed like he was worth the money. Along with the invoice, he had attached a progress report of each student.

Foster Magee would have approved, given the value he placed on his employees' well-being.

Focusing again on the figures before him, Travis

scratched his head. It was a good thing Ivy had agreed to come home. From what he was seeing, yes, what he had expected to see, the Lucky Clover would not be able to operate much longer.

He couldn't help but wonder what Ivy was doing. Was she exhausted and sleeping, or restless over the upheaval in her life. Things had to be overwhelming for her. The way of life she had known until now would be nothing like the one she was taking on.

The carefree river nymph he had first met now carried the fate of many on her shoulders. He would meet with a lawyer next week and make sure that even after her marriage to English, every inch of this ranch would remain her sole property and under her control.

He doubted English would fight that condition. All he wanted was the political advantage that being linked to the Lucky Clover would bring him.

"Thank the good Lord!"

Travis spun in his chair to see an angel standing outside his window.

"Ivy?"

"Yep, it's me." She lifted one leg over the windowsill, not seeming concerned that her sheer sleeping clothes slid up over her knee. "Sure am glad you're up late."

"What are you doing out there?"

"Getting dad-gummed lost, is what."

"But it's after midnight."

She shifted her other leg into the room. When she stood the gown settled modestly about her bare toes.

Not so modestly, it hugged the curves of her womanly shape.

"I just sneaked into my sister's bedroom. Got lost trying to find my way back inside the house." Placing her hands on her hips, she stared down at him with a frown. "Didn't much like what I saw in there."

"Is Agatha ill?"

Since Foster had passed, he hadn't seen much of Agatha. Being busy running the ranch, he'd relied on Hilda's reports.

There had never been any reason to doubt her judgment. She always seemed dedicated to Agatha.

"Can't rightly say if she's sick or not. It was dark and she was asleep. But she was skinny as a minnow."

Travis stood up, rolled his shoulders to stretch.

"Señora Morgan sends up plenty of food."

"Anybody ever see Hilda give it to her?"

"She takes meals in her room. But, Ivy..." For a moment his attention wandered, watching the play of lamplight on her hair. Gold shimmers weaved in and out among the strands falling over her shoulders. "If she's overprotective I'm sure it's out of concern."

"I still don't trust her. She was up there rocking back and forth and mumbling something. Then she sang a baby's lullaby to no one at all."

"She lost twin babies before she came to the Lucky Clover. Could be she was just looking back and remembering."

"It was downright odd, is what it was. And my sister looked like a ghost. When was the last time she was out in the sunshine?"

He didn't know.

The thing is, Ivy's sister had always been sickly, even as a child. It didn't seem so odd that after her fever she was even more so.

"Speaking of health." He took her by the shoulders, turned her toward the door. The urge to spin her fully toward him, to press her close and trace the curve of her waist, made his fingers itch. "You…umm…need to get some sleep. Tomorrow I'm showing you around the ranch and there's a lot to see."

She reached up and patted his hands. He wondered if she could feel how tense they were. How they nearly twitched with temptation.

"Good night, Travis." She stepped beyond his reach.

Even though he no longer had his hands on her, his gut twisted. Ivy would be completely unaware of the fact that with each step she took toward the door, the fabric of her nightclothes swayed over the round curve of her bottom.

"Sure do wish there was a swimming hole close by." Ivy turned, grinned and winked at him.

Hell in a basket! he cried out, but only inside his brain. Ivy Magee could no more be his than the moon.

Chapter Eleven

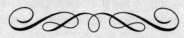

Walking into the kitchen before daylight, Ivy kicked the hem of her gown with her fancy shoe. How a body was supposed to go riding about a ranch in this getup was hard to imagine.

As soon as the horse started to trot, the dad-gummed bustle was going to spring her out of the saddle. It only made things worse that the dress was yellow. Every bee and hornet on the Lucky Clover would mistake her for a daisy.

But today of all days, Antie had insisted, it was important to look the lady.

Gathering proper manners, Ivy smiled at the women bustling about the kitchen by lamplight.

"Good morning." She nodded, thinking that they must have been up and busy for a long time since the kitchen was already filled with delicious aromas. Kind of reminded her of the *Queen* in that way. The boat's cook was always up well before daylight.

Now there was a comfort.

"Good morning, Señorita Ivy." Mrs. Morgan returned her smile. "What brings you here so early?"

"Food. I'm so hungry I could eat a bear." Oh, no, that

was not a ladylike response. Antie would take a switch to her if she knew. "I'd like a bite to eat if it's not too much trouble. Mr. Murphy is taking me riding about the ranch this morning and we are getting an early start."

"Ah, and you look so pretty. But you are going to visit ranch families, not neighbors. Your gown will be ruined."

Isn't that exactly what she'd told Antie an hour back? Looked like Antie was no more used to ranch ways than Ivy was.

"Laura Lee," Señorita Morgan said to a girl removing a tray of biscuits from the oven. "Fetch your spare riding skirt, and a blouse for your lady boss."

"Yes, ma'am." Laura Lee turned to Ivy with a smile. "I do believe we are of a size."

Laura Lee returned a moment later with a grin and an armload of clothes.

Gosh almighty if there wasn't a skirt cut like pants so a woman didn't have to break her neck trying to ride with both legs on the same side of the saddle. Ivy was only now beginning to get the feel of riding a horse as it was.

"I thought you'd need these, too." Laura Lee handed her a pair of tall black boots, polished to a shine.

Her first inclination was to hoot out loud but she caught herself. Still, clothing that was commonsense and pretty at the same time was something to hoot about, maybe even dance a jig over.

"Thank you, Laura Lee. I'll return them to you clean and unharmed."

"You'll do no such thing, Miss Magee. This is a gift and a little thanks for all you are doing for us. I can replace these clothes easy enough, but our ranch, our home, it can never be replaced."

"I'm mighty—" Dash it! "Quite grateful. Thank you."

Being one person in her mind and another coming out of her mouth was plum difficult.

But dunk her in the muddy river if she wasn't going to do her best to become a lady for the sakes of these women who were freeing her from the dainty gown and helping her into the amazing trouser-skirt…and feeding her while they did it.

She understood why they seemed so happy.

Ivy, of all people, knew how important home was.

The last thing Travis expected when he'd knocked at Mrs. Flairty's front door was to hear a scream, to see blood running from the woman's hand when she opened it to them.

Ivy recovered from the shock quicker than he did and led the injured woman to a chair.

Pulling up a stool, she sat down across from the cowboy's wife.

While he watched, his stomach rolling over, Ivy turned the wounded hand this way and that, examining the gash that the kitchen knife had made. She didn't flinch or turn green, like he reckoned he was doing.

"I should have been paying better attention," Mrs. Flairty said, grimacing.

"I know it hurts, but after a good cleaning and a few stitches it will heal fine. I've seen much worse leave barely a scar." Ivy smiled while she spoke, giving reassurance to her. And to him.

"You have?" Mrs. Flairty's eyebrows rose in her pale face. "I wouldn't think a lady like you would have occasion to."

"Well I…" Ivy glanced quickly at Travis. "This won't

take long. Tell her a funny story, Mr. Murphy, while I work."

"Once upon a time…" There was a river nymph swimming naked in the river—"There was a horse who—well he…"

"That's all right, Mr. Murphy…I'll just remember what it felt like to give birth to Sally. This will seem like a scratch compared to that."

Just as well, he had no idea what funny thing the horse was going to do. Unable to watch Ivy stitching the wound, he looked out the front door at clouds gathering in the western sky.

The tour of the ranch was going better than he could have hoped for. Ivy played the part of a lady well. But she was who she was. No matter how refined she acted, her friendly spirit, her kindness, shone through.

At the schoolhouse she had played tag with the children. When she assured them they need no longer worry about losing their homes, she accepted their sticky hugs and kisses with genuine happiness.

When he took her on a tour of the bunkhouse, she didn't turn up her nose at the ripe scent of so many men living close together.

Out on the open range, cowboys tending their herds spotted her and came galloping in to express their gratitude. When occasionally they punctuated their joy with a cussword, her cheeks did not flame. Travis wondered if maybe masculine language made her homesick for the roustabouts on the *River Queen*.

She didn't show it if it did.

"There now," Ivy said. "Keep your hand clean and it will heal just fine. Mr. Murphy? Would it be all right if we send over dinner from the main house for the next week? I don't want these stitches coming loose."

"That would be fine, Miss Magee."

If Foster was looking down, he would be right proud of his heir for watching out for the families of his cowhands.

Ivy stood and removed the blood-soaked apron she had put on but did not return it to Mrs. Flairty.

"I'll bring it back in a few days when I check on your hand."

They left a few moments later with a cake wrapped up in a towel and a bushelful of thanks.

"You were wonderful, Ivy. Cool as a stone in cold water."

"I wasn't the one being sewed up. She was the cool one." Ivy grinned, her smile free of mannerly restraint. "I've seen worse on the *Queen*. Are we ready to head home? I want to see my sister in the light of day."

"I'd like to show you one more thing."

"There's more?"

"I think you'll like it and it's not far—less than an hour's ride."

Half an hour in, the clouds lowered, blackened. Fat warm raindrops pelted down. The ground smelled fresh and damp. He breathed in deep, saw Ivy doing the same.

The trouble was, this time of year a refreshing rain could turn dangerous in a hurry.

"See that tree off yonder? There's a shelter shed."

By the time they reached it they would be soaked to the skin. He only hoped they would miss the bruising hail that was probably coming.

"Better shed those wet clothes, Ivy." Travis shucked his boots off, then his pants and shirt.

Ivy's mouth went a little dry; her cheeks warmed. Even though he kept his red underwear on, it was plastered against his skin, so as far as modesty went, they didn't provide any.

Not that she hadn't already seen his backside in the natural, but here, confined in this tight little room, everything seemed more intimate.

Since her underthings were sheer to start with, she figured she better leave her clothes on.

"I don't mind being wet."

Travis worked on building a fire in the small hearth. Try as she might to look away from his backside, shifting with his movements, it was plum impossible.

"You'll mind being sick."

That was the gull-durned truth. She didn't much cater to being sick.

"You just keep your head turned that way, Travis Murphy."

"I've seen you in less."

"From a distance…and I wasn't beholden to another man then either."

"You aren't beholden to him yet."

"Might as well be, with all these folks depending on me."

Travis sat down on the floor near the hearth, his back dutifully toward her.

"Join me." He beckoned a moment later with a wave of his fingers.

"You hungry? We can eat my cake." She'd made sure to bring it inside after they secured the horses in the shelter attached to the shed.

"I could eat the last crumb."

"It's my cake, Travis Murphy. Don't try and take more than your fair half."

Lightning scattered overhead, followed by pounding thunder.

Ivy sat down, facing away from him. The heat of the fire warmed her right side, smoothing away the bumps that the chill had pebbled under her skin.

She broke the cake then handed Travis his share.

"How long do you reckon we'll be stuck here?" she asked, as if this wasn't a downright cozy place to be.

"An hour, maybe two."

"No reason not to be comfortable, then." Sitting on the hard floor for two hours was bound to cause backache.

Pressing back, she leaned into a cushion of warm, firm muscle.

"It's better this way, don't you think?"

She felt his lungs expand. He grunted an answer, which could mean yes or no. After a moment of staring at the flames, he nodded.

"Are you homesick, Ivy?"

It took a moment to answer over the lump swelling in her throat. She tapped her fingers on the floor, noticed it then forced them to be still.

"I miss my uncle something fierce."

"Are you sorry you came? Now that you're here and have seen the place?"

Hail beat suddenly on the roof, pinging so hard she wondered if it was sturdy enough to hold off the storm.

Travis moved his hand along the floor. His long pinkie finger lined up with her slender one, grazed it.

For some reason that made her heart feel all plush, like it was a cat lying in the sun, stretching and content.

No one could accuse them of inappropriately holding hands, but—gosh almighty—they might as well be for all the awareness there was in the touch.

So no, she wasn't sorry for this time to be alone with Travis before everything changed. She cherished it.

"Sometimes, there is no going back, as much as we might think we want it." She leaned her head back. His shoulder blade shifted. With her eyes closed she listened to hail drumming the roof, to wind moaning under the eaves. "I used to look out at the Missouri, with the green trees reflecting on the water, dragon flies darting about and the sky so clear and blue…then I'd think, *Dear Lord, have you ever made anything so beautiful*? Well, a minute later we'd round a bend and there would be snow-capped mountains so tall and majestic looking, and I'd know that He had. Yes, I am homesick but I wouldn't change the choice I made."

"I only hope you always feel that way. I'm responsible for bringing you here. I don't take that lightly, honey. I want you to be happy."

"You did what you had to do, same as I did." His finger stroked the top of hers. "And you never know, Travis. Maybe William English is the one man meant for me. And you can take the credit for my happiness."

Unless, of course, that one man turned out to be Travis Murphy. Blisterin' day! If he was, she was in some kind of terrible trouble.

"I—" Travis seemed to lose track of what he wanted to say because he was quiet for a long time. "I want that for you. It's more important to me than you know."

Oh, great blisterin' day!

"I promise he won't be unkind to you." Travis wrapped his finger about hers, squeezed. She felt his deep inhalation. "If I hear he is, I'll shoot him."

Of course, he didn't mean it about shooting anyone, but the sentiment made her feel reassured. Travis was a good friend.

One who held her finger to finger, who didn't turn to gawk at her soaked underthings when he could do so, one who she suspected would return her to her uncle if she asked it of him.

Of course, William English would have to be some fiendish soul in order for her to ask that of Travis.

Now, more than ever, she knew that Agatha needed her, that Mrs. Morgan needed her, and Laura Lee and the schoolchildren, the stable boys and—

Thunder sounded more distant now, like it was moving toward the east. Folks in the main house would be directly under the worst of it. She wondered if her sister was frightened. Did her nurse reassure her or ignore her?

"Where was it you were taking me?" she asked in order to send her thoughts another way.

"That's a surprise for another time. I won't ruin it by telling."

"Did you eat all your cake? I plumb forgot to save some for Little Mouse. Like any sensible soul, she's partial to cake."

"How is she adjusting to life on the ranch?"

"She's happy enough exploring my room. For her, home is in her little cage or my hat. Doesn't matter much where they are."

"I wonder what will happen once you share a room with Engl—" Suddenly, he turned. She felt his eyes upon her back. Felt it when his fingers brushed her neck as he shifted her hair from her back to her shoulder. "...to your mouse, I mean. Don't know how he'd feel about a rodent."

The heat of his breath grazed her ear. Scoot away, scoot away, her brain screamed. Fickle female that she was, she turned her head so that her mouth was close to his lips.

"I'm good at keeping secrets," she whispered, her

breathing oddly shallow. "He'll never know…about my mouse."

Gosh almighty he smelled good. So manly and virile.

With a deep inhalation then a long exhale, he slid away from her, only keeping hold of the hair still twined through his fingers.

"Some secrets just show, even though we don't mean them to," he murmured.

He was right of course, so she unwound her hair from his fingers and scooted farther away.

But his gaze glanced quickly over her, just as hers lingered on him.

"I think the storm's moving on," he said.

But he was wrong. She feared that it was only beginning.

It had been a long time since Travis had taken dinner in the formal dining room.

While Foster was alive, dinner in this vast room was commonplace. Travis often ate here with his boss and whatever guests he was entertaining.

After Foster passed away, though, meals at this table became dreary. More often, he ate in his office or in the kitchen with the Morgans.

But this afternoon, when he'd blown in the front door with the wind at his back and Ivy clinging to his arm, he'd found Mrs. Morgan merrily setting the table with all the best china and silver.

The house now had a mistress. Apparently, Mrs. Morgan was determined to fuss over her.

This evening Travis, Madame du Mer and Ivy at her mannered best, gathered at one end of the long table.

"How do you do, Mr. Murphy," Ivy greeted him with

a nod as though they had not just spent the afternoon together in their underclothes.

"I'm delighted to be having dinner with two such lovely ladies," he answered in kind.

"I trust you had a pleasant day?"

"You ought to know, Ivy, I spent it with you."

Ivy sighed. Madame frowned.

"I reckon I know you did, but tarnation, I need to make polite talk or Antie will skin me alive."

"Antie will be disappointed." Antie arched an eyebrow. "The staff must understand that their mistress is a lady."

"The staff is not present, Madame du Mer," he pointed out. "Perhaps Ivy can be herself for a while."

"This is who our *petite* is now."

"Antie is right, Travis…that is, Mr. Murphy. If I am to make a success of things. I need to live this role."

He ought to be glad of that. It's what he wanted, but for some reason dinner didn't seem as appealing as it had a moment ago.

For some reason? He damn well knew the reason. Eleanor Ivy Magee, his river nymph, was changing into William's prairie queen.

All of a sudden the gravy on his potatoes seemed lumpy, the meat tough. Something wrong was wriggling in his heart—a vain hope that William would change his mind.

Eleanor Ivy Magee had come to mean too much to him.

One of Mrs. Morgan's serving girls carried in a dessert tray. She set a piece of cake in front of each of them.

"Thank you, Laura Lee," Ivy said with a formal, but warm smile.

"My pleasure, miss."

Laura Lee, blushing from the apparent gratification of serving cake to the boss lady, half skipped from the dining room and into the hallway.

In a bit of bad timing, she nearly collided with Hilda Brunne in the hallway, carrying a tray of food.

"You clumsy oaf! Have a care for your betters!" Hilda glanced sidelong into the dining room, spotted Travis and smiled at him as though she had not just scolded the kitchen girl. "Sweet thing that you are, Laura Lee."

Ivy stood suddenly, her chair scraping across the floor.

"Mrs. Brunne," she said mildly, but Travis figured she was as hopping mad over Hilda's rudeness to Laura Lee as he was. "If you want to keep your position at the Lucky Clover, you will treat your fellow employees with respect. If that meal is for my sister, you may leave it here. And bring Agatha down. She will dine with us tonight."

Hilda's eyes narrowed at Ivy defiantly. That was something Travis had not seen before. He'd heard stories once in a while from others, but with him she had always been professional, even sweet natured.

"I'm sure you mean well, Miss Magee, but routine is routine. I will not have my… Miss Magee's stomach soured by the change."

"I insist," Ivy answered, her smile sweet but determined looking.

"Good evening to you." With that, Hilda presented her back then continued down the hallway toward the back stairs.

Ivy sat back down in her chair with a thump. She drummed her fingers on the table, her eyebrows arched high in her forehead, glancing between him and Madame.

"Blisterin' day! That woman gets under my skin."

"She has no culture," Madame declared. "How is she to care for a young lady?"

The big clock at the far end of the room ticked away two minutes of silence during which Ivy's face became increasingly flushed.

"I've been here for more than a day and still haven't met my sister."

All of a sudden Ivy lurched to her feet, gathered up her skirt and looped it over her arm. With an abrupt spin, she went after Hilda Brunne.

Blisterin' day indeed!

Chapter Twelve

Hilda's rush down the hallway was slowed some by the food clattering on the tray, but she was still a good distance ahead.

And she was quicker than Ivy would have given her credit for. Maybe she was younger than she let on.

Hilda made it to the door. While balancing the tray on one hand, she dug into the pocket of her stark black dress and retrieved a key.

With a backward glare, she slipped inside.

Ivy heard the lock slip into place.

If she had to break down the door, she would not be denied seeing Agatha.

She pounded on the door. The impact made her bones hurt, a splinter jabbed her palm. It didn't matter. She'd chew through the blasted wood if she had to.

"Open the dad-gummed—" Ivy caught herself, took a breath. She was the one in charge, the lady of the ranch. "I insist that you open the door."

The only answer was silence, then the sound of the tray being slammed down on a table.

Ivy had never considered her temper to be out of the

ordinary, no hotter than anyone else's. But it flashed through her now as hot and quick as a boiler explosion.

She raised her foot, ready for another attack on the door.

She heard a jingle.

"No need to break a foot, Ivy." Travis handed her a ring of keys, the one she needed pinched between his fingers.

She drew in a composing breath, went up on her toes and kissed his cheek. "Thank you."

Antie stood beside him, frowning. Ivy reckoned she ought to have kept that kiss in her mind, but she was downright grateful to have the key.

A lecture was coming later, she saw it in her teacher's severe expression.

Ivy shoved the key into the lock, turned it. She shoved the door, felt the resistance of someone pushing. Suddenly, it swung open wide.

"You have no right," Hilda hissed.

In the soft glow of the parlor lamp, Ivy saw her sister sitting in a chair—too thin, too pale and very frightened looking.

Ivy had every right—and obligation—to protect Agatha.

Still, setting straight who had what rights would wait for another time.

"Agatha," Seeing the apprehension in her sister's eyes, she approached the chair slowly. She knelt down beside it. "It's me… Ivy."

"Mother Brunne?" Agatha cast a frantic look at her nurse.

Mother? If Agatha really had put Nurse Brunne in their mother's place, Ivy would have to deal with the woman more subtly than she wanted to. She'd have to bide her time, send her packing when Agatha was ready for it. But oh, how she wished to do it now.

"I'm your sister, Ivy."

Agatha's hand trembled. Ivy touched it, stroked it gently. But her sister jerked away as though she had been burned. Then she started to weep.

Hilda reached for a bottle on the table and took the stopper off.

"Take your medicine like a good girl, Agatha."

Agatha tried to push it away. "No, mother, I don't like it."

"You must. You are too frail for all this agitation."

Before Ivy could grab the bottle, Hilda pinched Agatha's hollowed cheeks and forced her mouth open. She poured what was in the bottle down her throat.

"Good girl," Hilda crooned. "We'll both sleep the better for it."

Sooner than Ivy would have expected, Agatha's eyes took on a faraway look then her eyes fluttered closed.

"What have you given her?" Ivy swiped the bottle out of Brunne's hand and sniffed the rim.

"Nothing harmful." Hilda glowered at Ivy over the rim of her spectacles. "Laudanum is a common treatment for the frail of spirit."

"Ivy," Travis took her by the elbow. "Your sister is asleep. There's nothing to be gained by staying."

Sure would be if that balcony was not outside the window.

But Travis was right. A confrontation with Hilda Brunne would help nothing at the moment.

"We'll speak of this in the morning, Mrs. Brunne," Travis said before going into the hallway.

"Oui." Antie shot "Mother Brunne" a scowl then followed Travis out of the room.

Ivy lingered behind in the doorway.

"I suspect that you do not have my sister's best interests at heart. I will not allow you to harm her."

"Harm my sweet Maggie? You are the one who used to pull her pretty red hair, Bethy." All of a sudden Hilda Brunne frowned, shook her head then blinked. "Ivy I mean… I simply misspoke, but the truth remains that even as a baby you were a troublesome one."

"I reckon you are going to find me even more troublesome now."

Guilt kept Travis from falling into bed and into the arms of oblivion where, he imagined, he had been for too long.

Why was Agatha really frail? It was true that the near-fatal fever had left her bedridden and the doctor warned them that it would take her a long time to recover. But had Hilda Brunne kept her weak intentionally? It made no sense why she would have, and it wasn't unheard of for women to be kept content by a dose of laudanum now and then.

With a good night's sleep impossible, he did what he often did when worried. He walked.

Out among the trees and the stars, he listened to the wind blow the treetops, seeking peace of mind.

"She's scared of me, Little Mouse."

Ivy's voice came from behind a tree a short distance away. The white ruffle of her nightgown peeked out from behind the trunk where she sat on the ground.

He ought to do the sensible thing and hightail it for the house. He knew how sheer that gown was, even covered by a robe but—

"It's festering me, wondering how long Agatha's been getting poisoned."

That very thought was festering at him as well. Had he been blind when it came to Agatha's care? Had he simply assumed that Brunne knew what was best for the young woman she'd raised?

"Ivy?" he called, but quietly. "What are you doing out here?"

"Grumbling to my furry friend."

"You decent enough for company?"

Wind shuffled the leaves of the trees but Ivy remained silent.

"My clothes are dry," she said at last.

Taking that as consent for company, he walked around the tree trunk, sat down beside her.

If he kept his gaze on the full moon peeking through the leaves, maybe he could sit here without feeling things he had no right to feel. Remembering things that would only cause him heartache.

Things such as how his river nymph had looked, naked in the moonlight that first night. He tried not to recall how she had smelled fresh and green with the Missouri as her perfume.

"You're worried," he said.

"Would be, I reckon, if I wasn't planning on taking charge of my sister's care."

"You're angry."

"Sure am. There's some things I don't understand." He heard the fabric shift across her chest when she shrugged but didn't dare look at her.

"Like how we didn't notice what was happening with her?"

"My pa...he should have."

The mouse crawled upon his knee. He touched the small white head with his thumb.

Odd that a wild creature could be so tame, so charming even.

In a way, the critter was like Ivy. A free spirit who had come to abide by the rules of society.

He couldn't help but wonder if English would ever know who Ivy really was, if he would come to love her like he—

With a start, he jerked back from finishing that thought.

Hell's beans! Just because he refused to think something didn't mean that he didn't feel it.

Double damn hell's beans!

"Your Pa began to take sick a short while after Agatha's fever. It was a slow sickness, but as he got weaker he trusted Agatha more completely to Brunne's care."

"Sounds to me like she's always been sickly."

"That's what everyone said. I was just a kid and accepted it. But I remember thinking maybe she was overprotected more than sickly. When I became a cowhand, all I saw were cattle for long periods of time. I'm sorry, Ivy, we all just trusted what Hilda told us, that Agatha was frail and the excitement of being out and about would harm her. It could be true, I reckon. I'm just sorry I never questioned anything."

"It was my pa's place to worry, not a boy finding his own way." Ivy shook her head. Her hair shimmered in the moonlight when the strands shifted. "Wonder how long she's been taking that laudanum. It could be to blame for her sorry state as much as the fever."

"I ought to have paid more attention, Ivy. I'm not a boy any longer."

She punched him in the side with her elbow. The wind caught a wisp of her hair and blew it across his chest.

"I reckon I noticed that, Travis."

It would be so easy to reach for her, feel what was barely hidden under her nightclothes and show her the man he had become...but that way lay disaster for everyone he loved.

If he had betrayed Agatha by his inattention, he would not do so again by forfeiting the only home she had ever known.

Ivy was meant for William English, not Travis Murphy. He made this a litany in his mind, repeating it over and over.

Because day by day, it felt more like Ivy was meant for him—for Travis Murphy and no one else.

"If you want to terminate Hilda's employment, I'll do it."

"Can't rightly see how we can. Looks like my sister thinks the witch is her mother. I wonder what the sudden separation would do to her."

"I'm sorry for that, Ivy."

"Why? I don't hold it against you. I just can't figure how my father could have quit seeing her when it seemed he cared so much for everyone else."

She lay her head on his shoulder, sighed. "Folks are just complicated I reckon."

"I think his true love was this ranch," he said.

The thought was unsettling because English was much like Foster in his dedication to a goal. Would Ivy be someone that her husband barely noticed?

If he were free to wed Ivy, Travis would be aware of her every moment of his life.

Coming downstairs the next morning Ivy found Travis pushing the parlor furniture against the walls.

"Antie's ordered dance instruction before breakfast."

"I already know how to dance."

Dance lessons were not on her mind just now. Her sister was.

"Show us, *ma petite*," Antie said, coming into the parlor carrying a tray filled with coffee and sweets. "We will see where to begin."

Wasn't this a waste of time? She was nearly as good a dancer as she was a gambler. All the men on the boat said so.

"All right, give me room."

Travis and Antie took a few steps back.

"More room than that."

Antie placed the tray on a table then the pair of them backed up to the wall.

If dancing was what they wanted, dancing they would get. The sooner they witnessed her skills, the sooner she could deal with her sister's welfare.

She began as she always did with a wide grin and her toe tapping. Next, she slapped her thighs and stomped out a rhythm, which was plum hard to do in this dress. When she shouted her ending "Yee-haw," she was nearly breathless. Dancing a jig was a world easier in trousers.

"That was…" Madame stammered. "It was quite…"

"Rousing." Travis clapped three times. "Lovely…energetic."

"Seems to me the pair of you wouldn't have your mouths hanging open if you thought so."

"So full of youth and energy," Antie said. "But when you become Mrs. English, the dances you will need to know are a bit, well, different."

Fancy is what she meant. She'd heard of elegant dances, even seen them done a time or two. Right now it all seemed so frivolous given that Agatha was upstairs being drugged.

"Monsieur." Antie nodded to Travis. "You will show your partner the position to begin."

Travis stepped forward, gave her a polite nod, then placed his big, warm hand on her waist. If she didn't have other things on her mind, she might enjoy learning to waltz, after all.

Next, he took her hand, placed it on his shoulder and smiled. She could hardly object to that and was surprised that her instructor in all things respectable was not raising a fuss.

He trailed his fingers down her other arm, his touch as soft as a secret whisper. This did make Antie tsk-tsk. But when Travis took her hand, held it out and up, her teacher nodded her approval.

"I didn't reckon a cowboy knew how to waltz."

"It's the Westernized version. It wouldn't do in royal circles."

"I doubt we'll be dancing with the king of England anytime soon."

Antie began to count out time. Travis led her this way and that. She stumbled into his arms two times by accident, then twice more on purpose.

It hadn't been a lie when she said she was a good dancer, so she caught on to the cowboy version of a waltz quickly.

After an hour she was comfortable, feeling the count of the steps, imaging them to music.

It seemed as natural as a bee gathering pollen to be held in Travis's strong arms, to let him glide her about the parlor in a melodic embrace. Well, melodic in her mind since there was no fiddler at hand.

She could only wonder if getting lost in one's partner's gaze was a common part of the waltz, or perhaps this was special to her and Travis.

More than special. Compelling, intimate, and something she doubted she would feel when the time came to dance with her future intended.

"Très bien, ma petite." Antie shooed them apart. "Mr. English will be pleased. Now you may eat."

Ivy blinked twice, clearing the dreamy haze swirling in her brain. She'd been so caught up in Travis that she'd plum forgotten this morning's goal.

"Gosh almighty!" She grabbed three pastries off the tray. "I'm having breakfast on the east porch with my sister."

"I'll help you bring her downstairs." Travis followed her up the rear stairway. "What did Mrs. Brunne have to say about this?"

"I reckon we're about to find out."

It sure did feel reassuring to have him at her back.

If Ivy still had trouble maneuvering in the restrictive clothing, it was not apparent in the moment.

She looked like an avenging angel in red plaid charging up the steps and brandishing croissants.

Couldn't rightly say she sounded like an angel. With every step she built up a bigger head of steam. Words that she must have learned from her river friends trailed behind her.

Approaching the door to Agatha's room, she balled her fist, raised it to pound on the door.

Half a second before impact she dropped her hand and spun toward him.

"Better calm me down before I scare my sister again."

He wasn't sure calming was possible, or if he should even try. It was becoming apparent that whatever fury Ivy released upon Hilda Brunne, the woman probably deserved.

It angered him that her smile had deceived him over the years. The woman he'd known was congenial. Although, thinking about it now, she had become that way after Foster died and he took over.

Had her smiles all been a ruse to make sure he did not see the person beneath it? A twinkle to blind the eye of the boss?

Taking Ivy by the shoulders, he drew her away from the door. It might not be wise to let the nurse know they were outside.

"Act like you would around your mouse. Calm voice, tender touch."

"I feel more like a lion than a mouse, but I'll try."

The sound of Brunne's voice came through the door, muffled, the words indistinct.

Quietly, Ivy cupped her hand and put her ear to the door.

He did the same. Amazing, he could hear each word clearly now.

"My sister is home, Mother. Last night I was afraid but—"

"And you were right to be, Agatha. She wants nothing to do with you. She is not your true family. The only one you can count on is me. Tell me you know that."

"But Mother Brunne—"

"Repeat it, Agatha, I am the only one who truly cares about you."

"You are the only one who truly loves me, Mother Brunne. I know that but... I have a sister!"

"Yes, one who is simply here to marry that William English. She's as stiff-nosed as he is."

"I think he's as handsome as a prince."

"How would you know that? You've never met him."

"I watched him from the balcony when he used to come and visit Papa."

"Don't you go getting any ideas about a handsome prince. Why do you think your father never let you attend any of his soirees? Never introduced you to Mr. English?"

"Because he knew you'd never be a fit wife is why. Agatha, my sweet pet, the sooner you understand that it's only you and me, the better off you will be. Don't be fooled—if your father truly loved you, he wouldn't have given everything to your sister."

Travis shook his head. That was not the reason she did not attend the parties. Foster had wanted her to. It was Mrs. Brunne who had insisted that she would suffer for it.

"I don't care about that. I'd be afraid if the ranch belonged to me. Aren't you grateful that Ivy's come?"

"Hardly. She'll try and come between us. Break us apart and rip out our hearts. Don't think that because she claims to be your sister that she won't toss us out on our ears. She has the power to keep me away from you forever. Never forget that."

"I'm scared, Mother. How will I survive outside my room without you?"

"You would not survive, my pet. Without me you will die."

"Maybe not if I had a husband, a strong and handsome one who loved me."

"Mr. English, you mean. You are not a fit match for him. Don't forget what the doctor told me."

"I remember, Mother. It would be the height of folly for me to marry. I would not survive the year."

"Repeat it."

"But what if he was wrong?"

"Repeat it four times—you must accept this."

Agatha did repeat it four times.

Travis had been with Foster and the doctor during Agatha's illness. He had never said anything close to that. All of a sudden he wanted to break down the door with his fists, even though Ivy had the key. He would demand to know why she was making this up.

"That's a good girl. Now give Mother a kiss on the cheek. And remember, as long as you hold on to foolish dreams of Mr. English being your prince you will be unhappy."

"You are right, I suppose. I'm not fit for any man, let alone Mr. English."

"The sooner you face that fact, Maggie, the better off you will be. Mother Brunne would not tell you anything that was not for your good."

Maggie? Who the hell was that?

"Take your medicine now, Agatha, my pet. You'll forget all about a handsome husband."

"Of course, Mother."

During the conversation, Ivy's shoulders had slumped. She'd sagged against him and he'd felt her sorrow. Now with talk of laudanum, she jerked and pushed the pastries at him.

Reaching into her pocket, she drew out the key. Quietly, she opened the door.

"Miss Magee will eat breakfast downstairs this morning," she stated.

"I forbid it." Hilda stood in front of her charge, her arms anchored across her bosom.

Ivy swept past her, swiped up the bottle of laudanum from the table. She carried it to the chamber pot and dumped the contents in.

"You have no right!" Hilda screeched.

"You will find, Mrs. Brunne, that I do."

"Let's see you manage her, then."

Agatha knelt beside her sister's chair.

"Are you frightened of me?" she asked barely above a whisper.

The fact that Ivy was petting Agatha's arm did not appear to reassure her sister. With her breathing quick and her eyes wide, she stared at Ivy in dread.

It was odd; Agatha should have been pretty, like Ivy was, but instead everything about her was dull.

Her delicate features added up to beauty. Her green eyes and red hair did, too. But Agatha was faded.

"Would you like a pastry?" Ivy held out a croissant with chocolate drizzled on top of it.

"No, what is it?" Agatha touched it cautiously with her fingertip. "Is this a forbidden thing, Mother?"

"Evidently, I am not the judge of it. It must be up to you to decide, Agatha."

"But I can't! I need you to tell me what to do."

"Can you stand?" Ivy asked, stroking her sister's hair with a light touch.

"Mother?"

"Travis, will you carry Agatha downstairs?" Ivy asked.

"But I'm not allowed." Agatha's fingers clutched the arms of her chair until her fingertips blanched. "Things are not safe down there. I could be hurt, or take sick."

"I promise you won't be hurt," Ivy cooed. "But Agatha, you are sick already. If you stay in this room, without sunshine or fresh air, you will get even sicker."

"Will you let me carry you?" Travis asked, fearing she would say no. He didn't want to pick her up against her will, but he would if that's what Ivy wanted.

Tears welled in the corners of Agatha's eyes, but she nodded her head one time.

"You, Mrs. Brunne, may spend the morning removing these oppressive drapes from the windows and getting rid of the laudanum," Ivy ordered.

The glare that Hilda stabbed Ivy with surprised him. Although, after all he had just heard, it should not. How could he have lived in the same house with this woman and not known her?

She had deceived him is how. It did not make him feel much of a man to have fallen prey to her artifice.

"When you have finished with it, you may remove the pictures from this room and put them in Agatha's."

Where was his Ivy? This Ivy was not the carefree nymph of the river. The woman now giving orders was her father's child, clear and simple. No one, he decided, could be a more fitting heir.

Chapter Thirteen

Even though Agatha was not sitting in direct sunshine, she blinked her eyes as though the morning light was too bright.

"I reckon it's been a while since you've been outside." Her sister's pale skin said so even if Agatha did not answer the question.

People in the process of performing this and that morning task walked on the path below the porch. It didn't escape Ivy's notice that they seemed surprised to see Agatha out of her room.

Moments ago, Travis had set Agatha down on the chair then gone off to see to his chores. His absence was for the best since his presence seemed to make Agatha nervous.

Then again, everything seemed to make her nervous. Even the croissants on the plate setting on the table.

"You can eat that. It won't hurt you."

"I'm not hungry."

"Would you like to walk in the garden?" There was a pretty one, just down the steps. Roses, lilac and daisies bloomed along pathways and around benches. "We can sit if you feel weak."

"I shouldn't."

"You'll be safe, I promise."

"Walking is difficult for me. I won't manage."

"Have you tried?"

Agatha shielded her eyes, gazing out at the garden.

"When I was little I used to sit in the garden sometimes. But I mustn't risk it now."

"I imagine that's what your nurse says?"

Agatha nodded, glancing apprehensively at the pastries on the dish.

"The truth is, the more you do it, the easier it becomes. Let's try. You can hold on to my arm."

"Mother says I'm not to trust you."

"I'm sure Mrs. Brunne cares for you deeply." Gulldurn it, Ivy doubted that was true. If it was, it was in some twisted way. "But she is mistaken. Agatha, I'm your sister. There's no one in this world you can trust more than me."

Agatha looked down at her lap.

"I've read about sisters in books. I wanted one for the longest time."

"So did I. I think that I remembered you. Not with memories exactly, but my heart remembered how it felt to be with you."

Agatha sighed, nodded. "I used to play that I had a sister. Mother always got ill at ease when I did. Finally she forbade it."

"Why does she say you shouldn't trust me?" Ivy picked up a croissant, licked the chocolate on top. "This is delicious—and I didn't keel over when I tasted it."

"Once you have taken my inheritance, you will toss me and Mother Brunne out with nowhere to go."

"Gosh almighty, Agatha! I will never do that. The only reason I agreed to inherit the ranch was for you...

and all these other folks, but mostly for you. I was happy where I was."

"You really are my sister?" She glanced up from her folded hands.

"Yes."

"I never knew about you until Travis went to get you."

"You came as a surprise to me, too."

Once again, Agatha stared down at her hands in silence.

"If I can prove to you that this here pastry won't hurt you, will you try one little bite?"

"I don't see how you can, but I might. As long as you don't tell Mother Brunne."

"This will be our secret. It would be nice to have a secret between sisters, don't you think?"

Agatha began to smile but halfway into it she stopped. "Mother says I must never keep secrets from her."

"I'm going to prove that this pastry will not hurt you." Ivy opened the pouch she had designed to wear at her waist. "I have a small friend. She's partial to sweets."

"You can trust her not to lead you wrong."

Ivy took the mouse out of her pouch then held her in the palm of her hand. The little critter stretched, yawned, sat up on her hind legs to lick her fir. Ivy couldn't help but kiss her between her cute pink ears.

"You kissed a mouse!" Agatha looked shocked.

Ivy wanted to cheer. While revulsion was not quite the emotion she wanted to elicit, it was better than fear which was all her sister had expressed so far.

"Can't help myself sometimes. She's just so cute. Here, Little Mouse, show us we have nothing to fear from pastry."

Ivy broke off a crispy nibble and gave it to the mouse.

"You see? She gobbled it down and wants more." Ivy

broke off another small bite and handed it to Agatha. "Your turn."

Agatha stared at it for a moment, sniffed it. "I suppose you wouldn't have let her eat it if it would harm her."

"I wouldn't give you anything harmful either. Do you trust me in that?"

"I want to maybe, but Mother says...I don't know what to do."

Giving a quick nod, Agatha appeared to make up her mind. She stuffed the pastry in her mouth whole and chewed slowly.

Three seconds in, she smiled. Ivy wanted to weep on the spot. How long had it been since Agatha had smiled? Given that her nurse was keeping her drugged, it had probably been a good long time.

Just as soon as her sister was strong enough, as soon as she recognized Hilda Brunne for the nasty, controlling woman she really was, Ivy would terminate the witch's employment.

It was a true shame she had to bide her time on this. But wait she would, and make sure the woman did nothing more to harm Agatha.

"I've never tasted anything so delicious!" Agatha looked at the remainder of the croissant with longing.

"Hasn't Mrs. Morgan ever sent treats with your meals?"

"Yes, but Mother eats them all in order to protect me."

"Blazin' day, sister, what is she protecting you from?"

"From becoming even more sickly. Sweet things rot the brain. So does spice of any kind."

Those things also made eating pleasurable so that one didn't end up thin as a rail like Agatha was.

"So Mrs. Brunne eats the things that taste good so that you won't suffer?"

"She does love me."

"The thing is, Agatha, I don't see Mrs. Brunne turning sickly from eating those things. Don't you wonder why?"

"I…"

With a trembling hand, Agatha picked up the rest of the croissant, licked off the chocolate like she'd seen Ivy do. She brushed the crumbs off her fingers. "I'd like to hold the mouse, if you think that would be all right?"

As if Little Mouse understood Agatha's need, she scampered onto the offered hand.

"Her feet tickle my palm." Agatha glanced at a child running along the path with a chalkboard tucked under his arm. "I hope no one sees. Mother will worry. I'll need to take a large dose of the medicine."

"Do you trust me at least a little bit?"

"Maybe I shouldn't, but I might…just a bit. So far I don't feel ill from eating the pastry like Mother always said I would."

"A little bit of trust is a good start, I reckon. I've told Mrs. Brunne you are not to have the laudanum. Will you tell me if she asks you to take it again?"

"I'll try, Ivy. I will, but it does make me sleepy and sometimes I can't make a clear thought."

"Now that I'm here, things are going to change for you. You might not be comfortable with it all at first, but in the end, you will be healthy—strong and not frail. You'd like that, wouldn't you?"

"I'd like to come down and watch the parties."

"How would you like to dance at one?"

Agatha shook her head, no.

Ivy reckoned she'd pushed too hard, made her sister skittish. But in time Agatha would be dancing.

As long as William English was pleased with Ivy, still

wanted to marry her after he met her, she would have the time she needed to make her sister strong.

Everything depended upon him accepting her.

Between now and the barbecue, when she would meet him for the first time, she would work as hard as a bee in summer to become a lady William would be proud of.

The heartache was, a bond with William English meant growing away from Travis.

Ivy sat upon her horse's back, gazing at rolling, golden land that seemed to stretch all the way to eternity. She breathed in the scent of the grass, listened to the distant bellow of cattle and the faraway shouts of cowboys who were well beyond her view.

Even the brush was alive with the twitter of small birds hopping merrily from twig to twig.

In June, she'd been positive that no place would ever be home but the *River Queen*. But now, here it was August and the big house to the east, looking like a pearl in the distance, was beginning to capture a place in her heart.

One day she expected to be as comfortable on horseback as she had been on the deck of the riverboat.

Of course the wide and muddy Platte would never be the equal of the great Missouri.

Even though she was coming to accept the changes in her life, find joy in her days even, she would always miss that wonderful river.

But life was opening up in a way that made her heart nearly sing out loud. Agatha was beginning to show interest in life outside her room.

If Ivy ever questioned the wisdom of having mice for pets, and she couldn't recall that she had, she did not do so now.

Affection for the docile rodent was what had convinced Agatha to regularly leave the safety of her room and venture into the sunshine. It seemed that her sister had a fondness for animals that had never been allowed to blossom.

The outings had been few and short, always accompanied by the hovering shadow of Mrs. Brunne. Still, it was a beginning.

Truth to tell, it wasn't only the mouse helping Agatha find life beyond her familiar walls, it was anticipation of the barbecue which Agatha intended to watch from a dim corner.

Ivy only wished she could watch from a corner, too. She didn't feel half ready to play her role.

Becoming refined was not as easy as putting on new clothes. There was learning to walk, talk and subtly flirt—and all at the same blamed time.

The flirting was what had her most worried. It was as natural to her as icicles hanging from the smokehouse during a heat wave.

Coquetry was the reason she found herself out here alone.

As much as she needed to learn how to charm William English, she sure as blazes couldn't practice on Travis.

If she batted her eyes at him, sighed in a way to make her bosom rise…well, blazin' days if she wouldn't want to feel his hands upon it.

It was a wicked thing to want and she knew it. But lately it was plum hard not to imagine. Maybe if his hands weren't twitching at her ribs during dance lessons she would not have pictured it at all.

But his big, bold, cowboy fingers were twitching. Subtly so Antie wouldn't notice, but still, they were.

He wanted to touch her bosom. She wanted him to. The secret was there between them.

"Gosh almighty, what a pickle," she murmured. "How's a body to learn how to attract a man and keep him away at the same time?"

Antie had told her what to do, lower her eyelids while looking into his eyes—a plum tricky thing to do in Ivy's opinion—and most important to sigh with the bosom. Look tantalizing and virtuous all in one demure little package.

It was all a bunch of monkeyshines, but here she was trying to learn it.

With a sigh—of resignation, not seduction—she slid off the horse then tied it under the shade of a tree.

"Why, it's a pleasure to finally meet you, Mr. English. I've heard so many wonderful things." She blinked and sighed but had the feeling that she resembled a grunting owl. "How lovely to finally meet you at last, sir. Mr. Murphy has had so many kind things to say about you."

Danged sigh was still wrong.

She knew what the trouble was and the realization made her cheeks flame.

When she performed this trick for real she would be wearing an immodestly-cut gown. She'd spent the better part of an hour trying to convince Antie to sew lace into the bodice but she staunchly refused.

There was only one thing to do. Ivy opened the top of her shirt and pulled it wide. She shook her head. Even with her chest exposed to every hawk in the sky, this was not how her bosom would look in the gown.

They'd be more pushed up. She reached both hands under her camisole and lifted.

Yes, a bit better, but she was still lacking the mood for the sigh.

What she needed was inspiration. It flashed through her mind, and not at all unwelcome. River green eyes, heated with admiration stared at her.

She sighed. Her bosom heaved in the exact way Antie had instructed.

It made her feel…pleasant.

Even though she wasn't bathing naked in the beautiful Missouri, she did enjoy the way sunshine filtering through the leaves warmed her exposed skin.

Since no one was around for miles upon miles, she popped her breasts out of their binding. Stepping from shade to sunshine, she extended her arms. With her eyes closed, she turned in circles.

Warmth kissed her skin, a breeze softly petted it and rustled the grass all about. She'd left her hair unbound this morning, but now she lifted it to better feel the sunshine on her neck.

Something was peculiar. Nakedness that used to have only to do with freedom and being close to nature felt different.

Now, being naked led to thoughts of Travis, which made her nipples twist under the sun's kiss. Down low in her belly, things began to churn.

It did feel right nice. She sighed again, ignoring the stir of her horse's hooves in the brush, his soft whicker.

This time she knew she had captured the spirit of the sigh.

Still, she doubted she could do it in polite company… to a stranger.

"Ivy?"

Travis had been checking on the herd. On the way back to the ranch he'd ridden over a rise and seen Ivy in the distance near a tree with her arms stretched wide.

It had looked like she was in some sort of a trance. Not wanting to disturb her, he'd approached quietly.

What he hadn't seen from afar was that she had pushed her blouse off her shoulders, baring her chest to the warmth of the afternoon.

It wasn't right to stand ten feet from her, staring in silence, but his voice seemed to have dried up along with his manners.

Ivy Magee, the intended of William English—not of Travis Murphy—was beautiful. The river nymph had morphed into the meadow nymph.

As proof, an orange butterfly fluttered over the tip of her nose, which was pointed skyward.

Eyes closed, she sighed, smiled and the tips of—

"Ivy?"

"Travis!"

She covered her chest with her palms, but her hands were smaller than—

Lightheaded, he spun about, stared hard at the distant house shimmering in the heat. "I'm sorry for gawking, Ivy. It's just that…the truth is…you are a beautiful woman…and I—"

Have wanted to see you like this from the first night?

The thought of William being the one to be with her intimately stabbed his gut.

"My behavior was beyond rude."

"Reckon I ought to have been more careful," she gasped.

Against all that was proper, he turned back around. Three strides were all that separated him from his dreams. From holding Ivy close, kissing her, touching her with love and forging a soul-deep bond.

Her back was toward him. He could tell that she was buttoning up her shirt.

Taking the three strides, he wrapped his arms about her, tugged her back against his chest. He squeezed his eyes shut because she had only fastened three buttons. The weight of her bosom lay on his forearm.

So light that it might have been a stirring of air, he felt Ivy's hand on his arm. She traced her fingertips over the coarse sweat-dampened hair.

"I want you, Ivy." His voice was harsh, strangled sounding. Maybe he was being strangled since he was having trouble breathing.

"I want you, too."

He opened his eyes, saw a strand of golden hair falling across the swell of one fair breast. His nose grazed her cheek. He caught the scent of wild grass in her hair, felt the sun warming her skin.

"There will be no going back from this, Ivy. If we take this step—if I make you mine—I won't give you up."

When she sighed, he felt the press of her back against his chest and smelled the sweet warmth of her breath.

"I know…but then think about everyone, about the Lucky Clover," she whispered, her breath short and husky sounding.

"And about Agatha," he added. But what he wanted was to lay her down in the grass.

Ivy stepped out of his embrace. "You'd best get going, Travis."

He didn't want to—and knew that she didn't want him to. But what they wanted didn't add up to much in comparison to what was at stake for everyone else.

What was the need of two people in comparison to the needs of so many?

And what was to say that Ivy would not be better off

with English? William offered the security of wealth along with a high social standing.

"If things were different…" He stared at the sunshine curls shimmering on her back. "I—"

"But things are not different." She spun about, blinking away the moisture standing in her eyes. "I'll see you at dinner, dear friend."

With a nod, he turned, stalked toward his horse.

They still had friendship between them, even though he'd come within a hair's breadth of ruining it.

He would not risk breaking that bond again.

Chapter Fourteen

Kneeling on the front porch, Travis watched a drip of paint roll down the banister he was painting. He wiped a bead of sweat from his brow with his forearm.

Even in the shade of the big trees, it was hot as a blister.

Heat didn't wilt anyone's enthusiasm for getting the ranch ready for the big barbecue, though. High spirits and excitement had folks buzzing about like happy bees.

It sure wasn't a secret that Ivy was going to meet her Prince Charming and save the kingdom.

Plenty of guests were invited, mostly the wealthy members of the Cheyenne Club, many of them also voting members of the legislature. Neighbors were invited, too, since everyone was anxious to meet the heir to the Lucky Clover.

He'd seen Ivy an hour earlier when she'd brought Agatha outside. Step by patient step, she'd led her sister down the porch stairs and into the sunshine.

It seemed to Travis that a lifetime of being made into an invalid might be an impossible thing to come back from. Ivy was fighting to heal her sister, but even as determined as she was, he was not convinced it could be done.

The sad truth, Travis was coming to believe, was that from the time she was a little thing, Mrs. Brunne had been making Agatha dependent upon her. It was hard to imagine why she would do it, what she had gained by it.

He turned his attention back to getting the porch ready for the party but the repetitive nature of the chore allowed his mind to wander.

Wander to Ivy, and the change in their friendship. They spoke, they laughed and still practiced dancing under the watchful eye of Madame.

But when their eyes met, their gazes did not linger. And if they came upon each other with no one around, one or other of them would find something urgent to do somewhere else.

He only hoped in time, after she was wed to English, the easy manner between them would return.

Right now, he missed the Ivy he had met on the *River Queen*.

These days she acted the woman she was being groomed to be. The real Ivy seemed buried under society's rules. How many days had it been since he'd seen her quick grin and heard her carefree laughter?

Too many, was how many. He jabbed a glob of paint on a spot he'd already finished. Better get used to it, he thought, smoothing out the mess he'd made on the wood.

At least he hadn't made a mess of everyone's future. It had been a close thing the day he had come upon her practicing an enticing sigh.

In that moment, he had come too close to forgetting everyone but her. He'd wanted to lay her down in the shade, make love to her then ride away into the sunset, just the two of them, to a place where the only thing that mattered was what was between them.

In the end, he'd remembered what was required. So had she. Duty came before love—funny how in its way that was also love.

A flash of blue a short distance away caught his attention. It was Ivy, sitting down on the blanket beside her sister.

He watched her, ignoring the paint dripping down his wrist. She hadn't bound her hair this morning. It lay in a carefree tumble down her back. From this distance he couldn't hear what she was saying, but he could see her touch Agatha's lank hair and shake her head.

Agatha shrugged, keeping her gaze on her folded hands.

The sisters were sunshine and shadow, but sunshine sure was trying to chase away those clouds.

If he had his way, he'd stand in Ivy's sunlight until he was burned.

Sure was a damn good thing he'd never told her that he loved her.

Didn't mean he didn't, it was just a good thing he'd never said so.

Sitting on a blanket in the shade with Agatha, Ivy tried not to openly stare at Travis while he painted the front porch.

Gosh almighty, it was a hard thing to do. He'd snatched off his neckerchief and tossed it aside. Then he'd unbuttoned his shirt and yanked it out of his pants.

It was a shame—a plum shame—that the day was so hot and he had to get half-naked so that sweat glistened on his skin.

It took all she had to pretend she didn't notice.

But after the misstep she had come so close to making, she'd been careful to steer as clear of him as she could.

Which wasn't easy since they lived in the same house. When it came to Travis Murphy she trusted her self-restraint about as much as she trusted ants not to invade a picnic.

She forced her attention back to where it belonged—to Agatha who ignored the lunch plate that Ivy had placed on her lap.

"You need to eat." Ivy lifted a chicken leg and waved it in front of her sister's nose. "You won't get strong if you don't."

"She will never be strong no matter how you try and force it." Hilda Brunne, who was never far away, sat against a tree smacking her lips over her own lunch.

As always, Ivy did her best to ignore the dark, hovering presence.

"I feel sick to my stomach, Ivy." Agatha pushed the chicken leg away. "I'd eat it if I could, but I can't."

"You're bound to feel unwell for a while. But only until the laudanum gets out of your system—after that, you'll feel better than ever. Trust me."

Agatha's glance slid toward her nurse.

"It's your fault she's doing so poorly. It's also your fault that I'm not getting my rest. If you hadn't thrown her medicine away we'd all be doing fine."

Did she really believe that? Some folks did.

Laudanum was considered an acceptable cure for all kinds of ailments.

In Ivy's opinion, it was gut rot!

During her time aboard the *Queen*, she'd seen many a soul ruined by the drug, hands and gamblers alike.

"Maybe you'd like to take your lunch to another tree,

Mrs. Brunne." If Ivy were free to be herself she'd have a few ringing words to say to the nurse. Instead, here she sat, lady of the land, acting cool and refined.

"I hope you are not going to let that vile rodent loose. Agatha can speak of nothing else."

"I was about to, if she can manage to eat a few bites." It might not be right to push food on her when she looked so pale, but her sister could not spare another pound. "What do you say? Three bites? You don't want to look like a ghost at the barbecue."

"I won't mind. I don't want anyone to really see me. I only want to watch close-up. I do want to see the mouse, though."

Agatha took a small bite of the chicken, then chewed slowly while she frowned.

This was a beginning, at least. Ivy drew open the string on the mouse purse. Little Mouse ventured out, sniffing the air and nosing about for crumbs.

Mrs. Brunne stood up suddenly and backed several yards away. "Filth! If it gets close to me I'll stomp on it and don't think I won't."

"Mother doesn't mean that, Ivy." Agatha cast her nurse an uneasy glance. "I'm sure she doesn't."

Ivy rose then followed.

"I'm sure you do mean it," she murmured. Nurse Brunne would harm innocent creatures and with a big wicked grin on her face while she did it. "But I won't allow it."

Hilda narrowed her eyes, smiled and ground her boot on a flower that had been waving its delicate yellow petals above the grass.

"Stop me why don't you?"

A twig cracked in the grass.

"Why, Mr. Murphy," Nurse Brunne said turning. "How lovely to see you."

Ivy could not say that in the moment she even recognized this woman of smiles and friendly wishes. The way Hilda Brunne could be one person, then a second later as the need arose she was someone else; it made Ivy's gut curl.

Before Travis had a chance to respond, Brunne had already hurried up the stairs and gone into the house.

He made to go after her but Ivy caught his arm. "Let her go. A confrontation will only upset Agatha."

"It gnaws at me, Ivy—being blinded to the fraud she was."

He reached up as though he wanted to cup her cheek. Ivy gazed down at the crushed flower because if she looked up she would see his damp, bare chest. She would throw herself against it and hold on tight.

"It gnaws at me, too." The poor flower was crushed beyond hope. "Because when you look at it, I'm every bit the fraud she is."

"Never think so, Ivy. You are the finest lady I've ever met."

Four days later, dressed in her party best, Ivy still felt like a fraud.

Sitting on a stool while Antie tied a ribbon in her hair, she gazed up into her mentor's face. She was a beautiful woman for her age—for any age.

"I wonder, Antie, why haven't you married again. I reckon Madame means you were?"

"One short and beautiful marriage was enough for me. My husband died suddenly, in an accident. I suppose I've been looking for a man to live up to his memory.

This is a difficult thing, living up to a memory. I fear it cannot be done."

If that was true, Ivy had little hope that her marriage to William would be as it should. Travis, her memory of him, would be a ghost standing between them.

"I'm not going to fool anyone, Antie." Ivy pressed her palms against the waist of her blue gown and stared down at the bustle of activity going on below her bedroom window.

William and party were due to arrive soon. "I'm a river gal. You can polish fool's gold all day long and it's still not the real thing."

"You do not need to fool anyone, *ma petite*." Madame went up on her toes and pressed Ivy's cheek with a kiss. "You are a beautiful woman—twenty-four karat."

"But I'm not who Mr. English is expecting." A thousand knots in her belly tightened. "I'm going to let everyone down."

A young woman carrying a checkered tablecloth passed by below. She spotted Ivy, smiled and waved.

"You look like a princess from a fairytale, Miss Magee," the woman called.

In the distance, Ivy heard fiddle players practicing tunes. Tunes that she was going to have to dance to... with William English.

"Wish I'd stayed on the *Queen*."

"And never have met your sister?"

Never have met Travis?

"I reckon I wouldn't go back, but gosh almighty, I'm nervous!"

Off in the distance Ivy spotted dust rising on the road.

A small boy ran across the yard and into the house. From below she heard his voice shouting to Mrs. Morgan that the first guests were coming.

Moments later a parade of kitchen girls hustled past carrying covered platters of food. The aroma drifted up.

"I'd lose my breakfast if it wasn't trapped in this here corset."

"Let us go down to greet your guests, *ma petite*."

"Will you be close by?"

"*Oui*, but you will not need me."

One of the stable boys had seen Ivy standing beside her bedroom window and pronounced her a princess walked out of a fairy tale. Mrs. Flairty told Travis she agreed.

Young Mac Johnson had seen her, too. Setting up tables, the kid's eyes had been dreamy looking. Even Slim, the Lucky Clover's head wrangler was convinced that William English was going to throw himself at Ivy's feet.

Waiting for her now at the foot of the stairs, Travis had a lump the size of the ranch in his belly.

He didn't know why. Ivy would play her part well.

Hearing a rustle of skirts, he turned, looked up.

Princess, queen, angel in blue—all of these words fit the vision coming down the steps toward him.

When the lump in his belly grew heavier, he knew why.

It wasn't for dread that William would not find Ivy acceptable. It was dread that he would.

With a death grip on his self-control, he extended his hand to Ivy.

She lay her fingers across his palm. He quashed the urge to pick her up and carry her away to— Hell, anywhere but here.

"You ready to meet William?"

"If I don't throw up all over his shoes, it'll be by the good Lord's own grace."

Going outside, Travis wanted to yank his collar open. It was one of those hot August afternoons when clouds pressed so close to the earth that a soul could hardly breathe.

If he knew Ivy at all, she would be mentally cursing a blue streak at her dress and the stifling underclothes.

Outwardly though, she smiled. She greeted guests who gathered about the food-laden tables. She nodded to the kitchen girls running here and there while they kept the platters filled. She patted the heads of the children of the hands who had been warned to stay away, but willfully dashed up to grab treats.

He supposed that William would be where the men were gathered to hear music and drink. When a man had his eye on the territorial legislature, he'd need to shake a lot of hands.

Come late September, very likely Ivy would be standing beside him.

Travis had promised her that he would be there to help, to run the ranch for her like he'd always done, and he would. But damned if it wasn't going to be the hell of a hard thing to see her with English, to know that one floor above his office she would be sharing a bedroom with the man.

He must have cussed under his breath because Ivy gazed up at him, one brow arched and half a smile tugging at the corner of her mouth.

"Is something amiss, Mr. Murphy?" she asked.

Is something amiss? This was not the voice of the Ivy he knew. His Ivy would have asked if he had a bee in his drawers.

Which he most definitely did and it felt damned amiss.

"There's William, standing over there by the punch bowl."

Her fingers clenched on his arm. "Here we go then, Travis. Wish me luck."

William English looked up from a conversation he was having with another dapperly dressed fellow.

His gaze held Ivy's as though he already knew who she was.

And why wouldn't he know, she wondered? How many strangers would be clinging to Travis's arm in a death grip? Although he wouldn't be able to tell it was a death grip from this distance, but it was nonetheless.

He also wouldn't know that Travis held on to her just as tight.

Mr. English smiled at her, nodded.

Ivy glanced up at Travis, subtly shaking her head. *Run away with me* was what she was thinking.

Travis blinked. Just there at the corner of one eye was the slightest hint of moisture. Then he nodded, just as subtly, reminding her they must do this.

Drawing upon weeks of training, she summoned the prim and proper Ivy. She returned William English's smile, mouth closed and lips sweetly curved. He would never know how hard it was to ignore the tickle of sweat dripping down her ribs.

Mr. English excused himself from his companions and made his way across the yard toward her.

Sure was a handsome fellow with his dark hair and deep blue eyes. He was taller than most of the gents gathered about. If duded-up good looks could win a legislative seat, he'd probably get every vote.

Travis shook hands with him, gave him a tight-lipped smile. Ivy figured he ought to look more welcoming than that since William English was about to save the Lucky Clover from ruin.

Everyone liked to give her credit for that happy event, but she was not the one with the money—her intended was.

"Ivy, this is our neighbor, William English. William, this is Miss Eleanor Magee."

She wondered if the politician noticed how clipped Travis's words were while he...while he gave her away.

"Such a pleasure to make your acquaintance, Mr. English." She extended her hand. He bent over it.

"I am honored, Miss Magee."

"Mr. English is running for office, territorial legislature of Wyoming."

This was a fine dance of words. She knew who he was, where he lived and why he was here. He knew why he was here as well, and he knew that she knew.

"I hope to serve our territory with dedication." It had to be a trick of light, but it looked like one of his eyes twinkled. Or maybe just a plain trick, one that politicians were accomplished at. "I hope I can count upon your support?"

"I'm certain you can, as long as you convince me that we stand on the same side of the issues facing our wonderful territory."

"Perhaps later on we can take an hour and I'll tell you about my views."

"There's Peter Pottsmith waving at you," Travis said. "Looks like he wants your attention, William."

"Will you save a dance or two for me after dinner, Miss Magee?"

A dance or two tonight was a small demand of her time. But what he was really asking for was her life— every living, breathing moment of it.

She could give him this, she had to give him this! Lives would be ruined if she did not.

A pair of laughing children brushed past her skirt then snatched a treat from the pastry table. At four years old, the boys hadn't a care in the world.

"There's nothing I would like quite as much, Mr. English."

If her actions kept those little ones secure in their homes, then her statement was not a lie. There truly was nothing she would like more.

But looking up at the tense set of Travis's mouth while he watched William walk away to greet Mr. Pottsmith, she knew there was one thing she wanted as much... though she couldn't have it.

Watching rain drip down the window, Travis turned his back on the party going on behind him. There was nothing he wanted more than to scour away the image of William holding Ivy in his arms while they two-stepped about the parlor room.

The dancing was meant to be done on a wood dance floor set up in the paddock, but the sky had opened up right after dinner so they'd moved the party inside and pushed all the furniture to the walls.

Beyond the trees, he watched lightning spread over the land. He prayed that his cowboys would find shelter and the cattle not scatter. It wouldn't be the first time a herd had been spooked by a storm.

Suddenly the scent of the Missouri River and a dash of lavender filled his senses.

He turned, hoping to see Ivy coming toward him with her smile bright and aimed at him.

But no, the dance had just spun William and Ivy past him.

Her smile was for English, and his was for her.

Looked like they were getting on just fine. He ought to feel happier about that since it had been his idea to transform Ivy into a mesmerizing society belle.

He'd sure as hell accomplished his goal, but damned if he was pleased about it.

Glancing away, his gaze settled on Agatha where she sat in a dim corner watching the dancers whirl past.

Ivy had been the one to dress her for the party rather than Hilda. The difference showed. Not just in the brighter colors, but in Agatha's expression.

She was still too pale to look healthy, but just now, watching the dancers whirl past, the emotionless gaze that was typical for her was replaced with interest.

Ivy had been right to toss out the laudanum, to insist on taking Agatha outside and into the sunshine.

Could it be possible that Foster's daughter was not destined to live life as an invalid as everyone had been led to believe?

Would someone so irreversibly feeble be tapping her toe along with the music?

Hilda Brunne emerged from the deep shadow behind Agatha, looking dour, as usual. With a frown she pointed at Agatha's tapping shoe.

Hurriedly, Travis cut across the floor through a dozen couples who hopped, stepped and glided about the parlor.

"Agatha." Stepping between her and Brunne, he nodded and extended his hand. "Would you honor me with a dance?"

"You know she can't, Mr. Murphy. Why torment her?"

Hilda leaned close to Agatha's ear and whispered, but not so quietly that Travis didn't hear.

"You will break your leg if you try. They will blame it on me and send me away. Do you want to lose the only person who loves you? Answer me—say the words."

"Mrs. Brunne, fetch Miss Magee a glass of punch."

She had better not try and lace it with laudanum. Now that he had the measure of her, he would be sniffing to be sure.

"Why I'd be delighted to do so if that is what Agatha would like." Brunne shot Agatha a brief glance, clearly warning her to refuse the punch. "Would it please you, my pet?"

"No…I…I don't believe it would."

"Fetch some for both of us, Mrs. Brunne."

"Oh, yes, my pleasure." Nurse Brunne hurried off. He doubted that she knew he heard her mumble a curse.

"Why would you say you didn't want the punch when you did, Agatha?"

"Oh, but I didn't want it. Not much anyway. Mother says—"

"I overheard Mrs. Brunne say that she is the only one who loves you."

Agatha looked hard at her hands folded in her lap.

"That's not true. Many people love you, Agatha. They always have."

Agatha glanced up, frowned at him. Apparently she didn't believe him.

And why would she? Her mind had been poisoned and under his watch.

If it wasn't for the fact that Agatha depended upon Hilda Brunne, clung to her and put her in the place of her dead mother, he would have sent her packing weeks ago.

"Are you sure you wouldn't like to try a dance...just a step or two?"

"Oh, no...I couldn't."

"May I sit beside you, then?" Without waiting for an answer, which might be a refusal, he pulled over a chair.

"You seem improved. I'm happy to see it." One had to look hard to see the improvement, but it was beginning to show.

On the far side of the room he watched Ivy and William finish their dance. It took only half a second for another neighbor to slip in and whirl her on to a polka.

English began a circle about the room, shaking hands and courting votes.

"I'd like to ask you something, Agatha."

"Yes?" She clenched her fingers together in her lap.

"It has to do with your nurse." Green eyes, pretty green eyes—he noticed for the first time—glanced at him then away. "When you are alone, is she kind to you?"

"Mama Brunne wants what is best for me."

"We all want that. But I wonder if I've failed you over the years...allowed Mrs. Brunne—"

"I can be difficult but Mama takes good care of me."

"I've been thinking. Now that Ivy is here and caring for you, I'd like to terminate your nurse's employment."

"But...you can't!" Her cheeks blanched of the little color they had. "I might die without Mother's care."

"This is what she tells you?"

"Yes. Everyone knows it."

"Ivy doesn't. You trust her don't you?"

"I'm beginning to, yes. But Mama Brunne has been with me my whole life."

"All right." It went against every good instinct he had, but he said, "As long as you want your nurse here, she will stay. But the moment you change your mind, or you feel uncomfortable with her, will you tell me?"

"I would not want to say anything wicked about Mother, but yes, I will."

"Sure you don't want to dance?"

"No, I— Look, here comes Mr. English."

All of a sudden the blush returned to her cheeks, brighter than before.

"Good evening, Miss Magee," William said, stopping before her and extending his hand as he had to everyone. "You look fetching this evening. Just the sight we need to chase away this dreary storm."

Travis saw the ghost of a tremor shake Agatha's hand when the politician closed his fingers about it.

"I believe this dance was meant for us."

"I'm not fit enough. I'd only fall and everyone would see it."

But she would be fit enough if it weren't for Hilda Brunne's dark care. Anger built a slow throb behind his temples.

"I won't let you fall. I promise."

Agatha shook her head but English did not relinquish his hold on her hand.

"Come now, Agatha. It will please your sister to see you enjoying yourself."

"Oh, just for a moment then…"

William placed one hand under her elbow and lifted her carefully from her chair.

She wobbled a bit but William kept a steady hold on her. To Travis's astonishment, Agatha smiled. Brightly, genuinely smiled. From across the room, he saw Ivy take notice. He felt her elation.

Returning, punch cup in hand, Hilda's mouth creased, her eyes narrowed behind her glasses.

I blame you for this, was what her expression declared.

"How nice to see Agatha having fun," was what she said to him.

Chapter Fifteen

Gull-durned shoes were making her feet numb. If only she could get away for a moment and set her toes free.

Looking about at the folks having a lively time in the parlor she knew that was not going to happen. A gully washer of rain pumping down outside sure didn't dampen the spirits inside.

Folks seemed happy as could be, eating and dancing, making her acquaintance. Or at least the acquaintance of the woman they thought she was.

Even though the hour was late, no one seemed ready to take to their beds.

Especially Agatha. One brief dance with William, only a few gentle steps in time to the music, had pleased her to the point where she actually defied Brunne's attempt to make her go upstairs. The defiance was not great and it didn't last long, but it was the first time Ivy had noticed her sister genuinely strain against her nurse's control.

There was no holding back a grin about that. She did cover her mouth though so no one would know the real Ivy was dancing a jig inside her corset.

"Miss Magee?" William English's rich, cultured voice came from behind her. "Might we speak in private?"

Schooling her smile, she dropped her hand and turned.

"Of course, Mr. English." They could speak, but privately? That seemed unlikely with so many people about. "If you don't mind going through the kitchen, I know a spot where we will be able to hear one another."

"Actually, I'm partial to kitchens. Especially on rainy evenings. Please lead the way."

Ivy led the way past half a dozen busy cooks to the back porch where a double-sized swing was sheltered from the rain by a wide overhang.

When they were seated with a polite distance between them, William cleared his throat.

"First, I'd like to say that your father was a good man. You have my condolences." Rain pattered beyond the porch. A breeze carried the scent of wet mud and freshened shrubbery.

Ivy tried not to ache for the Missouri, but it was a plum hard thing to do.

"Thank you. I wish I had known him."

"We spoke of things…of the Lucky Clover's future, before he passed."

"Yes, that was why Mr. Murphy brought me here. I understand what is at stake."

The hopeful future legislator let out a sigh.

"Are you agreeable to the proposition then?"

"It's an unusual situation, Mr. English." The faces of cowboys, their wives and children—and her sister's face, flashed through her mind's eye. Travis's grin pushed at the corner of her consciousness. She slapped it away. "But yes, I am agreeable."

He nodded. "I'm grateful. Would you mind calling

me William? I think it is appropriate under the circumstances."

William. This was the beginning then.

"I imagine you have questions about me?" That interesting twinkle flashed in his eye. "Ask me anything."

"Well, William, I do have a question. I understand that you need an appropriate wife. One who will increase your chances of winning this legislative election and in time the one for governor. My property will give you that. I just wonder—do you really think people will vote for you because of me and my ranch? You're gambling quite a lot on the possibility."

He laughed, the sound deep and rich. "You are an elegant and lovely woman. I've noticed how people are drawn to you. Even without the ranch's reputation, I think you would garner more votes than I would."

Elegant? Lovely? An imposter was what she really was. How long into the marriage would he realize it?

"Why do you want to hold office so badly that you would marry someone you don't even know?"

He had said that she could ask him anything.

"Once you've heard a few of my speeches, you'll see it's because I want to represent the people of Wyoming, to lock horns with established government and make my constituents' lives better." He shrugged, arched his brows.

"And?"

"And I like being in charge. It used to drive my mother to distraction."

Could be he expected to be in charge of her, too. Some husbands did.

"Before you tell me you want to back out of the arrangement like your expression says you do, I'll make a

few things clear. I'm grateful that a woman of such uncommon grace and beauty will be standing beside me.
Beyond that, I won't ask much of you. I won't ask you to
live somewhere other than the Lucky Clover. I'll make
sure that you have the funds to keep the ranch going.
You will act as my hostess. I would like children, but I
would never force myself on you. Maybe once we are no
longer strangers? But I will be faithful to you—I would
not bring you shame. All I ask, for now, is that you put
on a good show for the sake of my career."

She was already putting on a show. He just didn't
know it.

"I know you need some time to think this over. Even
a marriage of necessity needs consideration. I won't
announce anything until you've had time to think it
through."

A strong gust of wind rocked the swing. William
steadied it by planting a shiny black boot on the deck.

"Can I hope for your answer in three weeks? Folks
will be making up their minds who to vote for soon."

"How do you feel about mice, William?"

"You have one you need me to stomp? I'm quick."

"Not quite, but since you've been honest with me, I
will be with you." To an extent. "I have a friend—she
lives with me...and she's a mouse."

His laugh rumbled into the night.

"I like you, Ivy Magee...I like you very much."

Three days after the barbecue Ivy was still haunted
by what William had said.

"He said, *I like you, Ivy Magee...I like you very much.*
He can't know that for sure, since he doesn't know who
I really am. I don't even know that anymore."

"You are my sweet *petite*." Antie tied a red bow in her hair at the nape and plumped the loops. "I will miss you."

Ivy spun on her stool. "Miss me? Why would you? I'm only going riding."

"You no longer need me." Antie stroked her cheek with the backs of her fingers. "I must find another position."

"I do need you!"

"You need to go for your ride in the countryside— forget your worries for a while."

That was not likely to happen, no matter how far or hard she rode.

All of her life she'd been honest in her words and her actions. It ate at her that she was being deceitful to William.

And to Travis. He had to know she loved him, but gosh almighty she would never tell him so. How could she when she was about to marry someone else?

Blazin' day! She did need that ride.

Standing, she kissed Antie's cheek. "Don't leave me."

Hurrying out the door and down the stairway, she brushed moisture from her eyes.

Running through bright sunlight, she crossed the paddock and opened the barn door.

Going from bright to dim, everything was deeply shadowed. She ran smack into a man's back.

"I'm sorry," she muttered as the man turned. He gripped her by the shoulders to keep her from falling backward. "I didn't mean to—"

The features of a handsome, familiar face became clear as her eyes adjusted to the light.

"Travis!"

She hadn't seen him since the barbecue. It had seemed

better to steer clear of him now that she was within weeks of making a commitment to William.

"Where are you going in such an all-fired hurry?"

Away from you, away from William, away from herself.

"Riding."

He nodded and dropped his hands. But she felt the heat when his fingers skimmed her arms, traced the mounds of her knuckles.

"I'll saddle your mare."

The very idea that she had been grateful for a month ago, hit her in the gut like a fist.

Travis would be here after her marriage.

He would saddle her horse, balance her accounts, and care for her cattle and her cowboys.

"I'm not sure I can do it," she murmured.

"You sit a horse as well as anyone on the ranch."

Oh! She hadn't meant to speak out loud. She would never point out the misunderstanding, tell him that she wondered if she could love one man and live with another.

She'd find out soon enough, since she would never terminate his employment. Why, she could no more ask him to leave the ranch he loved than she could abandon her sister. He belonged here more than she did.

"You and English seemed to get on well at the barbecue." Travis's voice sounded casual, but she noticed his jaw grow tense.

"We did." She nodded. "You were right when you said he would not treat me unkindly."

"I'm glad." He turned and lifted the saddle.

It wasn't right to yearn to touch his back where his muscles flexed under his shirt as he lifted the saddle onto the horse's back. She had to curl her fists into balls and tuck them under her arms to keep from doing it.

He finished saddling the mare, then he offered her a hand up. "All ready to go."

She meant to keep her eyes trained on the floor, to stare at the straw crushed under her horse's hoof.

But she didn't and Travis's gaze locked on hers, held.

She felt the moisture well again.

He reached as though he would wipe it away, but instead, he tugged the bow in her hair.

Sure was a bad idea to let him touch her while he helped her into the saddle, but she did it anyway.

Some things were going to have to change. Just not at this very moment.

"Have a good ride."

With a pat to the horse's rump he left the barn.

The masculine scent of him lingered. So did she, breathing deeply until the last whiff of him faded.

Outside the barn one of the hands raised his hat to her. Leaving the yard she guided her horse around the hill and toward the homes of the cowboys.

Mrs. Flairty, sweeping her porch, set her broom aside and came to her front gate. She waved her hand to show Ivy that it had healed nicely.

"I've something for you, Miss Magee, if you'll wait but a moment."

When she came back out of her house Mrs. Flairty handed Ivy a bag of cookies. "Something for your ride."

A quarter of a mile down the road six children, free of school for the summer, dashed toward her. She handed them the bag of cookies then turned toward open land.

The horse galloped for a bit then slowed when the wide, muddy Platte came into view. While it stopped to drink, Ivy watched the golden land rolling away in the distance. She breathed in the scent of dry grass twisting in the breeze.

Home.

A sense of belonging settled over her soul. For the first time, she recognized that as much as the *River Queen* was home, so was the Lucky Clover.

If protecting the ranch meant being who she was not, so be it. When the day came that she became Mrs. William English, she would give him no reason to regret the marriage.

So far, she had not crossed any forbidden boundaries with Travis from which she could not retreat. There was no reason they could not remain dear friends, just as they had started out.

After riding another couple of miles, with the sun shining warmly on her back and listening to the comforting sounds of cattle bawling in the distance, she was certain it was possible.

She could have both her home and her friend.

A movement caught her eye. She watched a man top the rise of a distant hill, leading a horse behind him.

Poor critter must have come up lame.

"Better go see if there's trouble."

She patted her mare's neck then urged her to a trot.

"Whoa!" She pulled the horse up short.

There was something familiar about the fellow. It was in the way his left side listed slightly forward when he walked.

It could not possibly be…but…she strained her eyes.

"Uncle Patrick!"

Within a minute she was upon him, bounding from the horse before it fully stopped.

"Ivy? That you?"

With a leap she was in his arms, hugging for all she was worth.

"Who else would it be?" She held him at arm's length. "Don't you recognize me?"

"Where's your braid? Your pants and boots?"

"Why this here's a riding skirt! And I like to wear my hair looser now that I'm not working the *Queen*."

Well, that was something. There was a thing about her new way of dressing she did like better.

"You look like a fine lady, honey." His bushy brows nearly met when they arched. "I hardly know you."

"You might see some strange things, but don't you be fooled none. I'm still me on the inside." She hugged him again, making sure his appearance was not a dream that she was about to wake from. "What are you doing here?"

"I needed to see that my girl was safe and happy."

"I'm safe."

"How about happy? I know what I did seemed harsh, but I only wanted what was best for you."

"I'm happy enough." There would be time to tell him about her conflicted emotions later. "Say, did your horse pull up lame?"

"Cantankerous critter. I can't get used to the feel of being on his back and I think he knows it. It's been him against me all the way from the Missouri to here."

Ivy slapped her knee. "You can pilot a big ole river-boat but not a little bitty horse?"

"Nothing little bitty about this beast."

"I sure did miss you." She flung her arms about his middle again, gave him a solid squeeze. "You fixin' to become a landlubber and stay? Could be you'll meet some sweet woman. We've got a few widow ladies working for the Lucky Clover."

"She'd have to be some mighty special gal to care for

this crusty old shipmaster. But I would like to stay, if your husband will allow it."

"I'm not married yet—but I'm the one who would do the allowing."

"He's a good man? You care for him? I've been worried I might have sent you away wrongly."

"You weren't wrong, Uncle Patrick. Sometimes change is good, for all that it's hard. Just wait until you meet your other niece! And as far as William English goes, I've only met him one time, but I reckon he's a sight more honest than I am."

"I've never known you to tell a lie in your life."

"Did you know I kept a pet mouse on the *Queen*, in my hat sometimes?"

"Lucky thing I did not, young lady!"

"You're going to see some things about me that might be confusing—but I'm still me under it all."

"I'm mighty glad to hear that."

Travis spread a blanket under the shade of the trees near the house then set a circle of chairs about the perimeter. It was noon, time for Agatha's daily excursion out of doors.

In a few moments Ivy would bring her out, walk her in the sunshine for a bit then bring her to the chairs where she, Agatha, Antie, and today Patrick Malone would have lunch.

Travis used to have lunch with the ladies on occasion. Now it seemed better not to.

Dry leaves crunched, the sound coming from behind. Travis turned to find Ivy's uncle steaming across the yard, hands clasped behind his back and a frown on his face.

Two days ago, Travis had been stunned to see the

captain walking beside Ivy when she returned from her ride in the pasture.

Stunned, but at the same time pleased. It would do Ivy good to have him here.

"I'm worried about my girl," Patrick announced.

"Which one?"

Patrick's mustache twitched in a sudden smile.

It was clear as morning that the captain had become devoted to Agatha the moment he spotted her gazing down from her balcony.

He had claimed that his heart had swelled near out of his chest at the first sight of his sister's other child, a young woman whose red hair and green eyes were a reflection of her mother's.

"Both of them and for the same reason."

"Hilda Brunne?" He guessed.

"There's something not right about the woman." He rocked back on his heels, drew one arm from behind his back and pointed at Travis with the pipe that he clutched in his fingers. "She looks at my Ivy with an evil eye. She's up to something, that one."

"She's jealous." But up to something? "I've known Mrs. Brunne for most of my life. I don't believe she is a threat to Ivy."

"And Agatha?"

"Agatha wants her here, needs her in an unhealthy way. Ivy is doing her best to make her independent, but I'm afraid it will take time. As soon as Agatha can handle it, Ivy will let Mrs. Brunne go."

"Just the same, I—" All of a sudden Patrick's expression went soft. "Why isn't that a picture to warm an old uncle's heart?"

Travis glanced up to see Ivy leading her sister down the front stairs. It was a slow and careful process, coming down but Agatha did show slight improvement from the day before.

Ivy was dressed in a sunshine-yellow skirt, while Agatha resembled a delicate rose petal in her pink one.

An old uncle's heart was not the only one warming up.

Travis's heart was melting right through his ribs watching Ivy urge Agatha to walk toward the blanket unaided.

Sunshine gilded her hair, made it shimmer. He thought it made her lips shimmer, too, but that might have been in his mind's eye since he was pretty sure he tasted lavender on his tongue, too.

"You all right, boy?" The captain peered hard at him. "You look like your barge has been run aground."

Travis shook his head, taking his emotions in hand. "It's a touching thing to see Ivy bringing her sister back to life—kind of chokes a fellow up."

Nothing could be truer. Every day, seeing it— Well, he loved Ivy all the more.

"You know, son, I need to thank you for all you've done for my girls. Coming to get Ivy, fixing her up with that English fellow—I'm downright grateful. I understand from Ivy that he is a decent fellow. That he's even accepting of her rodent."

"He is? I didn't know she told him about her."

Odd how he felt betrayed by that when he had no right to feel betrayed by anything.

"That woman coming down the steps, Ivy's teacher, sure is a pretty little thing."

Patrick's eyes seemed to glaze over as he stared at Madame du Mer through a haze of pipe smoke.

"You all right, Captain? You look like your barge has been run aground."

"I'll tell you, son. I'm mighty glad I came, even if I did have to pull that devil of a horse the whole way."

"Your sister spends too much time napping, it seems to me."

Standing beside Ivy at the corral fence, Uncle Patrick took a long draw on his pipe then blew the smoke into the cloudy afternoon.

"I told you about the laudanum. Once the poison is out of her body she'll get stronger. She's a mile better than she was when I got here. You'll see how she improves day by day."

Colts and fillies in the paddock stomped and whinnied when Travis and a pair of adolescent cowboys entered the pen. Their nervous prancing whirled up a dust cloud.

It wasn't so dense to keep her from seeing Travis slowly approach a colt, extending his palm in an effort to sooth the animal.

She sighed, wished— No, she did not, could not. William was coming tomorrow for his answer. His formal answer, at least. They both knew that she would say yes.

But tomorrow was not today. Today she was going to let herself look at Travis, watch the way he moved, let the gentle drone of his voice sink into her heart.

Today she was going to silently love him.

"Your mother grieved over leaving Agatha behind."

"I reckon she did what she thought she had to, and my father too, I reckon."

Ivy was coming to understand all too well how a person could want one thing but do another.

"You are the spit of your mother, you know—not in looks, mind you. You must take after your father in appearance, but your bright spirit is just like your mother's."

Ivy touched the chain of her necklace, followed the links until she felt the scratch of the engraved letters. That was all she had of her mama, a charm and according to Uncle Patrick, a bright spirit.

"Now Agatha, looking at her is like looking at your mother."

"She will look like her." Ivy thought so every morning when she studied the dining room portrait. "Once I get her healthy."

"I don't like to think of what would have become of her if you hadn't left the *Queen*. You are saving her life, Ivy, nothing less." Uncle Patrick took another draw on his pipe. "I only wonder about the cost to you, my little love. Do you still dream of being a river pilot?"

"I think about it, but I like it here. There's nothing I would change even if I could."

That was a gull-durned lie. She would change her last name to Murphy if it were in her power to do it.

Since it was not, she looked away from Travis's work-roughened hands lightly stroking the colt's neck and concentrated on the smoke curling out of her uncle's pipe.

In her mind she replaced Travis's face with William's. Gosh almighty, he was a handsome one, but somehow that didn't make her heart beat any faster, didn't warm her insides like when she looked at—

"I wonder if you're telling me the truth, girl?"

She swung her gaze toward her uncle but he was watching Travis spread a blanket across the colt's back.

The young cowpokes watched and did the same with other colts.

"There's truth you tell and truth you live, I reckon," she murmured.

He grunted, nodded.

The only thing she'd ever been able to hide from her uncle was the existence of Little Mouse.

"I got a fair amount of money for the *Queen*."

The thought shouldn't stab her heart. She had accepted the loss and moved on.

"I'm right glad of it, uncle."

"What I'm saying is that it might help you save the ranch without you having to sell your heart."

"It's in too much debt and the note is nearly due. The *Queen* can't save the Lucky Clover."

"Maybe not, but she should have been yours. I came to give you your inheritance."

"And to stay?" *Please, please stay,* she thought. Now that he was here she could not imagine being without him again.

"And to stay."

"The *Queen* was yours, Uncle Patrick. You worked all your life for her. I can't take the money."

It was useless to argue with the captain. She didn't recall ever coming out on the top side of an argument with him.

"Have any of the ladies caught your eye?" A change of subject was in order.

"One in particular. But she's a fine one. You can tell it from a distance. Too fine for this old man, I can tell you."

"Antoinette du Mer, you must mean."

"Antoinette!" Her uncle's gaze turned soft in a way she had never seen. "Sounds as pretty as a freshwater pearl peeking out of a shell."

"She's sweet on you."

"Bah!"

"It's true. She told me so herself. I reckon she looks as moonstruck as you do."

"So, tell me niece, how does a crusty old fellow go about courting in these parts?"

She sighed past the jab to her heart. "Just follows his heart I reckon."

What wouldn't Ivy give to be able to do the same?

"Reckon I better do some fast sailing in those waters. These old bones aren't getting any younger."

Chapter Sixteen

Sitting in the dark, Travis drummed his fingers on the office desk.

William English was coming.

Tomorrow there would be no party, just a private dinner to welcome the possible future legislator and someday governor. Then later, as much as his stomach clenched as he thought of it, there would be a private moment where Ivy would become officially engaged.

The way Foster had arranged things, Ivy would accept the proposal and English would hand over a sizeable gift. The Lucky Clover would remain solvent.

The only thing that might postpone his late boss's scheme was the weather.

Something wicked was brewing. It could delay William's arrival.

Not forever, though.

Through the open office window Travis heard wind howling low across the land. It moaned through the trees, shifting the leaves with its humid breath.

Travis wiped sweat from his brow with his sleeve then yanked open the collar of his shirt. It was hot as a branding iron in here. He had to get out.

Not wanting to walk through the house at this hour and wake sleeping folks, he climbed out the window.

Once outside and walking around the building toward the patio garden, he figured it wasn't much better out here as far as the temperature went. At least the wind dried his sweat some.

In the end it wasn't cool air he was seeking so much as peace of mind, a bit of solitude to set things right in his mind.

Far in the distance, cattle called to one another. He couldn't hear the cowboys on midnight watch singing to calm the beasts, but he knew what the songs would be.

Close at hand, crickets chirruped. A nightingale perched on the porch rail went through her song list, not seeming to be bothered by heat or wind.

Sounds of home surrounded him. The familiar lullaby ought to be bringing him comfort and yet—

"Travis?" From behind, a hand lightly touched his shoulder.

"What are you doing out here, Ivy?" he asked without turning around.

It was a damn foolish question. From the first he knew she found freedom in the dark of night. It could be that he'd climbed out his office window hoping he would come upon her.

Was she even wearing a stitch? She hadn't been that first time on the *River Queen*.

"Little Mouse was restless. I brought her out."

He felt the tickle of her touch as her fingers trailed over his shirt along his backbone.

Slowly, he did turn, found she was dressed, but not in much.

She had hiked the filmy fabric of her sleeping gown up about her thighs and tied it in a knot at one hip.

There was a lamp sitting on the bench. In the dim glow he saw sweat glistening on her long, lovely limbs.

Her hair shimmered, tumbling over her shoulder and down her chest. He wondered if the gleam was caused by heat or lamplight.

He touched it. Wasn't heat or lamplight to his way of thinking. It was magic—the midnight enchantment of a prairie nymph. One who was not yet committed to another man.

Twining his fingers in the curling mass, he drew her close to him. Felt the tickle of the fine strands that the wind blew against his face.

He lowered his mouth, skimmed her cheek with his lips and caught the scent of prairie grass on her skin as much as he did river water. His heart rolled over.

"Ivy?" He'd never heard his voice so harsh with anguish.

He felt the hitch in her breathing, the pressure of her fingers on the back of his neck.

Damned if he was going to go the rest of his life regretting that he had never tasted her passion. For this one moment he was going to pretend she was his.

He nipped her bottom lip—tasted woman, earthy and wanting. Drawing her close, he felt the curves of her body, plush and hot.

He kissed her softly, then deeply. So deeply that it might be his heart caressing her as much as his mouth.

Ivy tasted so damned female, completely sweet and—salty?

A teardrop moistened his lips. Cut his heart to the quick.

Ivy spun away. She dashed for the bench where she had set the lantern. Kneeling, she opened her hand. The mouse scampered out of a bush and into her waiting palm. She tucked it into the pouch and drew the string closed.

Grabbing the lamp, she stood. She held his gaze for only an instant. Just long enough for the lamplight to reveal tear tracks.

She swiped them away with the back of her hand. She touched her heart then pressed her fingers to her lips and blew him a kiss.

Then she and her light were gone, leaving him to stand alone in the darkness.

Sitting in the dining room the next morning with Uncle Patrick and Antie—two people she loved dearly—Ivy had never felt more alone.

The dismal sensation made her push her breakfast away, get up from the table and pace.

Travis never missed breakfast. In spite of the fact that Señora Morgan said he'd gone to tend some skittish cattle, she knew there was another reason.

One passion-filled kiss had doomed them. Given them a taste of life's beauty, a wonder that would be forever haunting and forbidden.

"*Chère petite*," said Antie, as she sat beside Uncle Patrick, a foot closer to him than she had last time they dined. Her uncle must be sailing that vessel of his swift and true. "Pacing will not bring your young man here any quicker."

This was true. But pacing was a release for strangled energy.

Stopping in front of an open window, the curtains blowing inward, she stared out. She couldn't recall ever seeing clouds so inky black and churning. Blazin' days if they didn't look angry.

Glancing back, she saw Antie and her uncle exchange a look…a tender look.

"I don't expect him at all…not with the cattle so riled."

"I believe Madame du Mer was speaking of Mr. English, my dear." Uncle Patrick's ham-speared fork paused inches from his mustache while he wagged his brows at her.

"Of course I mean William…" she said, even though in the instant she had nearly forgotten he was due to arrive this afternoon. "The weather is bound to make him think twice about venturing out, especially when a herd of spooked critters could trample him."

"My guess is he will be here. He wants to ensure he wins the election. And you, my little love, are the insurance." Uncle Patrick chewed the ham, swallowed.

Thunder rolled in the distance, still far off but coming closer.

"Mr. Morgan claims that with you on his side, it'll put our man out front. Did you know, Madame," he said, turning his attention to Antie. "That Mr. Morgan claims to have never made a wrong prediction in an election?"

"*Mais oui?* This must be true then with two such intelligent gentlemen in agreement. I can only wish to have your knowledge."

Had Ivy not been in such a turmoil, she would have laughed out loud. Antie was turning the very charm that she instructed on Uncle Patrick!

"This thing I do know," she said with a perfect smile and elegant nod. "Our *chère* Ivy will be a competent future first lady for Wyoming."

A competent first lady? All of a sudden she wanted to hightail it for the simple life aboard the *River Queen*.

She could not, of course. The *River Queen* was

gone—now a part of her past. William English was her future.

Ivy pressed the curtain to the sill to keep it from flapping at her.

She ought to bring Agatha down for breakfast, but her sister hadn't slept well last night; she had complained of her muscles aching and feeling nauseous. Agatha's body would go through difficult times, getting rid of Brunne's "tender" touch with laudanum.

As if thinking of the woman had made her appear, she did, sweeping into the dining room as dark and roiling as the clouds.

"Miss Agatha is asking for the mouse."

"Bring her to my room, if you will. She can play with her there."

"She wants her in her own room."

This was unusual. Mrs. Brunne did not allow the mouse in Agatha's quarters.

"I doubt if that's wise."

"Agatha needs calming. The storm's got her fidgety. Since you disposed of her medicine, it'll have to be that vermin to do it."

"How do I know you won't stomp on her?"

"And make an unholy mess under my shoe?" Mrs. Brunne huffed in disgust. "I think not."

It didn't feel right leaving Little Mouse in Brunne's care, but Ivy could not spend time with Agatha right now. She had to devote the morning to getting gussied up for her suitor.

A bolt of lightning hit close by. The house shook. Mrs. Brunne grabbed her chest, stifled a cry. She rallied quickly, though and straightened her shoulders.

"Tell my sister I'll bring her to her in a moment."

The nurse glided out of the dining room like her feet weren't touching the ground.

"I reckon she's riding a broom under that skirt," Ivy grumbled.

"I have a moment." Uncle Patrick slid Antie a quick wink. "I'll take the mouse to her. You ladies go get ready for Mr. English's arrival."

"You are our knight, our hero, Mr. Malone." Madame's chest lifted demurely. Ivy still hadn't gotten the right of that trick yet. "Our *chère petite* will be the most beautiful woman he has ever seen."

At one in the afternoon, Ivy gazed at her reflection in the long mirror. She did look beautiful, but it was all due to Antie's skills.

Her mentor had been quicker fussing over her than usual. She didn't need to guess why. She'd lay a big wager that Antie was meeting Uncle Patrick in one of the many secluded rooms in the big house.

Ivy had felt a bit guilty being pampered and gussied up, given that out on the plains the cowboys would be soaked to the skin while trying to keep the cattle calm.

As soon as she had William's money behind her, she would make sure they got extra pay for their dangerous work.

There was no doubt that this afternoon, it was highly dangerous. Children were forbidden out of doors, women as well. The only cooks working today were the ones living in the house.

Chances were, the struggle Antie had gone through getting her poured into this elegant blue gown with tiny pearls sewn at the neckline and the hem was wasted. All the pretty loops and whirls she had spun into Ivy's hair would be for naught.

If William did show up she'd be more surprised than a hen hatching a duckling.

Turning from the mirror, she walked to the window and stared out.

Miles away, she saw a funnel drop from a cloud. Sure did look like an elephant's trunk gracefully swaying this way and that. The tornado didn't quite reach the ground, but if it did it would be anything but graceful.

She'd never actually seen a tornado before, but their reputation was horrific. She feared for her cowboys, for her cattle and for William if he really was out in the elements.

But her hands nearly shook for fear of what might happen to Travis. Even with the money to keep the ranch solvent, the Lucky Clover would be nothing without him at the helm.

She would be nothing. Without her friend—no, not her friend—she might as well be honest with herself. Not that it made a whit of difference to what her choice must be.

She would marry one man, be fond of him even, but she would love another.

Agatha would be safe, the children and their families would remain secure and William, according to those who "knew," would win his election.

The price to be paid would be her heart—and Travis's. Last night, without a word being spoken, they had made the final choice.

Their kiss had begun as temptation, but ended as goodbye. Not goodbye, as in never seeing each other again. But as in, they had counted the cost and found it too high. This goodbye meant laying to rest any small dream of the life they might have shared.

In the end, by the silent language of touch and glance,

they had admitted their feelings for one another then backed away.

The love they felt for one another, they would give to others.

A soft knock rapped on her door. She opened it to find Laura Lee standing in the hall.

"Mr. English has come, miss. He's drying off in the parlor."

"I'll be down directly." She closed the door and heard the young woman's steps hurrying away.

Returning to the mirror, she looked herself over one more time, adjusted a curl that had escaped its pin in an attempt to be free.

"Not for you, my friend, and not for me."

It was time. She was as ready as she was ever going to be.

That didn't mean her hands weren't shaking, her nerves as jittery as the lightning scattering over the ranch.

In moments she would give William her answer and never look back.

When she opened her door, Laura Lee was standing there, breathless from a run back down the hall.

"I nearly forgot this, Miss Magee, in all the excitement of Mr. English's arrival, but Mrs. Brunne asked me to give you this note."

Travis closed the front door on weather that was more beast than element of nature. He kicked off his boots, shrugged out of his coat, then wiped his face on the towel that the housekeeper always hung on the coatrack for rainy days.

He'd sent many of the cowboys to the safety of their homes. God willing, the hands farther out would make it to the shelter buildings. While protecting cattle, keeping them from panicking and becoming injured was vital, the safety of the men was even more so.

At least the storm would keep William from coming today. He didn't know what difference a day made, why the delay made him happy, but it sure damn did.

He crossed the parlor barefoot on his way to the kitchen. Coming in he smelled coffee. A good strong cup would be the thing to balance his emotions.

Lightning blanched the room in bright light. Thunder pounded nearby, probably hitting land between the big house and the cowboys' homes. The livestock in the barn would be plenty spooked.

Within seconds, the room's light returned to the soft illumination of lamps.

A man sat on the couch. Laura Lee was handing him a cup of steaming coffee.

"William?" What the—? "What are you doing here?"

"Good afternoon, Travis." The man stood, extended his hand.

"You look half drowned." Travis returned the handshake. "Why didn't you wait for the weather to clear? Can I trouble you for a cup of that, Laura Lee?"

"I said I'd be here today." He shrugged.

"That was a risky trip. It wouldn't do anyone good to find you drowned in a gully."

"I've got a surefooted horse and here I am, no more than waterlogged, extremely waterlogged."

"Legislature's not going to vote for a foolhardy fellow."

"Neither will they vote for one who does not keep his word."

Laura Lee laughed, handing Travis the coffee. "The

both of you look like half-drowned cats. But if I had the power, you would have my vote, Mr. English."

"Thank you, miss. Keep that vote for when we become a state. I'll need all I can get when I run for governor."

"Where's Ivy?" Travis thought she would have been here in the parlor accepting a marriage proposal.

"I let her know Mr. English was here." Laura Lee said, frowning. "It was some time ago."

"Will you run up and check on her?" Travis asked.

It sure wasn't like Ivy not to come down promptly. She had to know what William had risked to get here.

His heart soared and sank at the same time, wondering if she had changed her mind about marrying English.

The front door crashed open, driven on a gust of wind. Agatha leaned against the frame, sliding slowly toward the floor while she tried to catch her breath.

Travis dropped his coffee on the floor, turned to go to her.

William was quicker. He swooped her up and carried her to the couch.

Laura Lee ran out of the room then came back carrying an armful of fresh towels. She knelt before Agatha, wiping her face and hands. Chafing her trembling fingers.

"What were you doing outside, Miss Agatha?" she asked.

Something was not right. Agatha could hardly walk the length of a room. What in the blazes was she doing out in the storm?

"Mrs. Brunne," she gasped. Not Mother Brunne? He could not recall her ever referring to the nurse as Mrs. A fist grabbed hold of his innards and twisted. "She's lured Ivy out into the storm!"

Laura Lee gasped. "I did deliver a note!"

"When?" he asked.

Poor Agatha looked like she was ready to shiver to pieces. She clung to William, her knuckles white on his arm.

"It's all right, Agatha. Don't be afraid," he said, patting her hands and chaffing them at the same time. "Everything will be all right."

He placed a quick, comforting kiss on the top of her head while he shared a sharp glance with Travis. They had both been out in the weather and knew there was something to be anxious about.

"About forty minutes ago," Laura Lee said.

"She…she…tussled with me and gagged me…shut me in a closet out of the way of anyone."

"Did she say anything?" William asked.

Agatha nodded her head. "She said we were going to be together forever. No one would come between us again. She means to harm Ivy—I know it!"

"How did you get out?" Laura Lee rubbed her hands.

"The closet has a transom window. I climbed on boxes and broke it."

"Looks like you cut your finger," Laura Lee said, then wrapped the towel around it.

Agatha shook her head. "She cut me getting me into the closet."

Travis ran for his boots.

"I can't believe you made it all the way down here on your own, Miss Agatha?" he heard Laura Lee say. "You are stronger and braver than anyone knew!"

He lurched into his wet jacket and slammed his Stetson on his head.

"I'm coming with you." William reached for his coat.

"No." He would make better time on his own, and besides— "I promise to bring Ivy back. The best way you can protect her is to stay here, to remain safe."

William nodded. He didn't look pleased about having to stay behind, but he would understand the need. Without him the ranch would go to ruin.

"God's speed to you, then, Travis."

From the looks of things going on outside, that was exactly what he would need.

Chapter Seventeen

Lightning exploded on a knoll a hundred yards in front of Ivy. Her mare pranced nervously, wanting to run for the safety of home but another blast hit the earth in that direction.

"There's a good girl." Leaning forward in the saddle Ivy patted the strong chestnut colored neck, felt the ripple of tension under her fingers. "We're nearly there."

Slowly, the lightning drifted east but the relief wouldn't last long. Another band was approaching from the west.

In the distance, Ivy spotted the shelter house that Nurse Brunne indicated in her note.

It looked no more than a blur in the downpour and strain as she might, she could see no sign of the nurse.

She was certain this was the spot. The note had been clear…about a few things.

"I have your sister," it read.

Ivy didn't know for sure if it was true, but she did know that Agatha had not been in her room when she tore down the hallway like a mad woman to look. And the window had been left open to the rain. If Brunne had taken her sister, it had to have been through the window and onto the deck, otherwise someone would have noticed.

The note instructed Ivy to come alone. If she didn't, the price would be tragic.

She had no option but to believe it. Even though Brunne might love Agatha in some bedeviled way, she was possessive when it came to her.

Just there! Ivy spotted a figure holding an umbrella.

Hilda Brunne stepped away from a tree a short distance from the stone building.

The nurse's horse whinnied from where it was tethered behind the tree. The poor thing sounded scared. Ivy's mare reacted to the call with an agitated sidestep.

"It's all right." Ivy crooned to her mount, but the mare was not comforted. And why would she be? "I'll get off and lead you."

"Gull-durned lunatic." Ivy stared at Hilda while she towed her mount through the mud and lashing rain.

Taking shelter under the tree was not wise. Ivy stopped several yards from the drip line. Even so, she was too close.

"Come nearer and we'll talk," Brunne shouted.

"Where's my sister?"

"I'm sure you would like to know."

"You'd best come out from under that tree if you have something to say, Mrs. Brunne. I'm not standing under it."

"The rain's not as bad under here."

"I'm already wet." Blazin' days if she was going to be skewered by lightning, too.

"Such a prissy little miss." Brunne stomped out from under the tree.

Ivy led her horse twenty feet farther away. Rain

hit the ground so hard it sounded like pennies being dropped on a wood floor.

Brunne cowered under the umbrella, letting out a screech.

"Where is Agatha?" Ivy had to shout above the noise.

"She's safe in the stone house, come and see. The three of us can have a nice, cozy chat."

Ivy's scalp prickled. The fine hairs on her neck stood up. Even the threat of lightning hadn't made that happen.

She couldn't go into the shed even if Agatha was in there. Clearly, Brunne meant to entrap her. The means to do it would be Agatha.

"Better say what you mean to before we both burn."

"You dying is what this is all about. I'm finished with your interference. I want you out of my way."

"I'm not getting out of your way."

The woman really was insane! Didn't she understand that whatever danger she put Ivy in out here, she faced as well?

"Maybe not by choice." Brunne tried to control the umbrella, but it tugged at her double-fisted grip. "But I'll make sure you don't take Maggie and Bethy away from me again. You won't leave me to die this time."

Maggie! Who was Bethy?

"I don't know who they are, Hilda. I only want to take my sister home where she'll be safe."

"That's what you said last time, Harvey…when I found my way home, you and my babies were gone. You thought that storm you abandoned me in would be the death of me, but it wasn't."

"I didn't take your babies!" The lightning that had been approaching from the west slid closer by the minute. It was almost like she could feel it shaking the ground. "I'm not Harvey. Look at me! I'm Ivy."

"Ivy!" Brunne swiped the water from her face with her sleeve. "I know who you are—you want to take my Maggie—no, no, my Agatha. I'll kill myself and her before I'll let you have her again."

"What happened to your babies, Hilda?" Maybe if Ivy seemed sympathetic, Hilda's sanity would return long enough for her to let Agatha go. "Was Harvey your husband? Taking your babies was a horrible thing."

"I never knew what happened to them until I found them here...no, not them. Ivy and Agatha." Wind yanked the umbrella from Hilda's hand, sent it sailing for a good distance before the tip lodged in the mud. "Then Ivy's mother took her away!"

"I'm Ivy. I'm home again!"

Hilda looked confused; she shook her head. "I think we might drown, but this time we will be together."

Apparently Hilda's mind was shattered to the point where she could not tell now from then, or her babies from Mollie Clover Magee's.

Judging by the way the ground vibrated, the band of lightning was closing in faster than she thought. From behind the tree, Brunne's horse shrieked.

"I'm not Bethy, I'm Ivy. Look at me, Hilda. I'm Ivy."

"Of course you are, come back after all these years to make my girl healthy so she won't need me anymore."

Could lightning really make the ground vibrate that way?

"Bring Agatha out. Let me see that she's safe. I'll go away. You can have her all to yourself again."

"Do you think I'm stupid?"

It sure wasn't easy trying to outwit a person whose wits were gone.

Ivy's patience was run out—and so was time. She

could hear the frizzle of lightning bolts, smell the sulfur when they stabbed the ground.

They needed to be away from here.

"Go back to the ranch house—go get your babies from Harvey before he sells them again. I'm taking Agatha!"

Wind blew her words sideways, but Brunne heard.

"Oh, my dearie, you think I'm insane."

"It's not insane to want your children. Go get them. They've been crying for you."

"I suppose my own babies are long dead. But, Agatha isn't. Do you think I would risk bringing her out in this weather? Her room is where she belongs, not out walking in the sunshine, dancing with a man who probably will dump her in the river. Your sister is safely locked in a closet."

It could be that Agatha was at home. Or she could be in the shed. It was hard to know with the way Brunne's mind wobbled between the present and the past.

Ivy turned toward her horse. She reached in her saddle pack for the ax she'd snatched while saddling up.

Her hand shook. It was one thing to bring a weapon but another thing to actually use it. Her intent had been to threaten only. The horse bumped her, knocking the ax from her fingers and into the mud.

She scrambled for it while Brunne slogged toward her.

Something was wrong, something more than rain, lightning and a provoked madwoman who had drawn a bag from her pocket and started swinging it over her head. It was lumpy and heavy looking.

Lunging, Hilda slammed the bag at the horse's flank. Ivy heard the clank of stones. The mare screeched then ran.

The ax was too slippery to grasp. It slid away and disappeared into the muck.

Brunne latched on to her arm, whacked Ivy's head with the stones. Stunned, she fell face first into the mud.

Jumping upon her, Brunne pummeled her again with the bag. Ivy rolled, shoved her off.

Kneeling in the mud, she couldn't catch her breath.

The earth under Ivy's hands trembled.

Brunne's head snapped up. She stared at something, past Ivy's shoulder. Her mouth opened in a scream but whatever horror she was looking at closed her throat.

Trying to rise, the nurse slipped. Her hands and feet scrambled for purchase. She shoved Ivy backward, stomped on her belly seeking something solid to push off from.

Gaining her feet, Brunne sloughed through the mud toward her horse.

Ivy pushed to her knees, swiped the mud from her eyes. Spinning about, she saw it.

A wall of cattle, caught up in a stampede. They would not miss her.

She couldn't move, couldn't blink. Not until Brunne's horse screamed, panicked and terrified.

The woman yanked the reins, trying to hold the horse still so she could mount. Her boot slipped in the stirrup, twisted and caught. She slammed down on her back.

"Don't struggle!" Ivy pushed to her feet, stumbled toward her cursing, screaming adversary. "You'll spook the horse even more!"

The frightened animal was the only way of escape— for both of them.

Brunne slapped at the prancing hooves. Terrified, the horse reared. It galloped away, dragging her, bouncing and jerking over muddy ground.

Ivy took a few steps toward the shelter house. It was

too far away. She would never be able to outrun the herd in order to get to it.

Still, running was her only choice. Gull-durned if she was going to stand here cussing while cows crushed her.

The one and only thing to do was hightail it across open land and hope the cattle changed course.

Something snagged her toe and nearly took her down.

The dad-gummed umbrella! She plucked it out of the muck. Wasn't much of a weapon, but if she waved the mangled thing wildly, it might encourage a beast or two to turn aside.

Step by sucking step she plucked her feet out of the mud. Too bad the muck didn't slow down the herd.

Sodden skirts dragged her down. Her clothes weighed twenty pounds more than they ought to. Images of women tumbling off the *River Queen*'s plank flashed in her mind.

If she had to do it over again, she wouldn't be so judgmental.

Too bad she'd set off in such an all-fired hurry and not taken the time to change out of her fancy engagement gown into something that was not about to kill her.

Moments ago, she'd felt the ground shuddering. Now she heard the snorts of the beasts, smelled their damp hides.

Travis had been pushing his horse hard, but drew it to a halt at the top of a rise.

He felt the stallion quiver. He doubted that it was caused by the harsh weather.

The animal was too well trained to be spooked by a storm, no matter that this one was more severe than most.

More likely it was caused by a stampede. He strained

his ears to listen over the smack of rain, the yowl of wind across open land.

He couldn't hear anything, but still, he trusted that the horse knew better.

Slipping out of the saddle he knelt on the ground, felt the faint rumble, as though an unseen train was plowing across open range.

He didn't know where Ivy was, but he knew where she should not be.

"Let's go, boy," he said while mounting.

Coming over the next rise, he nearly lost his breakfast.

"Ivy!" he shouted, even knowing she would not hear him, that his yell would not help her.

The herd could not be more than a hundred yards away...now seventy-five.

She could not hope to outrun them, but she was trying.

He raced his horse down the slope, toward the approaching carnage.

He watched Ivy stop, turn, then wave an umbrella.

"No, Ivy! No!"

All of a sudden, she rushed the herd. She wouldn't know that the stampede was mindless, it would not notice one small woman brandishing an umbrella.

He was too far away. Even if the horse sprouted wings, he could not reach her in time.

All at once lightning struck between Ivy and the herd. The animals channeled to the left and looked as though they might go around her.

She ran, stumbled, ran again.

Leaning low over the horse, he gave it lead to run flat out.

He was within shouting distance when the herd turned again, back toward Ivy.

He could smell the beeves now. The scent of fear lay upon them, overcoming any other instinct they might have.

Damn! He needed thirty more seconds to scoop her up and get her out of harm's way.

No matter how he cursed, those seconds were not coming. The poor horse was already pushing his limit.

When the cattle were nearly upon her, Ivy turned her back on them, went down on her knees.

Her eyes locked on his; she reached for him then covered her head and drew her body into a ball.

Racing forward, he plucked his rifle from the saddle sheath. The odds of bringing down enough cattle to create a barrier were slim. All he could do was pray... and fire his gun.

By the time he reached Ivy, he'd brought down one steer. Not enough.

He slipped off the horse, slapped it to let it know that it should run. No need for all three of them to die.

Standing over Ivy, his legs braced on each side of her curled-up body, he continued to shoot.

The steer that would crush them barreled forward, not even aware that they were in his path.

"I love you, Ivy!" he shouted. He felt her arm curl around his leg.

Lightning hit the ground between them and the steer. He felt the frizzle of electricity move through his body. The explosion of thunder brought him to his knees. He draped his body over Ivy's hunched form.

The herd split in two, going wide around them. Thousands of hooves pounding the earth made a terrible sound that he felt in his bones.

It was only a couple of minutes before the herd moved on but he'd never felt seconds that lasted longer.

At last the rumble in the earth faded. The herd would run on without knowing why then eventually slow and stop.

"Thank you, God, thank you," he murmured.

Ivy wriggled out from under him then slammed against his chest in a choking hug.

"Are we still on this side of the m-m-mortal coil?" she gasped.

"As far as I can tell." He ran his hands over her, feeling for injury. "Where's Brunne?"

Ivy shook her head.

"On the other side, maybe." Her voice trembled as hard as her body did. "She got...her foot stuck...and the horse—"

She paused, took several breaths but the shaking didn't quit. "I tried to...but..."

"Hush, now," he crooned.

Wrapping her up, he rubbed her back and arms to try and stop the shivering, but the chill went deeper than cold, deeper than his ability to warm her.

He whistled for his horse, hoping his well-trained friend hadn't gone too far.

Ivy nodded toward the shelter house in the distance.

"I have a better place in mind. It's not far."

At least it wouldn't be if the horse came back.

"See if...if... Agatha is in there!"

"She's safe at home, honey. Can you stop shaking? Breathe slow."

No...clearly she could not. But at least she was breathing. Against the odds, both of them were.

* * *

Ivy ought to be dead and was not fully convinced she was not.

Still, it wasn't likely that a body would be having a shaking shiver fit if she had traveled beyond the Pearly Gates.

Travis stood beside her, his knee brushing her shoulder where she continued to kneel in the mud, willing her legs to become firm enough to support her. He stroked his mount's wet mane, looking him over for injury. As far as she could tell, horse and man seemed mortal enough.

"You are a damn good animal," he said.

That was the plain truth. The stallion had run only far enough to avoid the stampede then galloped back again before Travis even whistled.

"Here." Travis stooped beside her. "Loop your arms around my neck."

He lifted her then placed her in the saddle, his hands gentle on her hip when he shifted her weight.

"You s-s-sure are—" Strong was what she wanted to say but could only stutter. He had hoisted a hundred and twenty-five-pound woman and her fifty pounds' worth of muddy gown onto the horse. Admirably strong—his muscles must be made of stone.

"Hush, honey." He climbed up behind her, drew her in tight to his belly and chest. "I'm taking you someplace I know of that's warm."

She'd be a hog-tied, flying pig if a place like that existed within miles of here.

Even if he did know a warm place, Ivy doubted she'd ever be warm again. The cause of her shivering came from her soul, not her body.

There were so many things she could not get out of her mind. The sound of Hilda Brunne's bloodcurdling screams, and cattle, the rumble of hooves pounding mud, the scent of wet hides. Looking up and seeing Travis racing toward her...fearing that his despairing expression would be the last thing she would ever see.

If she was laying a wager, she'd bet that she would never be warm again.

It didn't seem that time had passed, but all of a sudden Travis slid off the saddle.

"Here we are."

He reached for her but instead of setting her on the ground, he carried her into a cave.

It was dark inside, but warm. That was mighty odd. She'd never heard of a warm cave.

"Can you stand?" he asked.

Maybe, but maybe not. "Yes."

"Don't move. I'm stepping away but I'll be close by."

She'd cheated death once already today, she would not risk moving about in a place so dark she couldn't see her own nose.

Locking her knees, trying to stand without shaking, she listened to Travis's footsteps moving about. Sometimes it sounded like he was walking on dirt, but other times rock.

The cave smelled damp, but a different kind of damp than outside. Out there, the weather of nightmares continued to pummel the land.

She heard the strike of a match, watched the flare brighten then dim. The illumination revealed Travis's hand reaching for a lamp.

All at once the interior of the cave became engulfed in a soft, golden glow.

"Blazin' day!" A hot spring? Sure enough, she was a hog-tied, flying pig.

"I meant to show it to you before, but it never seemed the right time. I like to come here sometimes to soak away stress."

Steam curled up from the surface of the clear water. It churned, bubbled and called her name.

"Cut me out of this dress."

The way he stood there staring at her, she wondered if he was going to refuse. A full minute passed, then half a minute more. She was beginning to feel like a bug pinned to a board.

"Give me your knife, then. I'll try and do it myself."

All of a sudden he drew a breath, shuddered. If she didn't know better, she'd think he'd been gone a'visiting out of his body and just come back.

"I'm sorry, Ivy, I was just…" And there he went, looking far away again but he rallied quickly this time. "I'll do it. With the way you're trembling, you'll cut yourself."

He stood behind her. His fingers brushed her neck, rubbed the grit crusted on her skin.

"I don't see any way to do this that won't ruin the gown." She felt the warmth of his words skim her ear.

"It's ruined anyway." Besides, a destroyed dress didn't seem so awful. Not compared to what they had just escaped—what Hilda Brunne had apparently not.

"It was her own doing, but still…"

"You mean Hilda, honey?"

Ivy nodded, felt the weight of the dress fall away from her shoulders.

"We'll send someone looking for her just as soon as we can."

Ahhh! She was free to her hips. It felt good to just breathe.

"I feel horrible about it, Travis."

"Because you are a good person. Don't forget she brought this on herself—she made a choice and paid a price she meant for you to pay."

"As much as her mind was in a condition to make a choice. Say! How did you know what she meant? Let alone know where to find me?"

"Agatha. Seems like Hilda said a few things in front of her before she locked her in a closet. Your sister broke out then hunted us up in the parlor. She told us what happened. As far as knowing where you were? I didn't. I made a lucky guess."

There was luck, and then there was providence, destiny. It seemed a far fetch to believe he'd just happened upon her in the very instant she needed him. Sure was more to this than luck could account for, in her opinion.

"Hilda...she was crazy, Travis. She had her twin babies all jumbled up with me and Agatha. Couldn't tell us from them."

"The ones who died?"

"That's the thing. They didn't die. Her husband took them from her, tried to kill her. She substituted me and Agatha for her own babies. When Mama took me away... it did something to her. Made her cling to Agatha. It's why she kept her weak. To keep her always as her own."

"She never seemed insane—no one ever thought so."

"I reckon the worst of the demon in her lay quiet until I came home. It didn't fester until she thought she would lose Agatha to me. And this storm. I think it had something to do with pushing her past reason."

The dress hit the cave floor with a thud, followed by the corset that Travis had cut along with the gown. She stepped out of the muddy blue puddle still wearing her camisole and drawers.

She spun about. "Is my sister all right? Did Brunne hurt her?"

"She's worried about you is all, and about Little Mouse. Laura Lee was fussing over her when I left."

"Praise the good Lord!" Ivy nodded and kicked off her shoes. "But why is she worried about Little Mouse?"

"According to your sister, Hilda dumped her somewhere outside."

"She's a crafty little survivor. I'll find her." Ivy rolled her head back on her neck. Her shoulders went slack.

"Shed those clothes, Travis. They're in as sorry a shape as mine."

He plucked off his shirt. Ivy thought it best to turn around, find distraction by touching the water with her toe, because he looked fine without his shirt. Stripped all the way bare, he would be more than fine. She knew that from the first time she met him.

"I'm sorry, Ivy. I never expected to bring you home to this," he said, his voice nearer than what would be proper under the circumstances.

Circumstances being William back in the parlor waiting to become engaged.

She stepped onto a shallow rock under the water. Warmth rushed between her toes and up her ankles.

The water was clear and beautiful. It would be a shame to muck it up with the mud on her underwear.

Besides, how much difference was there between barely a stitch on and plain old bare?

She wriggled out of the bloomers and flicked them away with her toe.

Heavenly warmth crept up her thighs as she stepped deeper into the water. Could be that some of her shivering was due to being chilly, after all.

Lifting her camisole off over her head, she pitched it after the drawers.

Two splashes disturbed the water—Travis stepping in behind her.

"Ivy…" His voice sounded as heated as the water, her name on his lips as pleasant as the pulsing undulation on her skin.

Finding the deepest point in the spring, she turned. Water covered her from the neck down…but it was clear as a window.

She crossed her arms over her chest as Travis waded toward her. His arms weren't trying to cover anything.

Not that she minded—he was male perfection, muscular, powerfully graceful.

Given that he wasn't trying to hide anything, it was easy to see what was on his mind. His intention was evident.

Standing in front of her he touched her cheek, slid one finger under her chin and tipped it up.

She had nowhere to look but in his eyes. Unless she stared at his mouth, but that was not wise.

Being naked in the spring wasn't wise either but here she was and glad of it.

"You heard what I told you earlier?"

What he believed to be his last words?

"I love you, too, Travis." And with those words, nothing would ever be the same again.

"I'm done pretending you were meant for someone else."

Gosh almighty, there must be a dozen ways to shiver and she'd just discovered a new one.

Chapter Eighteen

Ivy opened her arms.

Shot him that wide and lovely grin of hers. The genuine one, the smile William would never see. There was so much of Ivy the man would never see.

But Travis had seen all of her: the hopeful boat pilot, the gambler, the river nymph, and the lady of impeccable manners and captivating charm.

He loved all of who she was. William could never fully love Ivy because he would never fully know her.

When the man took her to his bed, he would not be making love to the true woman.

Ivy deserved to be loved. To be touched and cherished, if it was only this one time, for who she was. And Travis was the one who needed to cherish her, body and soul.

Before it was too late.

Once they returned to the ranch, she would accept a marriage proposal. Until she did, she was free. What he did tonight would not be illicit.

Lifting her dripping hand from the water, she touched his cheek, stroked the line of his jaw.

"I've only ever been meant for one man, for you."

Delicately, she traced a line across his lips. Water dribbled down his chin then his neck. "All it took was nearly being crushed in a stampede to make it clear."

He kissed her fingertips then put one arm around her waist to draw her to him, flesh to flesh.

Not simply flesh to flesh, though. There was so much more to the intimate press of skin on skin. It was as if everything that had happened in the last several weeks had led to this moment of joining. Some people would call it destiny.

He trailed his fingers up her spine, felt a shiver ripple under her skin, heard the whisper of a sigh when she tilted her head back and gazed into his eyes.

"You know what I'm asking of you?"

She nuzzled her hips against his belly. "I'm not blind, Travis, I reckon I understand the message."

He laughed, couldn't help it. "There's that, but what I mean is we can never come back from this. No matter what happens, we won't be the same."

For a few hours of fulfillment, he was taking on a lifetime of regret and asking her to accept the same. But regret was in their futures, no matter what.

He sure as hell would rather regret sharing love than denying it.

"I want you to know how much I love you, Ivy. Just because you—" Speaking about her future with William at this moment seemed profane. Still, she should know. "I'll always love you, no matter if—"

"Hush." She went up on her toes, kissed his mouth lightly. "We won't speak of that. It's you and me, now. I'll always love you, too."

Travis cupped her cheeks with his big, calloused palms. He gave her a kiss so sweet it was nearly reverent.

Down below though, under water, things felt down-right carnal. His erection rubbed hot and heavy against her belly.

All of a sudden the gentle caress of the kiss changed, flared. Intoxication lit her up inside like the match had done to the cave. She glowed from the inside out, throbbed from the outside in.

He kissed her jaw, nibbled her throat, then his head went below the surface of the spring. Ivy watched, blear-ily fascinated by the way the dark, glistening strands undulated with the movement of water.

She was about to touch it when his tongue flicked the tip of her breast. His mouth covered it, suckling gently. Her fingers curled. Her feminine part clenched.

Anywhere he wasn't kissing, he was caressing with long, strong fingers and making her joints melt.

It was too much effort to force them to hold her up-right. She let go and slipped beneath the surface with Travis.

Warm water sifted through her hair, freed it of bits of dirt and grass. Travis slid beneath her; she saw his face through rippling strands, looking up at her and grinning.

Needing a breath, she broke the surface. Travis came up under her, scooping her into his arms when he did.

"My nymph," he murmured, his eyes emerald green in the dim light. "My sweet water fairy."

"Truth to tell, Travis, I'm not feeling quite so ethe-real. I'm about ready to melt out of my skin for wanting you to touch me."

"Truth to tell, I've wanted to since the first time I saw you."

"Better get back to it then."

Travis carried her to an underwater ledge. Water

lapped her shoulders with an erotic suckle, and made her impatient to feel Travis's lips upon her again.

Pressing on his shoulders, she drew herself up, braced her knees on his thighs. His hands curled around her buttocks, kneading. At the same time, he gave her what she wanted, made a feast of her, made her moan his name.

Lightheaded, she slid back down, her thighs splayed across his lap and water kneaded her exposed womanly part.

Travis cupped her head, his fingers tangled in her wet hair. He kissed her deeply. She felt the loving message to her soul.

And then, it was no longer water lapping at her intimate place. Travis touched, caressed…petted.

"You are mine, Ivy," he whispered into her hair, his breath coming in short gasps.

"Always yours."

She felt a change. The hard, hot tip of him pressed against her where his fingers had petted a second before.

He lifted her to a shallower rock. Pressing her down, she felt cool, smooth stone on her back. He crawled over her. The heat of his skin laved her breasts and her belly.

"Never forget, I had you first." With his big, firm hands, he spread her thighs and thrust into her, staking his claim. "I loved you first, my Ivy."

Not only first…always.

There had to be a way. She would make a way.

Beyond the mouth of the cave, Travis watched the wind blow the clouds away. The morning star hovered over the horizon, bright with the promise of a new day.

One that he was not eager to face.

Looking down, he watched Ivy sleeping naked in

his arms. He'd made his point, time after time during the night.

Ivy belonged to him, even if it was only for this brief moment.

Sitting on a shallow step he held her close, warm water their intimate blanket.

He'd tired her out, and wasn't sorry for it. He had time now while she slept to just look at her, to memorize the way her lashes curled in slumber, how a slight smile curved her pink, well-kissed lips, even now.

He caressed her all over with his eyes, keeping this vision of her for the future. Looking at her long, beautiful legs, he remembered how they felt locked around him when he came inside her. Watching her hands, one lying across her belly and the other splayed across his, he cherished the fire those fingers ignited in him.

Moving water shimmied her breasts. He felt them softly undulating against his chest. Just there! Her nipples tightened. He could only hope she was dreaming of him, that she would always dream of him.

He would see his angel every time he closed his eyes.

"Ivy," he murmured.

One more time, just one. Then he would let her go as he must.

Ivy hadn't expected to sleep the day away but it was late in the afternoon when she woke, near evening when she ventured outside.

It was unlikely that Travis had even closed his eyes. His day would be spent checking the ranch for damage and making sure no one had been harmed during the storm. No doubt he had organized a search for Hilda Brunne.

She couldn't help but wonder what it would be like

the first time she saw him. Would she leap into his arms in front of everyone? Or would she only blush and remember?

Last night she had gone into a cave a plain and prickly caterpillar. Several hours later she'd emerged from that sweet cocoon a butterfly.

Travis had the right of it when he said nothing would be the same.

Dinner was in a couple of hours. Not so long to wait to see his eyes shining at her in love.

Reluctant to dispel that image, she stifled a groan.

She approached a bush near the porch off the kitchen, then stooped down.

Unusual aches and twinges conjured up visions of declared love, of emotions spoken with touch rather than words. Sure was an odd state of affairs when something that smarted could make a body grin from the inside out.

Even though things had been a mite quiet between her and Travis on the ride home, it wasn't over regret for what they had done.

More, what they were going to do about it. She knew Travis was fussing about her marrying William, trying to convince himself that it was still the right thing to do. Ivy had been stewing over it, too.

Lord bless Uncle Patrick for sitting up with her all night long, talking and helping to put her mind at rest about the decision she'd made.

Moving aside a leafy branch she peered deep into the brush. All she saw were the dark green shadows of late afternoon.

"Little Mouse, come on out. I've brought you a treat." She set the cookie crumbs on the ground then leaned back on her heels to watch and wait.

"I doubt if she's in that bush, Ivy. I've already looked."

She glanced back, smiled. "Howdy—I mean, hello, William. It was kind of you to search."

"My guess is that Mrs. Brunne dropped her farther toward the barn." He crouched next to her, shaking his head while he moved another branch.

"I understand you held things together when Travis came after me, that Agatha begged you for laudanum to calm her nerves?"

"Poor girl was at her wits' end with worry. It's understandable that she would seek an old comfort."

"As I hear it, you put a book in her hands. I can't say how grateful I am that you were there to take charge. I'll always be grateful."

"I'm sure I mentioned that I like being in charge." He flashed a chivalrous smile. Gosh almighty, there was a twinkle in his eye! "And I'm grateful that Travis brought you home safely."

Ivy stood up gingerly.

"Were you injured?" William stood with her, frowning and slipping his hand under her elbow.

She shook her head, looked away. Not injured, just a mite sore.

"I like you, William." The longer she waited to say this, the more miserable the telling was going to be.

"I like you, too."

Blamed twinkle.

"You think you do, but the truth is you don't know me."

"And you don't know me, but that will come with time. I have every confidence we will end up genuine friends."

"Yes, I hope so." As long as he didn't hate her after she told him what was weighing on her heart. "But there's something I need to say...well to confess."

"Would you like to sit?"

She shook her head. "I feel like I've got ants in my drawers as it is."

"I beg your pardon?"

"You've been tricked, William. You think I'm a lady fit to be a politician's wife. I'm not. I'm no more than a river rat. Why, when Travis found me my greatest dream was to pilot a riverboat."

He lowered a dark brow. "You have lovely manners for a river rat."

"It seems I'm not bad at acting, either. Why the only reason I'm not cussing and tripping over this dang pretty dress…" She kicked at the hem. "Is because Madame du Mer is a patient teacher. Poor Antie had the devil of a time teaching me how to smile and speak correctly. And flirting? Well she nearly gave up on that. I could dance all right, but not like a lady."

William was silent for a moment, looking at her with a puzzled expression.

There was nothing for it but to give him proof.

"Here's how I really dance."

Ivy stomped, slapped her thighs and grinned like a loon. Lungs heaving, she finished the performance with a yee-haw.

"I learned from roustabouts and deckhands."

"You are a fascinating woman, Ivy Magee."

"I reckon you didn't have my kind of fascinating in mind when you agreed with my father's proposal."

"My offer stands. I know what our union means to this ranch."

"And I know what the ranch means to your career." She took a breath, let it out in a whoosh. "The thing is… I can't marry you. I meant to hold up my end of things but it turned out that I like you."

"I can't see how that's a bad thing."

"Look a little harder, Bill." He was, with both brows peaked high in his forehead. "I just couldn't carry on with things and you not knowing who I am. Deceiving you was gnawing at my conscience."

"All right, I imagine it was." He folded his arms across his chest. "Now that I know, I am still asking you to marry me. A union would benefit us both."

"There's another reason I can't marry you."

He sighed. His fists slipped to his hips. The toe of his shiny boot scuffed the dirt.

"Because you are in love with Travis Murphy?"

"Gosh almighty, how'd you know that?"

"It shows—whenever you look at him or say his name."

"I reckon I'm no good at keeping secrets."

"Neither is he." William shrugged. "I suppose there's no use trying to argue with a woman in love."

Funny, but William looked nervous. She'd never seen him look anything but confident.

"Something troubling you, Bill?"

"There might be." He withdrew an envelope from his pocket. "I met Travis in the hall an hour ago. He was setting this on the foyer table. He seemed in an odd way. Warned me that I'd better appreciate you. Then he asked me to give this to you. I don't like to say so, Ivy, but I got the feeling he was saying goodbye."

"I might like to sit now."

He could not be leaving, not now when she and Uncle Patrick had figured a way to save the ranch.

William took her elbow and led her up the porch stairs.

She plopped down hard on a bench and regretted it.

"Travis loves the Lucky Clover," she said when William sat down beside her. "I can't think of why he'd leave."

"I didn't read what he wrote, but I'd guess his leaving has something to do with that. And with loving you."

"Fool man probably knew I wouldn't marry you after last—"

A subtle smile twitched William's mouth. "My guess is, he believes things will be better all round if he isn't here. It's his way to give you, and everyone else, a secure future. The way I see it, he's giving up the thing he loves the most for the person he loves the most."

"Seems to me he might have said so to my face."

"He couldn't have gone through with it if he did."

"Well, I haven't read the letter yet. Maybe he's only gone off to herd cattle for a week."

"Maybe," William said, but his expression said he didn't believe it.

"You don't have to lose everything, Ivy. You could still marry me."

"That's a kind offer. Don't think I haven't wrangled with the idea for a long time. But you'd be sorry for it after a while. A man's wife isn't supposed to be in love with someone else. Would you mind being my friend and neighbor instead?"

"I'd be pleased to be your friend. I don't see how we'll be neighbors, though. The note is coming due. You'll lose the ranch."

"I won't! I've figured a way to pay it." Too bad Travis hadn't stayed long enough to find out what it was. Gull-durned man! "Did I tell you I'm a gambler?"

"You fascinate me, my friend."

"I can win the wings off a bee."

William laughed, his smile at her not that of a polished politician.

"Are you asking me for a grubstake?"

"Turns out I have one." She was more fond of William English than she expected to be, but it was a good thing she wasn't going to marry him. "I hate that I might have ruined your ambitions though. I know you need the ranch as much as I do."

"It's still a long time before Wyoming becomes a state and I can run for governor." He leaned sideways and kissed her cheek. "Maybe in the meantime, I'll find a woman of influence who will love me as much as you love Travis."

"I expect you'll find a dozen of them, Bill."

"Bill?" He clapped his hand over his heart. "I like it, Ivy. I'll pick the first one to call me by that name."

"This is better." Antie fluffed the sleeve of Ivy's shirt. Straightened the hem of her riding getup. "Now you are fit for traveling. I will burn those river rags while you are gone."

"Maybe just pack them away?"

It had been her intention to wear her boat clothes back to the *River Queen*. The blamed thing was, once she put them on, they felt wrong…all floppy and ragged. Even the flowered strip of fabric she used for decoration seemed dull.

Just went to show she was no longer who she used to be. She no longer had to put on the pretense of being a lady of high society, but neither was she the unfettered girl who had lived at large aboard the *Queen*.

There were times when she liked letting loose of her clothes and running free, but other times when she liked looking pretty, just with her stays not as tight as they might be.

"Go downstairs, now, *ma chère*. Your uncle will be waiting."

Curious. There was a blush on Antie's cheeks when she spoke of Uncle Patrick. Curious and wonderful!

"We won't be away long."

No longer than it took to win enough to pay the note and get back home.

Because this was now home to her as much as the *Queen* had ever been.

Even though Travis had gone away, there were plenty of folks here she loved and had a responsibility for.

As angry as she tried to be at Travis for leaving, she did understand. His note had been exactly as Bill had expected. He loved her, would always love her. But his sense of duty—his love of home and responsibility to the wishes of the man who had raised him like a son—went bone-deep.

She knew all about love of home.

And if she was going to keep this one for all of them, she would have to go away from it for a short time.

Gosh almighty she was a different gal leaving than she had been coming.

As Madame had predicted, Uncle Patrick was waiting on the front porch, impatient to leave. He must be even more anxious to see the *Queen* than she was…and she could nearly taste river weeds, hemp rope and old, damp wood.

Agatha sat in a chair beside Uncle Patrick. She looked apprehensive.

Ivy crouched beside her.

"Don't worry, sis, Uncle Patrick and I will be back quicker than a wink."

"I'm trying not to be a shrinking violet, honestly, I am." Agatha clutched the strings of Little Mouse's new pouch. She and Bill had located the sweet critter near the barn as he'd guessed. "But without Travis here, without you…"

"Laura Lee will be here for you. Whatever you need… She'll take you outdoors, make sure you get fresh air and exercise." Ivy patted her sister's hand, appreciating the brave smile she was trying to give. "Why, I reckon you'll be running when you come to meet me and Uncle Patrick when we get back."

"I hope to be. But Ivy," Agatha leaned close to her. "I'm worried about the laudanum. If you aren't here and I find some, I might not be strong enough to leave it be."

"I've searched high and low," Ivy whispered. "It's gone. Besides, it won't be long now before you get over the craving."

"What if Hilda Brunne comes back?"

Her sister no longer called the woman mother. After hours of talking about what had happened, of showing her that yes, Brunne had loved her but not in a healthy way, Agatha had come to see that Brunne had used her as a way of perpetuating a fantasy.

"We looked for days." They had not found her wounded, or dead. It did not mean that she was not. The ranch was vast. But Hilda's horse had not come home either.

Hilda Brunne's fate remained, and might always remain, unknown.

"Everyone knows to be looking out for her, but really she is gone." In one way or another.

Ivy felt confident in leaving the Lucky Clover in the hands of Slim Morgan. He had cared for things in the past whenever Travis was away.

"We'd best get going." Uncle Patrick lifted Agatha's chin between his thumb and finger, kissed her forehead. "When we return your home will be safe and free of debt."

Ivy removed her mother's necklace from her throat and placed it around her sister's neck. "Keep it for me."

"I'll meet you when you get back, Ivy. I'll be running."

Moments later, Ivy rode away from the ranch house—from her home—with Uncle Patrick at her side.

He'd gotten better with horses, but not enough to keep him from cursing his sore backside every other mile.

Chapter Nineteen

It was late September and still warm when Travis led his horse over the gangplank of the *River Queen*.

After he'd met with the lawyer and secured Ivy's interest in the ranch, he'd spent the rest of the month traveling with no real direction. When he heard there was to be big-time gambling aboard the *River Queen*, he'd headed north.

Couldn't say why, for sure. Maybe it was because he had nowhere else to go. Maybe because it was the *River Queen* where he first laid eyes on Ivy Magee.

No, not Ivy Magee any longer. By now she would be Eleanor Ivy English. For some reason he couldn't seem to get her new name out of his mind. It haunted him like a song whose lyrics one could not forget.

Looking up at the white, three-storied boat in the fading sun of the late afternoon, he knew he had come here because of Ivy. The question was, had he come to remember or forget?

He reckoned it didn't really matter. He had no trouble in remembering everything about her. As far as forgetting went, he was realizing more and more that it was not going to happen.

He'd seen her in a stranger passing on the far side of the street in the new town of Billings. He'd heard her voice coming from a saloon in Spoonlick. He'd listened to the rustle of her hair, her contented sigh under the stars on the wide-open plains.

Wherever he went, she was there. When he'd heard that the *Queen* was docking in Middle Creek, that the rich and influential were coming to gamble, he'd decided to make the trip.

He wasn't rich and he wasn't going to gamble, but there was something about being here that made Ivy seem real again.

For weeks she had existed as a wisp of memory. Unless he was asleep. Then she was there in his mind, under his hands, warm flesh and loving whispers.

Within a week of leaving home, he'd known he'd made a mistake. He was homesick and lovesick in equal parts.

Wandering about, looking for a new place to settle had left him empty.

Time to accept the fact that empty was going to be the way for him from now on since he could not go home.

The place would never be the same anyway—not with Ivy a married woman.

The fact that he was in love with her would only bring trouble. Didn't matter that when he had fallen in love with her she was neither married nor attached. She was now, and if he went home, everyone would see the truth.

They would also see a coward—at least Ivy would. He'd left the woman that he loved more than his right arm only a brief note in farewell. She deserved more than that.

But by damn, it didn't take much to imagine what

would have happened if he'd tried to say goodbye face-to-face.

One loving glance from her and he would have caught her up in his arms, carried her away on his horse and never come back.

That act of selfishness would have doomed every person on the ranch, from Señora Morgan's newest granddaughter to Agatha.

There was one thing that brought him comfort through his wandering. The knowledge that William and his money would be there to hold everything together.

To hold Ivy— The thought snuck up on him before he had a chance to block it.

"You need a room, mister?" A boy's voice called him back from the misery he was about to dive into.

Looking up, Travis recognized him. Tom was his name. Tom knew Ivy. He and the boy had that bond, although the kid wouldn't know it.

"No, I'll be staying down here with my horse."

"Come for a chance at the high stakes?"

Why had he come? He ought to leave.

"I might." He did need a reason to be here. Maybe that's why he'd come. Maybe he'd been longing for a game of chance and not even known it.

"I'm thinking I'll try my luck this time." The boy took the horse's reins from his hand, grinning. "Follow me. I'll get you settled in. Better watch out for me though, I might just clean you out tonight. I learned to gamble from a wicked-grand player."

Hell if the kid didn't mean Ivy. He'd seen her skills firsthand.

The kid settled his horse in a stall near the paddle wheel.

"I'll take that one over there," he said pointing a few feet away.

It was the place he and Ivy had lain back in the hay, talking and getting to know each other.

The boy raised one brow then the other. Probably thought he was touched in the head. He wasn't wrong.

When was the last time he'd had a shave or a haircut, even a bath with soap?

It didn't matter really. He'd rather wander around the boat visiting Ivy's ghost than visit the barber in town.

The wood step creaked under Ivy's foot the same as it always had. The *Queen* might have a new owner but nothing else seemed to be any different. For the most part even the crew remained the same.

Funny, but when she first came aboard, no one recognized her. They ought to have since she was standing beside Uncle Patrick. Maybe it was because they were so plum pleased to see him, they didn't notice her. Or maybe it was because she was wearing a dress and fancy hat with feathers and silk flowers on it.

Even Tom hadn't known her.

"Good morning, miss," he'd said, his smile as open and friendly as ever. "I'll be happy to escort you to your room."

"Gosh almighty, Tom!" She'd nearly slapped him on the back, but somehow, it hadn't seemed quite fitting, given what she was wearing. "Don't you know me?"

"Ivy?" He squinted his eyes, then suddenly they looked like they were going to pop out of his head. "Glory, it *is* you!"

It was hard to blame him for being so surprised. It wasn't only her looks that had changed. She was different inside.

The last time she had heard this stair squeal, she'd been a girl with no one to look out for but her own self; her own dreams were all that had mattered.

At the top of the stairs, she paused to listen to all the sounds she remembered. The shouts of the roustabouts, the whistle of the twin stacks, the call of shorebirds settling in for the night—all so dear and familiar.

She walked to the rail and looked at the mountain range to the north. Sun still glittered on the peaks, but lower down evening shadows took over the land. It wouldn't be more than a few weeks before snow dusted the peaks.

Everything was the same…except for her. She still had dreams, but no longer of commanding this wonderful vessel.

Tonight her dreams would be of a man who was gone. A man whom she loved and would probably never see again. The note of farewell he'd written had been fairly clear on the point. She was to marry another and no longer think of him.

"Thickheaded fool," she muttered.

"I hope you aren't speaking of me, Ivy."

"Why howdy, Captain Cooper." The new captain of the *River Queen* and a man she had known since her childhood leaned his elbows on the rail and gazed out at the mountain peaks. "I would never say that about you."

"You certainly do clean up well," he said. "What a lovely woman you've become."

"I'm still me, just all gussied up and mannerly. I'm hoping this here gown might give me an advantage tonight."

The gown she wore was a few inches shy of being modest, but she knew some of the men she would be gambling with. They might get distracted by the view.

One thing was sure. They wouldn't recognize her. If they thought she was only a lady looking for adventure, she might have an advantage.

"Your uncle tells me you need to win big in order to save your inheritance."

"There's plenty of folks who are depending upon me winning."

"Here's something you might be interested in, before you decide what to do with all that money. I'm selling the *Queen*."

"But you only just bought her! Why the *Queen* is as fine a boat as you'll ever find."

"That she is, but do you hear that train whistle off yonder? The rails are going to do in the river trade… mark my words."

"That's what Uncle Patrick always said."

But the *Queen* was for sale? She could have her old life back, her dear paddle-wheeled friend. Even if she only put her to dock and used her for gambling and entertainment, she would be home.

She could bring Agatha.

"It's tempting, and I won't say otherwise. I miss this old *Queen* and the wide Missouri. But the thing is, I'd miss the Lucky Clover as much. I never expected to take to being a landlubber, but gosh almighty I do."

Ivy closed her eyes, feeling the heave and roll of the deck under her shoes. She breathed in the lush green scent of the river.

When she opened her eyes she saw a man walking across the gangplank on his way to shore. His hair was ragged and so were his clothes. But his carriage looked familiar. Could be he'd been a regular on the *Queen* in days gone by.

"I wish you luck tonight, Miss Ivy, I surely do."

She looked away from the man's back. Funny how he made her feel so odd.

"I reckon I could use a prayer along with the luck. I'll need a heap of money. Sure do hope the gents came with their pockets full of cash."

"From what I hear, the safe is pushing at the rivets."

He kissed her cheek then climbed the steps to the pilothouse.

The safe was full and her nerves were taut. It was all adding up to a gripping evening.

What was Travis doing on this gripping evening, she wondered, the same as she did every sundown. Had the good Lord kept him safely through the day as she prayed He would?

Would the blamed man ever come home and find that she had kept the ranch without having to marry Bill?

If he did, would she shoot him or hug him to death?

All she could hope was that time would tell.

The trip into town had been worth it. Travis didn't feel so much like a bear now that he'd had a shave and a haircut.

Walking into the saloon of the *River Queen*, he felt the most human he had in quite some time.

Everything looked the same as it had last time he was in this room. Plush furniture scattered about offered the promise of a comfortable evening. The soothing golden light from the lamps gave the saloon an air of ease.

Even with all that, a tremor of excitement hung on the air. Tonight was a night for the rich and powerful to challenge each other, herd leaders coming together to butt heads and tangle antlers.

This early in the evening, though, it was the young

men who sat at the gaming tables testing their luck. The rich men would arrive later.

Travis spotted Tom and would have liked to sit beside him but the table was full. He joined another group and slapped his money down.

This was small change compared to what was coming later. But for Travis, an unemployed drifter, it was what he was comfortable spending.

After an hour of playing, he'd lost a few hands but won a few more. At the end of two hours, he noticed that those joining the game were gentlemen of better means. Not the high-class fellows who would be coming soon, but prosperous enough to make him cash in his small winnings.

He bought a beer and settled into an easy chair in a dim corner. He wouldn't mind seeing the moneyed folks shuffling their high-stakes chips back and forth. He imagined that at some point during the night there would be enough chips on the table to pay off the note to the ranch.

His imagination ran wild and he let it. Staring at the table as though this was happening, he saw himself laying down the last, winning hand, scooping up the chips, cashing them in then riding for home to save the ranch and claim Ivy as his own.

Too bad the ranch had already been saved and Ivy was already claimed.

All day long he'd been tickled by the strangest sensation. Whenever he rounded a corner, he felt that she might suddenly appear, wearing her red-flowered sash and floppy hat with a mouse in the pouch.

Memory was a powerful thing. Maybe he wouldn't feel so lonely if he got a job here, taking solace in whispers from the past.

Or maybe he needed to move on and find a life of his own.

For now, he'd sit in his corner and drink a beer while watching other men live their lives.

He must have closed his eyes, drifted toward a doze, because he was drawn slowly back to reality when the drone of conversation stopped.

"Good evening, gentlemen. May I join you?" The honey-sweet voice seemed to caress the room.

His eyes came into focus on a pink gown, sharpened on a mostly bare bosom.

"I've always wanted to play this game and well, now that I'm a widow there's no one to forbid me!"

Ivy?

His heart slammed against his ribs; his breath came in short puffs.

A widow? William was dead? He must be or he wouldn't be allowing her to wear that revealing gown.

What the damn hell? She'd barely had time to be a bride let alone a widow! The way she was smiling flirtatiously at every man at the table, she hardly appeared to be grieving.

He'd only half risen when a hand clamped upon his shoulder. "Sit down, son."

Patrick Malone, captain to his soul, would tolerate nothing but compliance.

"What the blazes is going on?"

"Sit quietly and you'll find out."

"But she's—"

"Trying to win her home," Malone whispered harshly. "If she knows you are here it will ruin everything."

He'd heard the *River Queen* was for sale. It was understandable that she would want it. But now that she was a rich woman—or possibly a rich widow—why didn't she just buy it? Why gamble away good money…dressed in that? If William was alive he sure wouldn't let his wife go out in public that way.

"I do know how to play," she said to the group of wealthy fellows seated at the table. Men with fortunes to spend must have come in while he slept. "My husband taught me by the fireside at night. I did win sometimes, but I fear that he let me. I would appreciate the chance to know if I'm really any good at this game."

As a group, they didn't seem to know what to say. They were stunned by her beauty, was Travis' guess.

Ivy did look like an angel, even if her halo was a bit off-kilter. Lamplight cast a glow on her skin and a glimmer in her hair. The sweet pink color of her dress gave the impression of innocence. The fit said something else.

Glancing over at Patrick Malone, he saw the man grinning.

"I brought some money." Ivy hoisted a lacy bag. She waggled it.

"Please." One man stood, pulled out the chair beside him. "Do join us, ma'am. Your company would be most welcome."

"You are beyond kind." Ivy clutched the bag to her chest as she sat, smiling sweetly at the men. "I can't tell you how happy I am to be here. Life at home has been so dreary of late with my…" Her smile faded, she sniffed.

"Think nothing of it, my dear," said a portly man with a wet, lecherous-looking grin. "Please do join us. You'll be a lovely addition to our little game."

Apparently, Ivy had finally learned to sigh the way Madame had taught her to.

The dealer dealt the first hand.

Ivy lost.

"Oh, dear. That used to be a winning hand when I played with Charles."

Charles! Who the blazes was Charles?

Travis glanced at Patrick Malone. The man was grinning—almost looked like he was proud.

Of all the— Wait a blamed minute! A niggling suspicion gathered in his mind.

Ivy was not here to soothe her grief over a dead husband. Unless he missed his guess, she was not even married. How could she be? William liked things to be under his control and clearly, Ivy was under no one's control but her own.

He turned to the captain, his mouth open to demand an explanation. What he got was a swift jab in the ribs, a firm headshake.

Ivy won the next hand.

"My word," she gushed, looking pleased and proud. "Next time I'll have to bet more money."

She lost the next three hands.

"I'm having such fun with you gentlemen." She clapped her hands then set out her largest wager yet. "I hardly care if I win or not."

But she did win.

"I suspect," Ivy said with a wink to her fellow players—to her victims, "That you let me win that one."

Maybe one or two of them believed it, given that they were smiling indulgently at her. Uncle Patrick would know better—so did Travis.

What Ivy's uncle knew, and Travis did not, was why she was here and where she had come by the funds to risk such high-stakes gambling.

Why the damn bloody blazes hadn't she married English like he'd told her to?

If it wasn't for the fact that the captain would lay him

flat if he stood up or made a sound, he'd leap from the chair and demand to know.

Unless he leaped from his chair and kissed her.

Ivy wasn't married!

She was not as lost to him as he'd believed she was, all those miserable wandering days.

After an hour of play, the men began to notice that Ivy's chip pile was growing while theirs were shrinking. A few of the adoring smiles began to sag.

"You look familiar to me," said the man with the lewd-looking mouth. Could he possibly connect the widow to Ivy Magee? "I wonder if we've shared a table before."

Ivy's chest rose then fell. Lamplight caught the fine sheen of perspiration on her skin and cast a golden glow on the swell of her breasts.

"I would never forget a gentleman like yourself. I'd never forget any one of you. Even if my memory did fail, I doubt we would have met in the past. Charles, as dear a man as he was, rarely let me out of the house."

Tsking and shaking heads circled the table.

And not only the table. The men gathered against the walls three deep, watching the competition, falling under the widow's spell, shook their heads.

She lost the next three hands. The smiles of her opponents returned. They must be too smitten to notice that even though she'd lost, her pile of chips didn't go down much.

After another hour, Travis figured the men should have realized they were being artfully played. The angel in the risqué gown had them so charmed they could not see that they were being beguiled out of their money.

Damned if he wasn't ready to slap his small winnings down on the table and surrender them to her.

At the end of three and a half hours of play, Ivy's opponents were sweating, drunk and broke…at least until they visited their bankers in the morning.

Ivy pushed a portion of her huge mound of chips toward the dealer and gave him her thanks.

"This has been such a delightful evening, my new friends." Ivy squeezed the hands of each of her victims. "I do hope we can play again next time."

"Naturally!"

"Oh, *delighted*."

"Most *charmed*."

The lusty goat licked his lips.

Travis started to rise but once again Patrick Malone snatched his sleeve.

"Don't let her see you. I've a thing or two to say to you."

And there was a thing or two he wanted to know.

An hour later Travis sat alone on a bench watching the river slide past in dark ripples.

Patrick Malone had told him the thing or two he needed to know—and a good bit more that he didn't want to know.

He'd learned how deeply the cursed note had hurt Ivy. Malone had been right when he'd called him a harebrained idiot for leaving it. It was a coward's way of dealing with goodbye. He should have told her face-to-face that he was going away.

For that, he took the blame. But he hadn't made a wrong choice in going away, no matter how painful the choice had been for them both.

Gambling was far from a tried-and-true way to earn money. If he'd known about her scheme, he would have forbidden it.

He would have—if he'd had the right to. Which he damned did not. The ranch belonged to her. The inheritance from the *River Queen* also belonged to her.

A niggling voice in his heart reminded him that her future also belonged to her.

But didn't she realize that if she'd done the safe thing and married William, the ranch's future would have been guaranteed, not left to luck?

If he'd been willing to throw himself to the lions, she should have been as well. Besides, William English, for all that he was a politician, was not a lion.

Travis covered his face with his hands, scrubbed his newly shaven chin. Inside he didn't feel newly anything. He was still the long-haired, harebrained saddle bum who Malone had nearly punched in the face for keeping Ivy out all night long after the big storm.

Only the knowledge that bringing Ivy home in the devil's weather would have been risky had kept Ivy's angry guardian from breaking Travis's teeth.

Well dang blast it! He'd done what he'd done. Ivy had done what she'd done.

The fact that she wasn't married didn't have him jumping joyful flips off a saddle—actually it did, but only in a small, cautious part of his soul.

Mostly, he doubted that Ivy would ever forgive him for what he had done. For the decision he had tried to take from her.

But damn it, he had a ways to go before he got over the fact that she had entrusted the fate of the Lucky Clover to the turn of a card…and done it wearing a dress that had left a few dozen men panting.

As far as he could tell, he was the last one awake on the *Queen*. Maybe he ought to leave his face in his hands and fall asleep right here on the bench. Let the sound of the lapping water lull him to sleep.

A splash brought his head up with a jerk.

Looking toward the sound, he didn't see anyone.

But there on the lower deck was the puddle of a scandalous pink gown.

Ivy stood naked on the deck of the *Queen*, feeling the soft breeze stroke the sweat of a hard evening off her body.

It had been a long tense fight for the Lucky Clover. One that at times she had feared she would not win.

Now it was hers. Agatha was safe and all her father's people were safe.

And Travis was still gone.

Raising her arms over her head, she dove under the cool green water.

Surfacing, she flipped onto her back and floated. The late summer sky was so full of stars it seemed like she ought to be able to reach out and grab one.

One bright diamond shot across the sky, then another, and another. Gosh almighty she could make a lot of wishes.

Funny how they would all be to see Travis again.

Curse the man.

Going limp, she let go of her float. She sank under the water, blew out a lungful of bubbles.

It would be a long time before she swam in this river again. Maybe she never would.

Shoot, if she'd married Bill, she'd have had enough money to save the Lucky Clover and buy the *River Queen*.

Stroking up, she broke the surface of the water.

"Couldn't rightly have done that to Bill," she sputtered, whipping the hair out of her face and looking at the deserted decks of the *Queen*. "Not loving Travis like I do. I could have had you and the ranch if I didn't…"

Maybe it was a strange thing to do, to talk to a boat, but this was the *Queen*.

"But all the having wouldn't mean beans. Not without him. But I reckon he's never coming back."

"I'm here," came a voice from behind her.

"Travis Murphy!" She turned, glared hard then back-stroked away from him. "You lowdown, note-leaving mudsucker. Get out of my river!"

He stroked toward her.

"I heard what you just said."

"Well I was about to say that I hoped you'd stay away."

She treaded water away from him faster, but still the distance between them was shrinking.

"You said you loved me."

"Doesn't mean a ding-dong, Travis. You said you loved me but ran away, didn't even stay to put up a fight for me."

"I did what I thought was best—for you, for everyone."

"Turns out you just wasted your time. I won the money for the Lucky Clover."

"You might have lost everything."

"Maybe, but I didn't run away. I took a risk and it paid off."

Only five feet separated his hands from her bare body. She didn't know what she'd do if he got any closer—kick him in a tender part, or grab him around the neck and never let go.

"You think I ran away?"

Three feet now.

"Hard and fast."

"There is no running away from you. I paid the price for leaving every time I thought of you and William together. My heart's been bleeding raw every minute without you."

"Well…good." Two feet now, and blamed if she wasn't the one who bobbed forward. "Go away, Travis."

"I've already done that. I won't be doing it again."

Reaching out, he tangled his fingers in her floating hair, pulled her gently toward him.

"I love you, Ivy. Don't turn me away."

"Looks like you've caught me." Water lapped between his chest and hers, the sound sucking and seductive. "And it turns out I do need a ramrod. My old one got confused. Got himself all turned around in what his obligations were."

"I reckon that fool got lost in the wilderness." One of his hands treaded water, but the other touched her bare waist, drew her in. "I'd like his job."

"Well, there's more to the position now. It's permanent, lifelong." She touched his shoulder, closed the distance so that her breasts floated against the hard plain of his chest. She felt a dusting of wiry hair scrape her skin.

"Marry me, Ivy. I love you so damn much." He kissed her with river water on his lips. He tasted like everything that was home. "I promise I'll never write you so much as a sentence on a wad of paper unless I'm standing there to read it to you."

"I couldn't marry anyone but you. That's why I had to take the gambling risk…figured I'd win though."

She kissed him back, hugging tight to his strong, warm neck.

"Are you saying yes?"

"Gull-durned right I am, cowboy."

"We'll go to town first thing in the morning, find the preacher."

"Why wait? Captain's got the watch. We'll wake Uncle Patrick and be married tonight, right on the deck of the *Queen*. But that will be second thing."

"What's first?" he asked, his grin crooked, seductive.

The thick, hard heat of him pressed against her belly, inched lower. She lifted one leg, wrapped it about his hip. She kissed his lips, his neck, then wrapped her other leg around.

Treading water with one hand, he cupped her bottom with the other. Giving her a squeeze and a grin, he drove into her.

She undulated her arms in the water, rejoicing in the wonder...the unbearable beauty of having him move inside her.

Tipping her head back, she opened her eyes and watched stars twinkle like diamonds from horizon to horizon.

Gosh almighty, wishes did come true.

Two weeks later

Ivy Murphy might have ridden her own horse. It would have been a mite more comfortable than squeezing into one saddle...but not nearly as interesting.

With Travis at her back, his arms around her and his hips pressed against her behind...well, it was a good thing that Uncle Patrick rode half a mile ahead of them.

She reckoned her uncle was wearing a grin of his own, now that Ivy was a married woman. It was what he had wanted for her all along. He'd sold all he had in order for her to get a husband, settle down respectably and give him grandchildren.

She figured she'd wait another month to tell him her courses were late. That would be a secret for her and her husband to whisper about for a while.

"Sure can't wait to see my sister."

She snuggled back against Travis's warm chest. The weather was beginning to turn. It was a fine thing to know she'd have a good, hot man to wrap her up on the cold nights ahead.

"Won't be long now, honey." He wrapped one arm about her middle, patted her belly. "If you listen, you can hear the cowboys hooting. They'll let everyone know we're coming."

"I reckon they'll be relieved to have you home. Mr. Morgan especially. I get the feeling he'd rather be wrangling cows than receipts and ledgers."

Rounding the bend, they passed the barn, came to the edge of the yard.

Señora Morgan and her girls gathered on the front porch waving their arms and aprons. Children ran in circles, chasing each other under the trees.

Young Jose Morgan was leading Uncle Patrick's horse to the barn. Her uncle must have rushed into the house.

He hadn't kept it a secret how much he missed Antie while they were gone. Every night around the campfire he'd talked about how sweet he was on her.

More than sweet, it seemed. He'd purchased a pretty gold band back in Spoonlick and was anxious to get it on Antie's finger.

But where was Agatha? "Please, dear God, don't let her be wasting away in her bedroom," Ivy prayed out loud.

"Amen," Travis added.

While Ivy frowned in concern at Agatha's second-story window, the front door swung open.

Everything inside looked black in the midday shadow.

Laura Lee stepped out, smiling broadly.

Antie and Uncle Patrick stepped out behind her, holding hands.

Great glory days! Her teacher was grinning with her mouth open…showing teeth!

Uncle Patrick hoisted their joined hands. The pretty band of gold caught a beam of sunshine.

Ivy slipped off the horse with a "Yee-haw!" Sure did feel good to be who she was and shout it out loud.

All of a sudden, the doorway became filled with color…bright sunny yellow.

Agatha stepped onto the porch.

Laura Lee clasped her hands to her heart, fairly dancing up and down in excitement.

With confident strides, Agatha stepped across the porch and down the stairs.

Ivy ran to her, arms open. Coming up short, she nearly tripped over her riding skirt because…

Because… Agatha ran toward her, not quickly but she was running!

She heard herself screech. If Antie winced, Ivy would never know. She was wrapped up in Agatha's arms, Agatha wrapped up in hers.

They rocked and wept.

All at once a pair of wonderful strong arms circled them both.

"If your sister wasn't crying all over you, Agatha, she'd tell you that you are going to need this strength you've gained. Nieces and nephews take a lot of running around after."

Ivy poked her husband in the ribs, waggled her ring at Agatha.

Looks like her husband wasn't a master of keeping things confidential.

Still, watching his beaming smile and then Agatha's great joy, she was glad he wasn't.

"Uncle Patrick! Come on over here," she called, waving her hand for him to hurry. "I've got something to tell you!"

Gosh almighty, it was good to be home.

* * * * *

*If you enjoyed this story,
you won't want to miss these
other great reads from Carol Arens*

*WED TO THE MONTANA COWBOY
WED TO THE TEXAS OUTLAW
THE RANCHER'S INCONVENIENT BRIDE
A RANCH TO CALL HOME*

*When Cord Winterman takes on a job as a hired man
on Eleanor Malloy's farm, sparks fly, and Eleanor
soon realizes she doesn't just need this enigmatic
drifter with hunger in his eyes…she wants him, too!*

Read on for a sneak preview of
The Hired Man
by Lynna Banning

Cord knew she was watching his every move, assessing
him, judging him. Eleanor resented his presence in
her kitchen, rooting around in her pantry and in the
cutlery drawers. But she wanted an apple pie, didn't
she? If there was one thing he'd learned in this life,
it was that you don't get something for nothing. No
rooting around in a pantry, no apple pie.

He worked on, trying to ignore her, and trying to
ignore the undercurrent of pleasure he felt knowing
that her eyes were following every move he made. It
made his chest feel as hot inside as he felt outside in
the stifling kitchen with the roaring fire in the stove
heating up the oven.

While the pies baked, the children drifted out the
back door to play in the yard and Cord warmed up

the coffee, poured two cups and carried them into the parlor, where Eleanor sat.

She looked up at him with a strange expression on her pale face. He sucked in his breath and waited.

"You're not just a hired man, are you?" she said. "I mean, that's not what you did before I hired you, is it?"

"I'm a hired man here," he said carefully. "I'm not sure what I'd be somewhere else."

She reached for his offered cup of coffee, then glanced up again. "Do you have plans for 'somewhere else'?"

He gave her such a long look that she lowered her eyes.

"I was planning to go to California, to the gold fields."

"What stopped you?"

He didn't answer for a long time, just focused his gaze out the window on the apple orchard. "To be honest, I wouldn't have stopped here if I hadn't been so hungry, even though I'd seen your advert in town. But then I came up on that little hill and saw all those apple trees covered with lacy white blossoms. Kinda made my heart feel funny, so I stopped and…well, you know the rest."

She paused with her cup halfway to her mouth. "How long will you stay?"

"It's April now," he said slowly. "I thought I'd give it five months, say till August, before I move on."

"Very good. Doc Dougherty tells me I should be completely well and strong long before August."

"Yeah? You gonna chop wood and hitch up the horse and drive that wagon to town and muck out your barn by yourself? You need some help out here, ma'am. Even if I'm not going to be here, you should have a hired man to help out."

She gave him a half smile and sipped her coffee for a full minute before she spoke. "I chopped wood and mucked out the barn before I fell ill, Mr. Winterman. I have been on my own here for almost seven years, ever since Molly was born."

Cord studied her. Her cheeks were getting pink. "It's too hard for a woman alone. That's most likely why you got sick."

"That is pure nonsense. I got sick because I fell in the creek while I was chasing the cow and took a chill. A week later it turned into pneumonia."

He stood up suddenly. Dammit, he didn't want to concern himself with her well-being. He didn't want to like her kids, and he didn't want to like her. But he did. And he had to admit it scared the hell out of him.

"Think I'll check on the pies," he growled. He moved into the kitchen and bent over the oven door, and when he returned he brought the coffeepot and filled her cup. He didn't look at her. But he did ask the question that had been niggling in the back of his mind.

"Do you and your husband own this place free and clear?"

"I own it. I removed Tom's name from the deed when he…when he left home to go off to war. It's been seven years now, and he is considered legally dead."

"You said you had a hired man before you hired me."

"Yes. Isaiah. As I told you, he didn't do much."

"Why'd you keep him, then?"

"He needed a place to stay and I needed someone to help about the farm. Molly was just a baby then, and Danny was too little to be much help."

"How'd you manage after this hired man, Isaiah, left?"

"I managed," she said in a quiet voice.

"And then you got sick," he observed drily.

She took a swallow of her coffee. "Well, yes, I did. Doc Dougherty came, and he sent a woman out from town, Helen, I think her name was, to nurse me and take care of Molly and Daniel. She stayed until I was strong enough to get out of bed. I am growing stronger with every day that passes."

"Mrs. Malloy. Eleanor," he amended. "Seems to me you're just hangin' on by a thread. You've got two kids. You owe it to them to take better care of yourself. That means no more milking and no chopping wood."

She pressed her lips into a thin line but said nothing.

Cord studied the rigid set of her shoulders and the white-knuckled grip she had on the handle of her china cup. "I get the feeling you don't take orders too well."

She gave him a wobbly smile. "You are most likely correct. I was a great trial to my parents."

That made him laugh out loud. "I bet you're still plenty stubborn when it comes to doing things your own way."

"Oh, maybe just a little." Her cheeks turned an even deeper shade of rose.

"Maybe you're more than a little stubborn," he said. "Maybe a lot stubborn."

"Oh, all right, maybe I'm a lot stubborn." By now her cheeks were flushed scarlet. "Now that you're here, I will take better care of myself. Especially," she said with a little bubble of laughter, "since you can bake an apple pie. Which," she added with an impish grin, "you have quite forgotten is still in the oven."

Instantly he wheeled away from her and strode into the kitchen. The pies were not burned, as he had feared, just nicely baked. He grabbed pot holders and lifted them out of the oven. Oh, man, they looked just right, golden brown on top with rich juice bubbling out the vents he'd slashed in the crust. They smelled wonderful! He was damn proud of them.

Eleanor followed him into the kitchen, cup and saucer still in her hand. "Who taught you to make a pie? Your mother?"

"No," he said shortly.

She looked at him with another question in her eyes, but he ignored it. Best not to dig around in those long-past years. No good ever came from opening a wound that had healed over.

He set both pies on the open windowsill to cool and stacked the mixing bowl and the paring knives in the sink for the kids to wash up after supper. Eleanor returned to the parlor, where she curled up on the settee and gazed out the front window.

"You don't like talking to me, do you?" she asked suddenly.

Whoa, Nelly. How'd she figure that?

"Why is that?" she pursued, her eyes on his face.

"Guess I haven't been around many ladies lately."

"Silence is perfectly all right with me," she went on. "I spent years and years not being talked to."

She closed her eyes against the late-afternoon sun's glare, and that gave him a chance to really look at her. Her lids were purplish with blue-black smudges shadowing her eyes. She might not be sick anymore, but she was obviously exhausted.

So even if she was as stubborn as three ornery mules, now she had a hired man to help her. He drew in a long, quiet breath. For the first time in longer than he could remember he felt needed.

And that, he thought with a silent groan, made him nervous.

Don't miss
The Hired Man *by Lynna Banning,*
available September 2018.

www.Harlequin.com

HHEXP46758

HARLEQUIN®

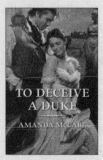

Save $1.00

off the purchase of ANY

Harlequin® series book.

Available wherever books are sold, including most bookstores, supermarkets, drugstores and discount stores.

- ✂

Save $1.00

on the purchase of ANY Harlequin® series book.

Coupon valid until September 30, 2018.
Redeemable at participating retail outlets in the U.S. and Canada only.
Limit one coupon per customer.

52615867

Canadian Retailers: Harlequin Enterprises Limited will pay the face value of this coupon plus 10.25¢ if submitted by customer for this product only. Any other use constitutes fraud. Coupon is nonassignable. Void if taxed, prohibited or restricted by law. Consumer must pay any government taxes. Void if copied. Inmar Promotional Services ("IPS") customers submit coupons and proof of sales to Harlequin Enterprises Limited, P.O. Box 31000, Scarborough, ON M1R 0E7, Canada. Non-IPS retailer—for reimbursement submit coupons and proof of sales directly to Harlequin Enterprises Limited, Retail Marketing Department, 22 Adelaide St. West, 40th Floor, Toronto, Ontario M5H 4E3, Canada.

U.S. Retailers: Harlequin Enterprises Limited will pay the face value of this coupon plus 8¢ if submitted by customer for this product only. Any other use constitutes fraud. Coupon is nonassignable. Void if taxed, prohibited or restricted by law. Consumer must pay any government taxes. Void if copied. For reimbursement submit coupons and proof of sales directly to Harlequin Enterprises, Ltd 482, NCH Marketing Services, P.O. Box 880001, El Paso, TX 88588-0001, U.S.A. Cash value 1/100 cents.

5 65373 00076 2   (8100)0 12376

® and ™ are trademarks owned and used by the trademark owner and/or its licensee.

© 2018 Harlequin Enterprises Limited

HHCOUP46758